W9-AKU-063

Rosemary Rowe is the maiden name of author Rosemary
Aitken, who was born in Cornwall during the Second World
War. She is a highly qualified academic, and has written more
than a dozen bestselling textbooks on English language and
communication. She has written fiction for many years under
her married name. Rosemary is the mother of two adult
children and has two grandchildren living in New Zealand,
where she herself lived for twenty years. She now divides her
time between Gloucestershire and Cornwall.

Acclaim for Rosemary Rowe's Libertus series:

'The story is agreeably written, gets on briskly with its plot,
and ends with a highly satisfactory double-take solution' Gerald
Kaufman, *Scotsman*

'A brilliantly realised historical setting dovetails perfectly with
a sharp plot in this history-cum-whodunnit' *Good Book Guide*

'Superb characterisation and evocation of Roman Britain. It
transports you back to those times. An entirely compelling
historical mystery' Michael Jecks

'The Libertus novels are among the best of the British historical
detectives. The characters are well formed and the plots leave
you guessing while giving you enough hints and clues to grip
your attention' *Gloucestershire Life*

'Libertus is a thinking man's hero . . . a delightful whodunnit
which is fascinating in the detail of its research and the charm
of its detective team' *Huddersfield Daily Examiner*

'Rowe brings to life a dark corner of the Roman Empire . . .
A tense, atmospheric thriller' Paul Doherty

'Lots of fascinating detail about what the Romans ever did
for us . . . History with an entertaining if murderous twist'
Birmingham Post

The Germanicus Mosaic

Rosemary Rowe

headline

First published in 1999
by HEADLINE BOOK PUBLISHING

This edition published in paperback in 2004
by HEADLINE BOOK PUBLISHING

10 9 8 7 6 5

ISBN 0 7472 6101 6

Typeset in Plantin by Avon DataSet Ltd,
Bidford-on-Avon, Warwickshire

Printed and bound in Great Britain by
Clays Ltd, St Ives plc

Headline's policy is to use papers that are natural, renewable and
recyclable products and made from wood grown in sustainable
forests. The logging and manufacturing processes are expected to
conform to the environmental regulations of the country of origin.

HEADLINE BOOK PUBLISHING
A division of Hodder Headline
338 Euston Road
London NW1 3BH

www.headline.co.uk
www.hodderheadline.com

For my mother

Author's Foreword

The Germanicus Mosaic is set in 186 AD. The Roman Empire was at its height, although the popular emperor Marcus Aurelius was dead, and his inept, corrupt and increasingly unbalanced son Commodus now wore the imperial purple. Most of Britain was a Roman province, administered at this time by a single governor; the quarrelsome local tribes had settled into uneasy peace, military roads now joined important centres, and Roman law prevailed, though there were signs of bubbling unrest in sections of the army. The province was an outpost of empire, fringed by insurgent tribes. There were constant clashes on the borders to north and west, and even in the rest of the island old Celtic ways were not entirely lost. Educated people spoke Latin, but native dialects still existed, and roundhouses and native farms and settlements (*oppida*) were found as well as Roman garrisons, towns and country villa-estates. Roman nobility (often holding high official positions) were the social élite, although many native men of wealth had important posts in local administration. The most significant distinction, however, was between free man and slave, although a man might move between these two conditions in his lifetime. There were many ways into slavery – capture in a military campaign or by slave-trading raiders, or a sentence to servitude following a criminal offence. Some were driven to it by want or debt, and some gamblers even staked their own freedom on the fall of a dice. Children of slaves were automatically slaves, and freeborn parents sometimes sold their children, often for a fixed term, either from economic necessity or in the hope of gaining advancement for them. For a slave who was manumitted (like Libertus) gained the status of his ex-master, and could become a full citizen, entitled to the protection of Rome. Some freedmen rose to positions of considerable wealth and status. Slaves could also occasionally serve out their contract, or buy their own liberty, but it was harder to escape from slavery than to enter it.

Many slaves led lives of drudgery, but others were highly regarded by their masters and might learn a trade or even keep the books. Of course, not all free men had the status of citizens and the lives of poor 'free' peasants and traders, scratching a living in difficult times, must sometimes have been harder than those of household servants who were sure, at least, of food and shelter. Citizenship was a prized possession, to be earned with difficulty by those not born to it. An auxiliary soldier, for example, was rewarded with his citizen's certificate on retirement, after twenty-five years of service. Unlike a legionary officer he did not receive a gift of land when he left the service, and if (like Germanicus) he desired a villa, he would have to find a way to pay for it privately.

The Romano-British background in this book has been derived from exhibitions, excavations, interviews with experts and a wide variety of (sometimes contradictory) pictorial and written sources. This is, however, a work of fiction, and although I have done my best to create an accurate picture, there is no claim to total academic authenticity. The existence of the British governor Pertinax, and the attempt by an army faction to have him accept nomination as emperor in place of Commodus, is historical, as is the existence and (basic) geography of the major town named in the story, Glevum (modern Gloucester), Corinium (Cirencester), Isca (Caerleon) and Eboracum (York). The god Nodens was an important local deity, and the remains of a substantial temple to him can be found at Lydney.

All other characters and places in the story are the product of my imagination, as are the details of the festival of Mars.

Relata refero. Ne Iupiter quidem omnibus placet. (I only tell you what I heard. Jove himself can't please everybody.)

ROMAN BRITAIN

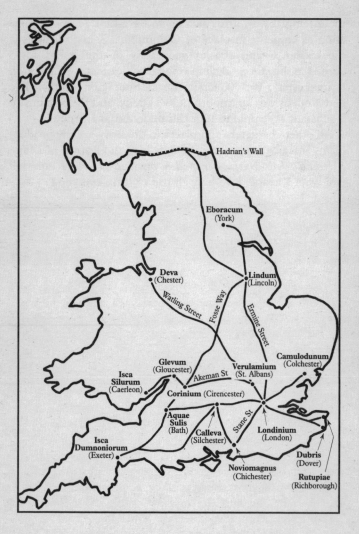

Chapter One

As soon as I heard the voice, I knew there would be trouble.

'Libertus? Libertus, the pavement maker? Are you there old friend?' There was no mistaking those patrician Roman tones. Marcus Aurelius Septimus was here, come to my dingy workshop in person.

I was kneeling on the floor cutting pieces of tile for a mosaic at the time, but I clambered to my feet instantly. 'Old friend' I might be, but nobody – least of all a mere freedman – kept the provincial governor's personal representative waiting, at least not if he was wise. Inwardly, though, I was cursing. I should have made a better sacrifice at the festival of Mars yesterday. It was only the third hour of the morning and already things were not looking good.

The arrival of Marcus worried me. Usually if he wants anyone he simply summons them to him. This is not a part of Glevum where wealthy Romans normally come calling – no sign here of the neat paved streets and fine buildings of the *colonia*, the retirement colony for veterans. This workshop is in the teeming, undisciplined outskirts, beyond the original walls, in one of the straggling, ramshackle streets which have sprung up around the town in the last hundred years. Even the

1

name 'workshop' dignifies the place – the back half of a poky room screened off from the open shop-front by a rough wooden partition, and shared with the fire, the cooking bench and the rickety staircase to the living quarters above – though the word impresses the customers. And doubtless increases the rent.

So I didn't have to be a rune reader to know that this visit spelt trouble. My own fault, I thought wryly, as I stripped off my leather apron and shook the marble chips from my hair and eyebrows. I had been tempting the Fates: humming to myself, permitting myself to be happy, or as happy as a middle-aged ex-slave has any right to be. There was food in the cupboard, oil in the lamps, and as soon as this mosaic border was finished (it shouldn't take more than a day or two) there would be money in my pouch. I was already making plans. I would indulge myself and take the time to walk the twenty-odd miles to Corinium: if one kept to the military road there was usually someone about, marching troops or army supply carts, so even a lone traveller was relatively safe from brigands and bears. I was looking for my wife. I wanted to trace a slavegirl called Gwellia who, I learned, had been sold at the slave market there a year or two before. Gwellia had been my wife's name. It was a faint hope, after twenty years of searching, but enough to bring a tune to my lips, especially when the day was fine and warm, and autumnal sunshine was slanting through the window-space, turning the dust-filled air to gold. So, I was humming.

But the gods had other plans. Here was Marcus calling me. Calling me 'old friend' too, which was a dangerous sign. That meant he wanted something.

'Old' friend was right, I thought, glancing at myself in the beaten copper of a pan. My knees creaked, the lines were etched in my face, and my hair was grey enough, even without the sprinkling of marble dust. Would Gwellia recognise me even if I found her, I wondered. Or I her? She was a mere girl when they snatched her from me. She would be thirty-eight now, and I was ten years older. Already older than most men in Glevum.

But my visitor was waiting, and I could hardly go out to greet him covered in dust. I picked up the amphora from the table and poured water over my head and hands to rinse them – a waste of good clean drinking water, but it couldn't be helped. I rubbed my hands hastily through my hair and straightened my tunic. Showing a decent respect for men like Marcus Aurelius Septimus is one of the more obvious secrets of long life.

'Master, hurry up. Here's Marcus come to see you.' That was Junio, my servant-cum-shopboy, scurrying around the partition from the front shop.

'I know.' I felt unreasonably irritated. 'Fetch him a seat.'

Junio grinned. 'You think I'd leave the imperial buttocks standing?' Marcus is rumoured to be related – distantly – to the emperor himself. There is probably no truth in it; Aurelius is one of the commonest clan names in the empire. Why should a cousin of Commodus consent to kick his heels in rain-sodden Britannia so far from the intrigues and comforts of Rome? But Marcus did come to this province with the governor and he has never denied the rumour. So, remembering that two previous legates to Britain have ended up as emperors in the past, I see that this household always treats him as if he were of imperial blood. One can never be too careful.

'I've put out the folding chair for him,' Junio said, keeping his voice low. We were speaking Latin, as we always did: Junio had been bred in captivity and, like me, found that the language of his masters came more easily to his lips than his native tongue. Now, however, he didn't want Marcus to overhear. 'And a stool for you. A lower one, of course. Now, should I bring some wine? It's the amphora he gave you himself, at Janus feast, so he can't complain of the quality.'

The boy was impudent, but I found myself grinning back. 'Do that. And mind you don't sample it on the way.' I aimed a playful cuff at his ear, and went out to the front of the shop. The shop-front was open to the street and the sudden light made me blink.

Marcus certainly looked imperial enough, sitting there with his jewellery and his dazzling white patrician toga, with its deep purple stripe; conspicuously affluent among the dusty piled stone-heaps of my shop-front and the noise and smells of the street. He looked so out of place there, between the tannery on the one side and the tallow makers on the other, that the passers-by, market women and street urchins and pie sellers, nudged each other and stared as they jostled past, and one man, leading a donkey weighed down with hides for the tanner's, was so busy gazing at Marcus that he missed his footing and sat down heavily in the mire.

Marcus, too, was surreptitiously examining the soles of his fine soft leather shoes. Stained and wet, I noticed, from the filth of the muddy gutters. That would not please him. Marcus was a fastidious dresser.

He looked up when he saw me and, managing a wan smile, extended a ringed hand. I knelt ostentatiously to press it, wishing devoutly that he had summoned me to him, as usual, not only for his sake, but so that I could make my obeisance on the comfort of Roman paving instead of having to kneel here among the stone chips.

'Libertus!' he said warmly, after a painful interval. 'Longinus Flavius Libertus, it is good to see you.' I rose thankfully to my feet, and sat on the stool as he indicated, but I was warier than ever. Using all my three names, the badge of Roman citizenship I had acquired with my manumission, was to accord me a most unaccustomed dignity. Longinus was my slave-name, I had adopted Flavius for my dear master, but I was glad enough to be called by my new cognomen, Libertus, 'the freedman'. My own name I had lost, years ago, with my freedom and my wife. But here was Marcus giving me my full legal title. Whatever he wanted, it was even more serious than I'd thought. What mischief were the Fates planning for me now?

'Excellence?' It wasn't my place to say more. Marcus would come to the subject in his own good time.

He was working up to it, one could see, fidgeting with his brooch and buckle and the seals on his finger; a good-looking boy, with his short, fairish curls, intelligent, hooded blue eyes and thin, ascetic face.

'So then, my friend, how goes the pavement?'

'Well, thank you, excellence.' I looked at him in surprise. Ordinarily conversation with Marcus began with a chronicle of his doings, or detailed exploits of the Fourteenth Legion, in which he had a cousin, and in which it was necessary to show the liveliest interest. Or, at the very least, the gossip from the Glevum guard-barracks: who had been promoted, who flogged, who found outside of the curfew hours cavorting with a girl – or boy. But a question about my pavement? Was this a delicate way of reminding me that I owed the Didio commission to his patronage? I said carefully, 'It is almost finished, and I believe Caius Flavius Didio is pleased with it.'

Marcus nodded. 'He is delighted. I saw him at the bathhouse yesterday and he was telling me of it. The finest paved courtyard in the Insula Britannica he says. He will pay you well.'

'Thanks to you, excellence.'

Marcus fiddled with his seals. 'But, Libertus, I have need of your advice. You remember Crassus?'

'Crassus? Crassus Claudius Germanicus?' That was a foolish question. What other Crassus could it possibly be? Another recent commission which Marcus had secured for me. 'Is he satisfied with the pavement in his new . . . librarium?' I hesitated deliberately over the word, and glanced at Marcus.

It was rather daring of me. Crassus was a Roman citizen and a wealthy one too. As a retired centurion from an auxiliary regiment he had earned his citizenship on retirement, as all conscript officers did after twenty-five years. He was looked down on, of course, by the 'old blood' but having acquired a thick skin along with his considerable fortune, he had bought up a tract of land near Glevum and built himself a villa to equal that of any patrician ex-legionary. A boor and a bully he might be, but the man had money and status and it was not for me to question it if he chose to call that tiny cell a 'librarium' simply because he had acquired half-a-dozen manuscripts in pots. Marcus heartily disliked the man, but my irony risked a rebuke.

I was safe. Marcus was laughing. He said, 'It was absurd. Crassus paid such a price for those manuscripts, but if one had given him laundry lists for the fullers, copied out on vellum, he would have been just as pleased with them. I presume the man went to school, like everyone else, but I am sure he never learned to read more than the company orders, and never opened a scroll for pleasure in his life. But he was very determined on his librarium pavement, I seem to recall.'

I nodded. Marcus wasn't really asking me, he had been present himself when the mosaic was ordered.

'Wanted it in a hurry, too,' Marcus went on, 'before his brother should visit. Did you manage to finish it in time?'

'I did. I finished it a fortnight ago. He professed himself very satisfied.' I did not add that I was never more pleased to finish a pavement in my life. I had scarcely seen my employer, of course, one rarely did on these commissions, but the whole household lived in terror of their master, and the once or twice I had glimpsed him myself had certainly sufficed. Crassus Claudius Germanicus was a singularly unpleasant man.

'Ah.' Junio had appeared with the tray, and Marcus took a goblet absently, and waited without glancing at the boy until it was filled. He sipped it appreciatively. 'A fair wine. Roman, is it? You didn't buy this from the market sellers.'

'Your gift, excellence.'

I took my goblet in turn, and sipped at it, though I had never learned to like the sour taste of wine. I preferred mead, or the honest ale or apple-beer of my youth. I waited, but Marcus said nothing more until Junio had disappeared. I was surprised. Marcus – brought up with a household of slaves – usually ignored the presence of servants.

Not on this occasion. Marcus watched him go. 'That slave of yours,' he said coolly, 'can you trust him?'

'Implicitly,' I said. 'I would trust him with my life.' That was true. I have done so, in fact, on several occasions.

'Because,' Marcus went on, as if I had not spoken, 'it

may be necessary for you to be absent for a day or two, and people may be asking for you. Friends, clients, acquaintances . . .'

I sighed inwardly. Not for my friends; a native nobleman who has been captured as a slave and been cut off from his family does not acquire many friends. But I had 'advised' Marcus before, and I was aware that his 'day or two' was more likely to be at least a week. That was the price one paid for having a wealthy patron. So much for Corinium, I thought, and there was still that pavement of Didio's to be completed.

I managed a tight smile. 'There may be customers, certainly.'

'Well, you know what Glevum is, Libertus. Rumours everywhere, and this is one occasion when I would prefer that your movements were not the subject of public gossip. Perhaps your slave could tell callers that you are away . . . have left town, on urgent business perhaps.'

My mind was racing. I did indeed know Glevum. Garrison for the local guard-force, and the chosen retirement place for every wealthy ex-legionary in the business. A model of Roman local government, and therefore, naturally, a hotbed of political and social undercurrents of all kinds.

I looked at Marcus warily. 'That could be arranged. And Caius Didio? He will be anxious about his mosaic.' I meant that I was anxious about it myself.

'Leave him to me,' Marcus said.

I nodded. I could guess now why Marcus had come to see me, and I did not like what I guessed. I did not like it at all. I had first met Marcus after the death of a wealthy landowner nearby, a politically sensitive matter, which I investigated for him, and since then Marcus had always turned to me when he discovered some 'accident' or fraud which appeared to compromise the dignity of Rome. My help in these matters, he always says, first earned me his protection and patronage, and my refusal to ask for money won his respect. I had an uncomfortable feeling, now, that I was about to be given another opportunity to win his respect.

'There is trouble, excellence?' I prompted, hoping that my dismay was not written in my face.

If so, Marcus was too preoccupied to read it. 'Trouble, yes. You are perceptive. It concerns Crassus. The aediles have been to see me.'

'The aediles? The junior magistrates?' For a moment, I turned cold. The aediles were concerned with commercial matters, and they could be ruthless. Marcus had many enemies amongst the market informers. They would enjoy making 'an example' of his protégé. I swallowed the rest of my wine in one gulp, before I could trust my voice to say, 'Has Crassus complained of me?'

I had reason to be wary. That pavement which Crassus had wanted laid with such indecent speed had not been of my own design nor even worked from a pattern book. I had been encouraging Junio to learn the art of pavement-making, and this was a small mosaic of his: a rather crude *Cave Canem* mounted on linen backing, a sort of apprentice-piece. When Crassus Germanicus had wanted an almost-instant pavement, it was that mosaic – with the lettering quickly altered from *Beware of the Dog* to *Art is Long* – which I had hastily cemented into place in his librarium.

'Has he complained of me?' I asked again. It had seemed amusingly ironic at the time, that ravening dog gracing the floor of the so-called reading-room; Crassus even seemed particularly pleased with it. But suddenly it seemed much less funny. 'It was pre-patterned work, but it was the only way to manage it in such a short time. He wanted the floor finished and ready in weeks.' I was gabbling in self-defence. 'It took me almost the whole time to flatten and prepare the place. The slaves had dug it over roughly and brought in a fresh layer of clean soil – it had been the slavegirls' room, you remember, and the floor was just trodden earth – but the floor was still hopelessly uneven. I had only enough time to roll out the mosaic and make it fit by adding an extra border at one end.'

Marcus inclined his head. 'No, he has not complained. On the contrary, he was bragging about it in the marketplace. You did well to finish it at all, especially with an additional border. I don't know how you managed.'

By using a template for the border pattern, was the answer – cutting the shape in wood and tiling up to it, and then filling in the space – but I wasn't going to tell him that. It had taken me a long time to work out a usable system, and it was a secret I guarded jealously. One day, perhaps, I would tell Junio. But not yet. In the meantime I was content to allow myself to breathe out. I had been holding my breath ever since Marcus mentioned the aediles.

'Why he wanted a librarium out there, off the back courtyard, and didn't include one in the public rooms in the first place, I can't imagine.' Marcus drained his wine. 'But then, I suppose, his brother came, and it was important to impress him. Anyway, he was satisfied. Has he paid you?'

'No.'

Marcus said, 'Ah!'

My heart sank. That was it then – not a complaint against me by Crassus, but a complaint against Crassus by his creditors. That was a blow. That commission had been worth many sesterces. But why all this talk of secrecy and discretion? I made a bold guess. 'So what do you want of me, excellence? Has Crassus Germanicus disappeared?'

Marcus looked at me, the hooded eyes very shrewd. 'Yes,' he said. 'Or no. He attended the festival of Mars yesterday . . .'

I nodded. 'I went out to see the procession myself.' Musicians, priests, sacrificial animals. The whole regional garrison, rank after rank, and following them, less firm of step but prouder than ever, the veterans: first the men of the Second Augusta, the Glevum 'colony', and then the retired officers from other legions and auxiliary regiments. And all of them, the whole procession from first to last, wearing the hammered mask of Mars. Even for a non-Roman like me it was a stirring sight: the breastplates and standards glinting in the sunshine, the plumes bobbing, and the heavy-soled hobnailed sandals ringing in unison on the paving stones. 'Quite a spectacle.' That was an understatement. I had felt like a child again, tiptoe amidst the jostling crowds – even the slaves had been given a holiday – eating hot pies from the street sellers with Junio, and pastries so sweet that the warm honey oozed out between our fingers as we ate.

'I saw Crassus myself,' Marcus said, 'leading a contingent.'

I too had seen the stocky, bull-necked figure striding out among the column of veterans. I said so.

'And that,' Marcus said dramatically, 'is the last time anyone saw him, it seems. He did not return to the villa after the procession. The servants were not unduly worried at first. You know how much feasting there is after the parade, and Crassus loved a feast.'

I nodded. 'A man of expansive appetites.' Germanicus was likely to have drunk himself stupid in some Glevum wineshop, and rolled into bed with a convenient 'barmaid'. I added hopefully, thinking of the money he owed me, 'Perhaps he will turn up, after all.'·

'He did not appear this morning,' Marcus said. 'Nor for lunch. In the end they sent out to find him. All his usual haunts – the bars, the baths, the market – but without· success. No one had seen him since the procession. Or his personal slave either. They both seemed to have disappeared.'

Something in his tone caught me. 'Seemed? Why the past tense, Marcus?'

'An hour ago the slaves went to stoke the boiler – the underfloor heating had been allowed to burn down over the holiday. They found a body in the hypocaust. That is what the aediles came to tell me. It will be a matter for the governor's court, of course, not the local ones. Crassus was a Roman citizen. But it is a delicate business. My spies tell me that Crassus Germanicus may have been . . . shall we say . . . a supporter of the army.'

This time, I groaned aloud. I knew what that meant. Commodus was not the most popular of emperors, and though he had taken the title 'Britannicus' most of the army here was in ferment against him, and had imperial candidates of their own, ready to step in when the time was right. The last thing I wanted was to be investigating that kind of political intrigue. If Marcus got me involved in this, I could give up worrying about getting to Corinium next week. Ask the wrong questions here and

I might never get to Corinium at all – or anywhere else either. And I had no desire to visit the netherworld.

'Excellence,' I pleaded, 'this is a question for the law officer.'

Marcus ignored me. 'I am on my way to the villa now. And I want you to accompany me. You see things which other men do not, Libertus. I need your pattern-maker's mind.' He favoured me with his most winning smile.

I said nothing.

'I sent word to expect us,' Marcus went on, as though there had never been the remotest likelihood of my refusing – as I suppose there wasn't. Marcus was a powerful man.

'Perhaps there is no mystery to solve,' I said, without conviction. 'Crassus Germanicus is a man of brutal temper. He has killed a man, and then run away. That seems the logical conclusion.'

'I said so myself,' Marcus replied, 'but the aediles thought otherwise. Still, we shall go and see. My driver awaits us. Fetch your cloak, and your strigil if you need one, and give your slave some story about being called away. A private commission for me, perhaps. That should put a stop to any rumours.'

A strigil, I thought. To use in the bathhouse so that I could wash and shave. Marcus did not expect me to return home in a hurry. I got to my feet.

'I will fetch my things.'

As I tied them into a cloth, I told Junio exactly where I was going and what I was doing. It was the only defiance I could think of. Besides, I felt easier that way. Then I went back to Marcus.

'All right, excellence,' I said, wearily. 'Let's go and find this body.'

Chapter Two

I had donned a toga, of course, as the strict letter of the law demanded. All male Roman citizens throughout the empire are supposed to wear one 'in public', but often I didn't bother. The edict is not much enforced, and a man in my position is more likely to be stopped and questioned on suspicion of unlawfully wearing the badge of citizenship, than for failing to wear it. Besides, frankly, I dislike the things: tricky to put on, hard to clean, and impossible to work in, because (as you will know if you have ever worn one) they force on the wearer that measured, upright gait which is the hallmark of Romans everywhere, otherwise the whole thing undrapes itself. But I do have one, for formal occasions – useful for impressing Roman clients – and today I was accompanying Marcus. Occasions do not come much more formal than that.

There were advantages, too, of a kind. The milling throngs in the street stood back deferentially to let us pass and the tanner's man – who saw me every day in my simple tunic and cloak – goggled openly. Only a plain unbleached white-wool toga, of course, none of Marcus' patrician stripes, but transformation enough. I sighed. Next time they wanted a contribution to maintain the neighbourhood fire-watch (one of the delights of living between a tannery and a candlemaker's was the constant interesting possibility of conflagration) they would expect an extra few denarii from me.

When we got to our transport, though, I was glad of my warm garment. Marcus had brought along a courier gig, light and fast, but desperately draughty compared to the covered imperial carriage I had been expecting. The driver was standing beside it, holding the horse, looking bored and perished to the bone in his thin tunic. I followed Marcus into the gig, as gracefully as my toga would allow, and gave the lad a sympathetic smile. It is one of the less recognised miseries of being a slave, that everlasting waiting.

The driver seemed to take my smile as an encouragement and we set off at a clip which set the gig bouncing. We took the shortest route, back through the town, and I appreciated once again the advantages of rank. No humble mortal like myself could bring wheeled transport inside the walls in daylight, or blithely propose to take precedence on the military roads. But with Marcus anything was possible.

Out of the East Gate, skirting the narrow tenements of the straggling northern suburb, away from the river marshes and up towards the high road that runs along the escarpment. Towards Corinium, I thought with a pang. It is a good road, kept up by local taxes for the imperial post – the military messengers – and, like all Roman roads, paved and straight. We made good progress, out past the burial sites which line the roadside these days (the Romans have made it illegal to bury the dead within the city), and were soon into open country.

We had seen nothing on the road, beyond a lumbering farm cart and a lone cloaked messenger galloping hell-for-leather towards Glevum, but presently there was a distant glint of bobbing metal ahead. I saw Marcus grimace. A cohort of soldiers on the march; auxiliaries recently relieved from Isca, probably. They would keep up a good pace, but they filled the road, and with their supply carts and camp followers up ahead (wives were not allowed, but many soldiers had families all the same) the whole procession could straggle for miles.

'There is a back way to Crassus' estate,' I said doubtfully. 'I learned it when I was staying at the villa. It is shorter, but the road is poor.'

That was an understatement. The road is villainous, one of the narrow, winding, unsurfaced tracks which used to serve as local thoroughfares before the Romans came. As a pedestrian, struggling to and from the villa with my mosaic pieces on a handcart, I had rather enjoyed its melancholy charm. There was even a ruined roundhouse halfway along it, presumably the homestead of the original native farmer from whom Crassus had 'acquired' the land.

In a fast gig, the journey promised to be exacting rather than melancholy.

Marcus had no such qualms. 'We'll take it,' he said, and I instructed the driver where to turn.

It *was* exacting – more exacting than a Roman tax-collector. We lurched perilously down the rocky track, the gig threatening to overset at every turn and with overhanging branches clawing at our faces, until we shuddered down a final hill and joined up with Crassus' wide and gravelled farm lane. We forked through the left-hand gate, round to the back of the estate into the farm and farmyard. Unchallenged. The usual gatekeeper was not at his post, and there were no land-slaves tending the animals or working the estate. Only a tethered goat looked up at us in surprise.

It was almost eerie.

We took the gig right to the inner gateway, and left the driver to wait (again). The gate was open, and we walked straight in, past the heaped woodpiles for the furnaces and the fruit trees neatly planted against the wall. We had almost reached the door to the inner garden before someone came scurrying to greet us: a big raw-boned man, wringing his hands like a soothsayer prophesying doom. I recognised him at once, as much from the fluttering hands as from the blue tunic: I had met him when I was laying the librarium pavement. Andretha, the foreman of the slaves.

He was breathless with self-justification. 'I have rounded everyone up, excellence. In the inner courtyard. The aediles left a guard.'

He led the way. They were all there. Not just the household, but anyone who had happened to be passing by when the discovery was made; all waiting, trembling with cold, fear and the bitter draught which always blew through the colonnades. I remembered it vividly. The librarium was in a tiny room leading off that courtyard.

Why is it that retired officers, especially foreign ones, insist on building country villas like this, on the Roman style? Lofty columns and courtyard gardens fed by the rain from the high sloping roofs might be very welcome and cool in the heat of Rome. Here, in the wet, cold winters of the Insula Britannica, despite all the paintings on the surrounding walls and the statues in little arbours, the effect was damp, draughty and dank. No wonder Crassus had arranged to have a private hypocaust and bathhouse installed. It wasn't just a sign of status; the underfloor heating made the front of the house – the owner's quarters – tolerably habitable.

'They are all here, all the household!' Andretha bowed

and bobbed his obeisance like a twig in a whirlpool. 'And anyone passing by the gate. I had them stopped and brought here for you, most respected excellence. One can't be too careful.'

I glanced at the huddled group. The outsiders first. Two turnip sellers, fuming at losing a day's trade at the market. A pedlar. A beggar. A soothsayer. Even, incongruously, a travelling merchant and his plump wife, conspicuous in British embroidered wool.

Behind them, the household. I recognised some of them slightly. Land-slaves in hessian aprons, rough tunics and with leather 'boots' roughly shaped and bound around their feet with strings; cleanshaven houseslaves in neat blue tunics; ageing slavewomen in shapeless sacks; and, in the corner, the two short-skirted, perfumed slavegirls with haunted faces and braided hair. The guards smirked, obviously imagining only too clearly what duties those two performed for gross, ugly Germanicus.

'They are all waiting, excellence,' Andretha was saying, over and over like a Vestal chant.

'I will speak to them later,' Marcus said. 'First, let us see this body.'

I could have shown Marcus to the spot myself. Out of the courtyard and round to the side of the house where the boiler room lay. Another large guard with a stave was standing at the entrance to the stoke room.

Marcus gestured him aside and we went in. It was dark and stuffy. The air was heavy with the nauseous, unmistakable smell of death, and still oppressively warm, although the fire had been allowed to die more than a day ago. The room was empty: nothing there but the great heaps of fuel and the open entrance to the furnace, its white embers still faintly glowing.

Nothing, that is, except for the body of a man. He was dressed in centurion's uniform – leather-skirted doublet, breast-armour, groin protector, greaves and sandals. A sword and dagger still hung at the belt and there were torcs of office around his neck. A beaten brass mask of Mars leaned drunkenly against the wall, and one dead arm still trailed against the crested helmet as if in some final gesture of farewell. The other hand, and the head, or what remained of them, were thrust into the open furnace. The effect was obscene.

'Examine it, Libertus.' Marcus seemed unable to bring himself to look too closely at that charred skull, the blackened, fleshless bones which had once been fingers and hand.

I bent forward and lowered the lifeless trunk gently to the floor. The legs and arms had been shaved, recently by the look of it, but the torso was short, stocky and disconcertingly hairy. The features had been consumed by the flame, but there was no mistaking the ring on the charred finger. Crassus' seal. I had seen it many times. Marcus, too.

There was one obvious conclusion to be drawn. Marcus drew it.

'By Mithras,' he exclaimed, 'the aediles were right! It is Germanicus! No wonder they couldn't find him. So! All we have to do now is find someone who wanted him dead.' He grinned at me as he spoke – that description probably encompassed almost everyone in Glevum. 'All right, let's go and see what these people have to tell us. We'll see them in the triclinium. I'm sure there will be a brazier in there, and if this looks like taking too long we can have some food served in comfort.'

'Naturally, excellence.' Andretha led the way. It wouldn't occur to Marcus that there might be difficulties for anyone in these arrangements. With the other servants under guard, Andretha would have to light the brazier and organise the food himself, to say nothing of the problems of the waiting passers-by who would have families concerned for their safety.

The dining room was a fine room. I had seen it before – painted plaster walls and a mosaic floor in a geometric pattern (not one of mine, but I recognised good work-manship). Marcus reclined on one of the gilded couches, and I perched on a bronze stool nearby.

The questioning began. The 'outsiders' were easily disposed of. The merchant and his wife had never visited Glevum before and had lodged at a nearby inn the night before. There would be a dozen witnesses who could swear to their movements. They had left their lodgings only an hour earlier, and it would have needed that time to get here. It was the same with the turnip growers; it was impossible for them to have been at the villa before the body was discovered.

The pedlar and the beggar were no more helpful. Marcus had them flogged, on the off-chance, but it did nothing to refresh their memories and in the end he let them go. The soothsayer did claim that he had important information from the omens, but when this turned out to be that 'the dead man was possessed of secret enemies' Marcus was so infuriated that he ordered him marched to Glevum and locked up for a week, though not in any expectation of learning anything more to the purpose.

We saw Andretha next. He was anxious and trembl-ing, swearing that the murderer could not possibly be anyone in the villa. I could understand why. Strictly, if a master was murdered by one of his own slaves, the whole household could be put to death, although the last time that sentence had been carried out in Rome there had been a major riot, so the law was not always implemented these days – provided the individual culprit could be identified. The chief slave, however, might still be found guilty of negligence, and he could pay for that with his life in some interestingly excruciating ways.

'No one in the household,' he protested again.

'All the same,' Marcus said, turning to me, 'any one of the servants might have done it, and no doubt most of them hated him. I suppose the land-slaves are less likely. They don't usually come to the house so it would be difficult for any of them to hide the body in the hypocaust.'

'Impossible, excellence,' Andretha said, hastily. 'If one of those roughly dressed fellows came anywhere too near the villa I'd have him caught at once and punished.'

'Unless,' I said thoughtfully, 'the house was empty, as it was during the procession.' Andretha gave me a poisonous look.

Marcus frowned. 'But during the procession, Crassus Germanicus was alive. I saw him with my own eyes.'

'And as soon as it was over,' Andretha rushed in with relief, 'all the household slaves came back to the villa together in the farm cart. No one could have come faster. I saw to that. I was in a hurry to make sure everything was properly prepared for Crassus' return.'

I could believe that. Failure to have the brazier lit and food and drink waiting would have resulted in someone feeling his master's lash. Crassus was not a tolerant man.

'I swear to you,' Andretha said, wringing his fingers, 'there were servants on watch for his return all night. I don't believe anyone could have come to the villa without being seen or heard.'

'And yet,' Marcus said dryly, 'someone did come to the villa. Someone brought the body back and put it in the hypocaust. If there was a watch, you'd have thought somebody might have noticed.'

Andretha was so terrified by this suggestion that he had failed in his duty, that he could not have made a sensible answer if he tried. He didn't try. He simply spread his hands hopelessly, as if there was no sensible answer he could make.

'All the slaves returned together, you say?' I put in.

Andretha nodded. 'Except Daedalus, Crassus' personal slave. Of course we expected that. He would have stayed with Crassus, to fetch horses or wine, and carry torches. See him home, guard him if necessary. Only, of course, he hasn't returned either.'

'So where,' Marcus wanted to know, 'is Daedalus now?'

An anguished look spread across Andretha's face. 'I don't know. Nobody knows. He was supposed to stay with Crassus. Do you suppose Daedalus killed him, at the procession?' He was grasping at straws. If Germanicus was murdered in Glevum, it was not his responsibility. His duty to guard his master against all comers was within the estate.

'As I remember,' I said, 'Daedalus was promised his freedom at the next moon.' The man had been boasting of the fact when I was at the villa. It had struck me as odd, at the time. Crassus was not the sort of man to manumit a good slave out of kindness of heart.

Andretha nodded eagerly. 'That is true.'

'Then surely,' Marcus said, 'Daedalus had less to gain than anyone from Crassus' death? He will be sold on now, or left to the next owner with the rest of the estate.'

'Or perhaps he saw his master killed, and fled in a panic?' Andretha babbled on. 'There are always brigands and cut-throats at these processions. That is more likely, if he failed to guard him . . .' You could almost see hope rising to Andretha's face. Cowardice from a personal bodyguard was not his responsibility either. 'Yes, excellence, it must have been that.'

I was thinking aloud. 'Then why put the body in the hypocaust? Why not just abandon it in the town? Why would Daedalus, of all people, bring it all the way back to the villa, where it was certain to be discovered and bring suspicion on him? Come to that, why would anyone? If a killer wants to dispose of a body, why not just push it into the river or bury it somewhere? Why drag it back to the villa and put it in the furnace? Unless Crassus did manage to come back here, somehow, and the murder took place in the villa after all.'

'He couldn't have done.' Andretha flashed me another venomous glance. 'There were people looking out for him from the moment the procession was over.'

'Well,' Marcus said, 'let's talk to them and see if we can throw some light on the matter. Starting with the gatekeeper, I think.'

Andretha went out, and Marcus turned to me. 'It is just as the aediles told me. You see why I am concerned? It looks like a political murder. It seems impossible for it to be a mere household affair.'

'Difficult, certainly,' I said. 'I'm sure that if Andretha knew anything about it he would probably have told us. If it was a household murder his one hope of clemency would be to turn informer. But why do you think it is political?'

Marcus looked around, as if the plaster walls might be listening, and said, sheepishly, 'Because Aulus the gatekeeper is an informer of mine. I have never trusted Germanicus – he always had far too much money for a mere auxiliary centurion.'

'He was a great gambler,' I said doubtfully, re-membering tales of several dice parties which had taken place while I was working at the villa. 'And doubtless the dice were on his side. Crassus was the sort of man who would ensure that.'

'He was famous for it,' Marcus said, 'or rather for his unexplained good fortune. Or so Aulus tells me. Apparently the Fates took a kindly hand, even in his army career.'

'Oh?'

'Yes, Crassus remained an optio for a long time. He wanted to be promoted to centurion, he kept grumbling that he was overdue for promotion, but it never happened. They said there was no post available, and then his commanding centurion conveniently died – a little too conveniently, gossip said.'

'You think he killed a senior officer?' I said. 'Surely not! That would be treachery.' I was not debating a moral point; that sort of crime carried an automatic death penalty, and Crassus had been very much alive, at least until recently.

Marcus laughed. 'I don't suppose he did it, in fact. The death was not especially suspicious, the man just suddenly fell ill one night and died. There are always unexpected deaths, through infections or poor food. There were rumours, but Germanicus had witnesses to say he was miles away that night, and he gained his centurion's baton. But whispers persisted among the company. At least, so Aulus tells me.'

'So what are you suggesting? That somebody believed the story and killed Crassus for revenge?'

'No. In that case someone would have stabbed him years ago – and it is probably nothing but rumour, anyway. If there had been any real suspicion he would have been executed then and there. But it gives some indication of the man. People believed it of him. And he may have old enemies, or old confederates, in the army still. Aulus informs me that twice in the last few weeks armed soldiers have come to the villa at night and Germanicus has gone out to meet them – having first ordered his gatekeeper away on an errand.'

That was seriously bad news. Even I knew that sections of the army wanted to overthrow the emperor and instate the legionary legate, Priscus, in his stead, while other sections favoured the governor, Pertinax, for the imperial crown. The complication, from my point of view, was that these two treasonable alternatives were not politically equal. Marcus was the governor's personal representative. He rose or fell with Pertinax. No wonder he was concerned about possible political conspiracy.

'How do you know this?' I asked, warily. If he was right I stood a good chance of ending up in the hypocaust myself.

'Aulus had the presence of mind to keep watch, and saw them. One man came each time, and Germanicus went out and was whispering to each of them in the lane. But here is Aulus, he can tell you himself.'

Aulus was unwilling. He was a great, coarse, lumbering bear of a man with a leering manner, shifting eyes and a nervous tongue which licked out and moistened his lips as he spoke. Serving two masters is always a dangerous task, but he told his story at last, glancing occasionally around him in case Andretha was lurking in the shadows. In essence, though, it was precisely as Marcus had said. He could add nothing, although he hedged the story round with excuses: it had been too dark to see in detail, and he had been too far away to hear. At least two visits, though, he was certain of that. One three days before the procession, and one a week or two earlier. A centurion on both occasions. He was unable to say if it was the same man.

About the disappearance of Crassus, though, he was adamant. It was exactly as Andretha had reported, and he knew absolutely nothing more about it. By the time Marcus let him go, Aulus was sweating.

'He's hiding something,' Marcus said. 'But we'll get the truth out of him. By flogging if necessary.'

I shook my head. 'I doubt it, excellence. By all means interview the household, but I don't believe flogging will help. No one saw this, except the murderer himself, and he won't tell you. Perhaps we should be asking in the town? Looking for someone who saw Crassus after the procession?'

Marcus frowned. 'Well, perhaps. But remember, I expect discretion.'

I sighed. The implications of that did not escape me. Marcus had no intention of demeaning himself by interrogating the townspeople at random. He expected me to do that, when I had finished here. In the meantime precious time would be passing.

'There may be someone who saw Daedalus, too. He is a missing slave, after all.'

That roused him. A runaway slave is a serious matter. 'You think he did it? You know the man, you were in this household for weeks.'

I laughed, shortly. 'I hardly knew him. I was in the librarium. A man who works for Crassus has little time for gossiping.'

'But you knew his reputation?'

I did. Crassus' favourite slave; clever, shrewd, talented – he had a gift for mimicry which made him a favourite for 'fashionable' entertainments – but ambitious too. 'He could have done it. He is calculating enough. But he had been promised his freedom. He may even have received it – it is not unknown for men to free their slaves at the festival, as a sort of sacrifice.'

'And then he turned on his ex-master? It is hard to see why, although Andretha might hope so. If Crassus was killed by a free man, it changes everything.'

'Why else would he disappear?'

Marcus raised his eyebrows, and voiced what both of us had been thinking. 'Suppose Germanicus threatened to refuse him, after all? Changed his mind about manumission?'

'And Daedalus killed him in a fury? Murder in the heat of the moment, that I can understand. But why bring the body back? And how? Dragging a corpse for miles is to invite discovery, and anyway they could not have returned here before the others. Crassus was in the procession. He would have had to wait till the end of the sacrifices, and they had no transport. The servants had the farm cart, and you heard Andretha – Crassus intended to hire horses when he had finished feasting.'

'He didn't do that,' Marcus put in. 'The aediles have already made enquiries. No one hired a horse, or a carriage. There were none free to hire immediately after the procession. He and Daedalus would have been on foot – unless they stole a nag. Or borrowed one. There was some itinerant pilgrim who passed this way on a mule, but they didn't hire that either, he was seen trotting back with it long before the festival was over. No thefts have been reported.'

'In any case,' I said, 'a man who wanted to hide a

corpse could hardly have risked stealing a horse as well. He'd have had half the countryside after him. No, I fear you are right. We must try to trace those armed soldiers. But – let us listen to the household first. There may be something we can glean from them.'

But no one – not the lute player, not the cooks, not the house-slaves or the dancing girls – had anything to add to the story we had heard already. Crassus set out early for the procession with Daedalus and had insisted on walking the three or four miles to Glevum because the day was fine and he intended feasting afterwards. It sounded daunting to me, walking miles in full armour and then taking part in a procession, but presumably it was nothing to an old soldier trained to march all day carrying his entire kit.

The servants had all travelled to Glevum together on the farm cart, watched the procession, and come home the same way, and no one had seen or heard anything of Crassus until the two men who stoked the hypocaust went down at midday to relight the furnace.

Marcus questioned them harshly, but they were unshakable. They had gone to the feast with the others and, having been granted a holiday from stoking, had spent the afternoon chopping logs for the extra woodpile in full view of the slaves carrying water and tending the inner gardens. The stoke-hole was round at the side of the villa and, with the furnaces out, no one had been near it. Equally, no one could have got to it from outside without being seen.

'So, we are back to politics,' Marcus said, over the bowl of stew and fish sauce which the kitchen had finally produced. 'It seems nobody in the household did it. Or all of them did.' He looked at me enquiringly.

I said nothing. I was trying to spoon up my stew

without actually swallowing any of the fish sauce – that horrible fermented stuff with anchovies in it that the Romans seem to put on everything. Furthermore, I was trying to do so without Marcus noticing. I gave him a wan smile.

Marcus said languidly, 'Or perhaps Crassus' death is just some punishment by the gods. It was the feast of Mars after all.' He finished his own stew and pushed the plate away. 'Well, I'll leave it to you, Libertus. I've done all I can here. Send to me, if you discover anything. I suppose we must allow Andretha to make arrangements for the funeral procession, so we will meet in three days, at least. In the meantime, I'll ask at the guardroom, and see if there is any information about those two soldiers. They must have been missed, they were out well after curfew. And now, I must get back to Glevum. My carriage driver will be anxious for his supper.'

Chapter Three

I lay awake for a long time, thinking. Andretha had shown me to a guest bedroom – a proper Roman bed with a stuffed mattress supported on a webbed wood frame – but for all the fine woollen blankets I slept less soundly than I might have done on my own humble pile of reeds and rags. This murder worried me. Not that I mourned Crassus particularly, but I dislike unsolved puzzles. Why bring the body back where it was certain to be found? And how? It seemed an impossible feat. And so deliberate, as though it meant something. Assuming, I thought drowsily, that Crassus hadn't crept home unnoticed and committed suicide by stuffing his own head into the furnace. Or drunk himself stupid, stumbled into the stoke room and died of inhaling smoke.

And then tucked himself tidily into the furnace, perhaps? Besides, how would he have got past the villa gates? A stocky man in full military uniform, complete with shield, spear, helmet and mask, is not easy to miss, especially when the whole household is on the lookout for him. And ten times more so if he is drunk. No, however he had died, someone else had put him in the furnace.

Tired as I was, that jolted me awake. How *had* he

died? You can't just stuff a healthy man into a fire and expect him obligingly to stay there. Yet there were no stab wounds on the body, and the charred skull bore no signs of a blow. Drink perhaps, to render him unconscious? Or poison? That was more likely; Crassus had a strong head for drink. In that case a woman might have done it. It would take a strong man to carry that weight any distance, but even a woman could have managed to hoist the top half of Crassus into the furnace, if he were already lying lifeless at her feet. But (I kept coming back to the same question) why do it at all? His sword was at hand. Even if the man was merely unconscious, why not simply slit his throat and run?

If I knew the answer to that, I thought, I would have the key to everything. And what about those confounded soldiers?

I slept fitfully at last, dreaming of furnaces.

When I awoke, morning was already streaming through Crassus' smart glass windows, the bluish green of their light criss-crossed on the bedcovers by the shadow of the supporting wooden grills. An interesting pattern for a mosaic, I had time to think to myself, before a timid voice addressed me.

'You are awake, citizen? Andretha bade me bring you these.'

It was a young house-slave bearing a wooden carrying-board. I had noticed him when I was here laying the librarium mosaic, a slight, dark-haired youth with dandified manners and a perpetually hunted look. He had interested me then, with his pale skin, anxious brown eyes, and general air of having learned to run backwards more quickly than forwards, but (since a pavement maker has little time for idle gossip, especially when he is working for Crassus in a hurry) I had never spoken to him until the interview yesterday with Marcus. For a moment I could not speak to him even now. I was too busy goggling at the array of toilet accessories laid out on his tray.

A phial of perfumed oil for cleansing, a fine curved strigil to scrape it off with, and even a sponge-stick for more private ablutions, in case I should have omitted to bring my own and wished to visit the latrine. And a fine bowl of rainwater, with fresh blossom floating in it, so that I could rinse my skin.

I grinned. All this luxury and a formal title, too! Andretha was certainly nervous. When I was working at the villa, walking the weary miles to and fro with my twist of bread and cheese in my pouch, I was lucky to get a grunt and permission to rinse the stone-dust off in the garden water-butt.

Now, though, I was no longer a simple craftsman. I was 'citizen', an associate of Marcus, in a toga and an imperial gig, and Andretha must be falling over himself to repair the damage. I suspected he had even troubled to take the chill off the rainwater. I trailed a finger in its cool depths.

The slaveboy misinterpreted the gesture and hastened an apology. 'I am sorry, citizen. We did not like to . . .' He trailed off.

Light the boiler for the bathhouse, he meant. It had not occurred to me. Even in my slave days I had never lived in a villa grand enough to have its own bathhouse. But of course Crassus had one. It was the kind of display of wealth and Romanness which he particularly enjoyed – and which, since he was ambitious, he probably needed. A citizen who possesses property in excess of 400,000 sesterces is, of course, eligible for election to the ranks of the *equites* and Crassus would have loved to become a knight. A display of expensive possessions was a first step on that ladder.

Hence the famous librarium pavement, of course, and the inlaid table I had seen in the atrium. That alone must have been worth a chief's ransom. It probably *was* a chief's ransom. After what Marcus had said about Crassus' reputation in the army, it was not hard to form a shrewd suspicion about how the centurion had amassed his wealth. Strictly illegal of course – serving officers are not permitted to take private bribes – but then, technically the inlaid table was probably not a bribe at all, but a 'gift'. With a sword at their throats it is astonishing how generous people can suddenly feel, especially if Germanicus' reputation for ruthlessness had gone before him.

I realised that the slaveboy was still staring at me, like a nervous mouse.

'Of course you could not stoke the furnace, in the circumstances,' I said lazily, as if a luxurious bodily dip in hot and cold water was a normal daily occurrence for me. 'In any case, I would like to look at the stokehouse again, and see the body before it is moved. There are one or two little details I would like to confirm.'

The boy shook his head apologetically. 'It is too late, citizen. Andretha has had the body brought into the house, to be anointed and washed for the funeral.'

That news brought me out of bed abruptly. 'Already?'

The slave took a step backwards, as if I had offered to strike him. 'Your pardon, citizen. Andretha asked permission last night, and his excellence Marcus Aurelius Septimus agreed. It was done at once. Andretha thought it was unfitting to leave the master in the stokehouse overnight, even under guard.'

I could see his point. It was undignified. And with the

stream running near the villa there was always the risk of rats. Or worse. Even this close to Glevum there were sometimes sightings of wolves or bears. One of them would make short work of a corpse, especially a tastily toasted one.

I nodded doubtfully. 'All the same . . .' Surely Andretha must have guessed that I would wish to examine the place in daylight, with the illumination of the morning sun? Or was this hurry to remove the body *because* he knew that I would want to view the scene?

I looked at the scented rainwater. Of course, this was a matter of life and death to him, so naturally Andretha was over-anxious to please. But was it my imagination, or was he trying a little too desperately, like a man who has something to hide? 'All the same . . .' I said again. I slipped off my under-tunic and began to pummel myself enthusiastically with the oil, thereby preventing the slaveboy from offering help, as he had obviously intended.

He began to offer explanations instead. 'There is much to arrange, citizen. Funerary libations, the funeral litter, musicians – professional mourners and an orator even, since there is no family to do it.'

'No family?' I queried, remembering the librarium pavement. 'There is a brother, surely?'

The boy nodded. 'Yes, citizen, there is. His name is Lucius. He was here a week or so ago. Andretha has sent a messenger after him already, but it is doubtful that he will come.'

I paused in my oiling to prick up my ears at this. 'They quarrelled?'

'No quarrel, no. Only they had been apart for years, and Lucius has changed. Completely. Crassus was . . .' He trailed off nervously, as if he had said too much.

'Crassus was what?' I demanded.

He dropped his voice, and whispered guiltily, 'Disappointed. He had been boasting for weeks about his brother's visit – the drink, the women, the banquets he would hold . . .'

I nodded. I had been a guest at one of Crassus' banquets. He had held it in Marcus' honour – another move in the game of seeking preferment. Marcus, knowing he wanted a pavement, had taken me as part of his retinue and gained me the commission. I had vivid memories of what Crassus' banquets could be like.

'But Lucius was not interested?' I prompted.

'The fact is, citizen, he has joined the new religion, the Christians, and he has given it all up – gambling, drinking, swearing, fornicating, everything Crassus was looking forward to. Dresses like a hermit and lives on alms. He spent his time here trying to persuade Crassus to repent.'

'That would not please Germanicus,' I said, keeping a straight face with difficulty. 'Sharing his villa with a fasting aesthete.'

Even the timid boy could not restrain a grin. 'Not quite that,' he said. 'Lucius has eschewed gluttony, but he praises God for good food, and is a trencherman yet. No rich sauces and conspicuous greed, but give him a suckling pig and fresh herbs and he will make a good meal of it – and wash it down with fine wine, too. He must have been a big man once, and he looks more Bacchus than beggar still. Crassus is no wraith, and there is nothing to choose between them.'

'Yet Lucius lives on alms?'

'Those who give them know, I think, what form their alms should take. Fresh-baked bread and honest oatcakes, and he has learned to feed himself with fish and fruits. The bounty of God, he says, though he will eat nothing that has been offered to idols. Refused a meal here – wood pigeon and partridge breast – because it had been offered at the household shrine. Crassus used that in the end as a way to get rid of him. He wouldn't attend a funeral where food was left for the afterworld, and libations made to the gods – especially imperial ones.'

I whistled. 'A dissenting Christian, eh? Be careful the emperor doesn't get to hear of that.' I was serious. Commodus takes emperor worship very seriously. He hasn't even waited to die: he's already decided that he is an incarnation of Hercules. Seems to believe it, too. Not like poor old Vespasian, exclaiming on his deathbed, 'Alas, I am becoming a god.'

I added aloud, 'There have been several Christians thrown to the beasts recently, for speaking out against the imperial cult.'

The boy nodded. 'Crassus knew that. He could not wait to get his brother out of the house. My master always wanted to become a knight, but if that sort of news got about, it would be the end of his preferment.'

'But they parted on good terms?'

'Crassus gave him money, and I even heard him promise help to found a church, once Lucius had found a site and patron. I think he'd have promised anything to get his brother away from here.'

'But you did not believe he would honour his promises?'

'I doubt it, citizen. Not while he lived, at least. He was always mocking Lucius behind his back, and he and Daedalus did a merciless and deadly accurate imitation of him. Anyway Lucius didn't want to stay. He wanted to be well away before the Mars parade. Pagan ritual, he called it.'

'I see.' I did see. A devout and practising Christian hermit who had been gone a week. A likely suspect for murder. I picked up the strigil. It was much better than my own. 'No other family?'

'There was a woman,' the boy said. 'She came here twice, claiming to be Crassus' wife. Said he had lived as her husband when he was garrisoned in the north, and had promised to marry her when he retired. She had found his whereabouts at last, apparently, and followed him. Regina, her name was. Poor lady, she was kind to me.'

'She stayed at the villa?'

'He refused to see her the first time, but when she came back and began to threaten to tell everyone in Glevum what had happened, he took her in and gave her a room in the villa for a month or so. She tried to plead her case, but he would not have it. Gave her money in the end, I understand, and perhaps that was what she came for, because she went off looking triumphant and we haven't seen her since.'

'When was this?'

'Oh, months ago.' He was frowning at me anxiously. 'Excuse me, citizen, but are you sure you don't want me to strigil your back? Or help you to shave? I have a novacula ready.'

Of course, he would have been waiting to assist me in my ablutions. I thought of that rough sharp knife rasping my skin and shuddered. In the hands of anyone less than expert, a novacula could be lethal. One false move . . .

'You shaved Crassus?' I asked, scraping the last of the oil from my skin and allowing him to rinse me off with a jug of water as I stood in the bowl. It was not as good as cleansing oneself in the bathhouse, of course, where the heat and steam open the pores, but I felt much refreshed. I towelled myself dry and reached for my toga. This time he did not wait to be asked, he came behind me and helped me to fold and secure it into place.

'Yes, I shaved my master,' he said.

I thought of Crassus as I had seen him at that banquet: small, squat and pugnacious with a square, blunt head like a battering ram; carefully cleanshaven, in the Roman fashion, but with hands and arms so disconcertingly hairy that he looked like a bear in a toga. There were fresh, bloody nicks on the side of his thick neck, then, as if someone had shaved him with an unsteady hand, and evidence of older scars on the cheek. 'Not an easy task,' I said, remembering that even though Crassus had been fresh-shaved there was still the faint blue of whiskers under the swarthy skin.

'No.' Almost unconsciously the boy's hand had risen to his shoulder, and I saw, under the neck of his tunic, the darkening shadow of a bruise.

'Show me,' I said. It was an impertinent request, but he obeyed, with that instinctive unquestioning obedience of slaves everywhere.

'My hand shook,' the boy explained. 'A day or two before the procession. I cut his cheek. It is nothing.'

Not quite nothing. His back, from shoulder to waist, was one red mass of weals and bruises. Small wonder the hand that held the novacula trembled in its work, if this treatment was commonplace.

'Did Crassus beat all his slaves like this?'

'Not everyone, no. Usually he had Andretha flog them – if the cook spoiled a meal, or one of the gardens failed to please him. But I was always there, you see, in reach. Besides, he knew I feared the lash. I am not . . . strong. Sometimes with others Crassus used more subtle methods – which hurt them more, often.'

'Such as?'

The boy glanced at the door-screen nervously. 'No, citizen, I should not have spoken. I was sent to help you shave and cleanse yourself, not to gossip.'

So it was Andretha who had been subject to these 'subtle methods'. I had been searching my memory for the boy's name, and now I found it. 'Well, thank Andretha,' I said, with forced jollity, 'but I think I shall forego a shave this morning, Paulus. It is Paulus, isn't it?'

He nodded.

'I want to see the body again before Andretha puts it on the funeral bier. These events will save him some of the grislier preparations. No eyes to close.' Paulus swallowed hard and looked so squeamish that I tried to make light of the horror. 'Though he will have to find some way to leave a coin in the mouth for the journey across the Styx. They say that failure to pay is one reason the ghosts of murdered men often come back. If Crassus did come back, however, perhaps he could help me by identifying his killer.'

It was a feeble attempt at levity but it had an unexpected effect on Paulus. He turned whiter than my toga. Fear of the dead, I wondered, or fear of the secrets that the dead might tell?

Of course, the barber was a member of the household and probably expecting general reprisals. 'Don't worry,' I said. 'We shall find the murderer without help from the afterworld. And Marcus is a fair man, he will only execute the guilty.'

It had been meant to reassure him, but Paulus looked more desperate than ever.

'What is it?'

He shook his head helplessly. 'I suppose you had better know. Someone else will tell you if I don't.'

'What is it?' I said again.

'The other day, at the festival of Mars, I wasn't with the others. While they were watching the procession, I slipped away.'

Now, why had Andretha not mentioned that? That sort of information might have saved his skin. 'To do what?'

Paulus shook his head stubbornly. 'I don't know. I just . . . wanted to be away. But someone may have noticed. The truth is, citizen, I missed most of the procession. I didn't return until they were getting on the farm cart at the gate. And Andretha must know it. So there you have it, citizen. I did not kill Crassus, but there is no one who can prove that.'

But Crassus was in the procession, I thought. And besides no man could have carried the body back here in that time. A foolish confession, but a particularly brave one, from a boy so timid. So why then did he avert his eyes as if he were lying?

'And?' I prompted.

He took a deep breath and by now his face had taken on the waxy creaminess of marble against the frame of his dark hair. 'And – there is no truth in the rumour of course, because it is expressly outlawed on pain of death . . .'

'But?'

Paulus gulped. 'But there are people in the villa who believe I am a follower of . . . the Druids.'

41

The Druids! The forbidden religion, which called for ritual human sacrifice.

'And are you a follower?' I asked.

'Of course not,' he said, and this time we both knew that he was lying.

Chapter Four

There was obviously nothing further to be gleaned from Paulus. He had taken a calculated risk, preferring to tell me this now rather than disguise the facts and have them beaten out of him later. He was probably wise. Someone would assuredly have told me, if he had not; one of the effects of possible 'blanket executions' is this peculiar willingness to inform on others. All the same, the poor fellow obviously felt that he had said too much already, and retreated further into himself than a Roman snail at the smell of cooking.

I could hardly blame him for worrying. Personally, I have no particular quarrel with Druids – at least none that I would want any practising Druid to hear of. There was a lot of learning and culture among the Druidic priesthood while it lasted, and if devotees did offer themselves as sacrifices from time to time, so that their entrails could be read, well, worse things happen every week in the arena. But our Roman masters have decreed against it, and who am I to question their judgement? Perhaps it *is* true that the Druids sometimes kidnap their victims. Marcus certainly thought so; if he heard there was a Druid in the house he would immediately suspect that the body in the hypocaust was some kind of bizarre ritual. Perhaps he was right.

I sent Paulus scurrying away to fetch my breakfast, and after that I dismissed him, to his evident relief. I was glad, really, to eat in my room unattended. It gave me time to plan my course of action. First, I wanted to examine the body; I was sure there was information to be derived from that. And then, Andretha. On his own, preferably. There was something in the man's over-anxious manner that I did not altogether trust. After that, I would wait and see.

I ate the bread and fruit, but wine, even watered wine, was too Roman for my stomach at this early hour. I opened the door-screen and Paulus leapt guiltily away from behind it.

'You need something, citizen?' What had he been doing there? Waiting for my commands, or spying at the door-crack?

'Water,' I said, indicating the empty drinking vessel. 'I need to keep a clear head.'

'Instantly, citizen.' He almost tripped over his sandal straps in his anxiety to be gone, but I detained him.

'If you see Andretha, tell him I would like to view the body, and to speak to him privately.'

Paulus paled, but said simply enough, 'You may do both things at once, citizen. He is in the master's bedroom, preparing the body for the funeral. Shall I fetch him?'

It was tempting. The idea of having the supercilious Andretha obliged to obey my summons was almost irresistible. But I thought better of it. I preferred to take the chief slave unawares. 'Fetch the water,' I said. 'I will go to him.'

'But, citizen . . .' Paulus began, looked agonised, and then trailed off. Shouldn't I go with you, he obviously meant, but lacked the courage to say so. It was not polite to wander about a strange house unaccompanied by at least a slave.

'Marcus has asked me to investigate,' I pointed out. 'I can do that best alone. You wait for me here.'

I made my way to the bedroom, following the pungent smell of candles and burning herbs. Andretha was, indeed, at his master's bedside. The armour had been removed and left neatly ranged by the wall. The body was now draped in a linen sheet from chin to ankles and Andretha was kneeling beside it, with a bowl of water at his feet. He squawked up at my approach, like a seagull surprised stealing honeycakes, overturning a small oaken chest and scattering half a dozen silver pieces in the process.

'You startled me, citizen, coming in unannounced.'

That was a rebuke, as near as he dared it. I grinned at him cheerfully. 'It is necessary that I work unobserved. As it seems that you do. Performing the ablutions already?'

Andretha flushed, but when he spoke it was with careful deference. 'Not the ritual cleansing, citizen, no. Only washing the dust and ashes from him, where he was lying on the floor. And finding his ferry fare, as you see.' He scrabbled after the coins, and thrust them back into the chest. 'I hope I have not offended, citizen, but it is hard to know how to proceed. His closest relative should close the eyes and begin the lament, but there are no eyes to close and anyway his brother is not here to do it. Yet it would not be fitting merely to ask the military guild. Crassus would not have wanted a common soldier's funeral.'

I wondered if Andretha always talked like this to guests – like an anxious politician on the steps of the forum. I made soothing noises.

He flapped his hands helplessly. 'I have done my best – sent a slave to fetch the anointing women, and find some professional mourners and musicians. They will provide a litter – at a cost. I am trying to prepare things here. He should be dressed in his best robes for the funeral. I have sent his sandals to the shoemender for fresh hobnails, he must be fresh-shod for the afterlife. I thought he had new ones but I cannot find them. I took off his uniform. I hope I did not exceed my duty, citizen. It was an awful task.'

It must have been. The charred skull was an even more appalling sight than I remembered. I hardly wished to look at it myself. I turned away and examined the armour. The leather skirt was burnished and I admired again the campaign seals on the chest-harness, and the intricacy of the gleaming breast-armour – the little individual metal pieces sewn to a fabric shirt, to afford maximum protection but allow movement to the wearer.

'Fine work,' I said.

'Yes, citizen,' the slave agreed. 'And such a waste. It was all ordered new for the procession.'

I was surprised. 'Where does a veteran obtain new armour? From the armourer?'

He flapped his hands again. 'I don't know that, citizen. I suppose so. A man with money might buy anything. There are those, too, who sell Roman armour which is not quite new . . .'

I knew what he was referring to. The insubordinate Silures on the western border had taken their toll of casualties recently. There was always a ready unofficial market for good Roman body-armour; helmets were prized trophies, and even the Silures themselves recognised good protection when they saw it.

'And the old armour? What became of that?'

Andretha shrugged helplessly. 'I don't know that, either, citizen. But those that sell, buy.' He flashed me a sideways look. 'Daedalus could tell you these things, citizen. If he were here.'

'Yes,' I said. I had not forgotten the missing slave. But Andretha had a point. Marcus, for instance, was inclined to overlook Daedalus. He was only a slave after all, and had no personal importance. 'I will ask him, when I can.'

An uneasy flush came to his face. 'You . . . know where he is, citizen?'

That surprised me. 'Do you?'

He shook his head hastily. 'No. I wish I did, I promise you. If I knew I should tell you at once, and you could fetch him here. He could do this, at least. This should be Daedalus' job, not mine. Crassus was fastidious. He would have no one but his favourite attend him when he dressed.'

I nodded. I wondered why Andretha had not delegated the grisly business of undressing the corpse.

'He was the personal slave, the favoured one,' Andretha said bitterly. 'Always a party to my master's plans. He would have known what to do. Should I cover the face, for instance? It is not usual, but what sort of spectacle will this be, in the funeral procession?' He shot me that look again. 'Citizen, I beg you to find Daedalus. He could tell you what happened in Glevum, and tell me what grave-goods to provide. If I guess wrong, Crassus will be a spiteful spirit.'

I could imagine that, too: Crassus, dead but intransigent as ever, refusing to cross the Styx without his favourite possessions. I said, 'Yes, we will find Daedalus, never fear.' I wished I could feel as confident as I sounded. 'Marcus is enquiring in the town. In the meantime, I wish to examine the body. What, apart from the uniform, have you removed?'

The briskness of the question had the desired effect. Andretha again became all apology and eagerness to please.

'Nothing, citizen, nothing. A few leaves and bits of dust and grit, that's all.'

'And blood? Was there blood anywhere?' This was something I had hoped to check before Andretha began.

'A very little dried blood on his legs, that is all. There is a graze, too. It had gravel in it, but that did not bleed, it seems.'

'Show me.'

He lifted the cover, instinctively moving the cloth so that it obscured that dreadful head, and I saw the body fully for the first time. It lay in a simple tunic, ready to be salved, dressed and perfumed to impress the lords of the underworld. It would not have impressed me, if I were Pluto. Deprived of his trappings, Germanicus looked diminished, puffy in death, and somehow insignificant.

Andretha showed me the graze, on the top of one foot and ankle, as if the body had been dragged, face down. The legs and arms were as I remembered – shaved, and nicked in a dozen places as if the barber had done his work clumsily. I recalled the bruises on Paulus' back. Was this where he had gained them? Cuts like that would rouse Crassus to a fury.

I thought aloud. 'Why did Germanicus have his legs shaved? He did not use to do so.'

Andretha was so anxious to answer that he visibly tried not to smirk. 'I think, citizen, it was your friend Marcus who began it. Something he said once, after a banquet in his honour, when Daedalus entertained the guests by doing an impersonation of Germanicus. Very like, Marcus said, except for the legs.'

I nodded. It was not Marcus who said it, in fact. It was me. It had been at that banquet I had attended with him. That must have been also the first time I saw Daedalus. I closed my eyes to remember it more clearly.

It was after the main meal. The peacocks, swans and gilded larks had been cleared away (Germanicus didn't stint himself when it came to a banquet) and the ducks' eggs and spiced meats were brought in. Then the lute player struck a chord, and a slave stepped forward – Daedalus, as I now realised, though the name was not mentioned at the time.

He was wearing a tunic, but after bowing he burrowed in a basket and wrapped himself in a piece of coloured cloth, not unlike a child's toga. Another burrow in the basket produced a pottery mask with flowing clay curls like a medusa. He buckled it about his head. There was an uneasy silence.

Then, 'Welcome,' he said, 'on behalf of the governor.'

I gasped with mirth. It was Marcus to the life. It was not tactful to be so openly amused, with my patron reclining by my side, but my laugh was out before I could stifle it. Fortunately, when I dared to look, Marcus was chuckling, too. All around the tables there was a ripple of delighted laughter as the act went on. It was merciless, but the slave's impersonation was excellent. Everything about him, the walk, the impatient tap of the baton, the lift of the shoulders, the voice even, had become Marcus. It was funnier as it became bolder, and soon the guests were thumping the tables. Marcus, mellow with wine, applauded as loudly as the rest.

Another chord on the lute. The man in the mask turned away, and adjusted his toga. When he turned back, Marcus was gone, and we seemed to be watching one of the other guests, one of the quaestor's clerks, a small, thin fellow with a high-pitched voice and an exaggerated manner. The clerk looked furious, but the masked actor only mimicked him the more. It was hilarious. The whole room rocked with mirth, though this time I did contrive to conceal my amusement. I sometimes have dealings with the quaestors.

But it was the third and last performance which I remembered most. Daedalus turned away, hunched his shoulders, thrust out his belly and lifted his chin – and now it was Crassus we were looking at. The man's neck seemed to have disappeared, and there was the pugnacious strut, the self-important swagger. There was an uneasy snigger.

'Silence, by Mithras, or I'll have you whipped!' the actor shouted, and the whole gathering collapsed in laughter and applause.

'Dangerous,' Marcus whispered in my ear. 'Crassus is not a man to mock in public. Or has he arranged this on purpose, to see who laughs the most? He would be a dangerous enemy to make.'

Crassus looked towards us and smirked.

'Now, since I am guest of honour, he will ask me what I thought of the performance,' Marcus grumbled under his breath. 'What should I tell him? That it was indistinguishable? It is hardly a compliment.'

'Not indistinguishable,' I said. 'Crassus is hairier. That slave's limbs are smooth.'

'You have sharp eyes, pavement maker,' Marcus said. 'It is true. But I can hardly tell Crassus that!'

'No,' I grinned. 'Tell him the actor's body is . . . balder.'

Crassus had taken it to heart, it seemed. I looked at the marks on those lifeless legs. 'And he has shaved himself from that day on?'

'Not every day,' Andretha said, 'but often, if his arms and legs were to be uncovered. Paulus would tell you.' He looked at me slyly. 'Or Daedalus, if you find him.'

'Yes,' I said again.

Andretha was still looking at me anxiously. 'You have seen all you need, citizen?'

'I think so.' I ran my eye over the body again, where it had been hidden by the armour. There was no obvious cause of death. So, it *was* poison, I thought. The only mark on the body was a weal on the side where the plate-shirt had buckled on. I let the sheet fall, revealing again that fleshless face.

Andretha gave me that flustered look again. 'If you permit, citizen – I must finish here and arrange the building of the funeral pyre.'

I looked at him sharply. 'Cremation then? I thought since his brother is a hermit you might have buried him, in the new Christian manner.'

Andretha furrowed his brow and fluttered his fingers in deprecation. 'This was his wish, citizen. At least, I hope it was. He said it before witnesses, so if I do wrong may Jove forgive me. It was when his brother was here. Lucius thinks of nothing but the afterworld, and was trying to persuade Crassus to do the same, but Crassus just laughed and called us all to witness that he wanted Roman rites when he died. "Throw me on the fire," he said. "I don't want to wake and find myself buried alive. And invoke all the gods you can think of, just in case. Including Lucius', if you must." He was laughing, but I think he was in earnest. Anyway, there is a shrine and niche prepared in the temple up at the spring.'

I nodded. Roman strictures on disposing of the dead apply to towns and habitations, not country land. There has been quite a fashion, when new villas are built, for installing family shrines somewhere, away from the buildings but within the estate. Crassus, no doubt, would have an elaborate one, complete with flattering statuary and complimentary inscriptions designed and at the ready. 'What did Lucius say?'

'He was angry, I think, that Crassus was mocking him. He said, in front of us all, that he would never attend such a pagan ritual.'

'He might change his mind,' I ventured.

'I doubt it, citizen. He is a man of his word. And in any case, there is scarcely time now. I sent to Lucius early this morning, at Marcus' suggestion, but he lives a long way off. The messenger has not yet returned and this body has been unburied for two days already. If we delay the rituals much longer the spirit will not reach the underworld.'

I sympathised. The company of Germanicus was unpleasant enough in life. The prospect of his presence, dead, was an appalling one. It was likely to be a wrathful presence besides, if he missed his ferry over the Styx. I'm not sure if I believe in spirits myself, but in Andretha's place, I'd be taking no chances.

'In any case,' I said, 'under the circumstances, a cremation would be best.' Burial, on the Christian pattern, was taking over from the Roman burning in some cases, but it seemed absurd to do anything else here, since the job was half done already.

'If you have seen enough, citizen, I must finish the preparations. The women will be here with the oils soon. I must arrange for the food and drink to be prepared, so the soul has enough sustenance for its journey.' No mean task, I thought, if Crassus' spirit was half the trencherman that the living man had been. Andretha would not want the spirit turning back because it was hungry. He added, 'And I must find the lute player and arrange a rota for the lament.'

I nodded. Once the anointing began the weeping and wailing would not cease until the funeral took place. 'Then I will leave you. I, too, have work to do.'

He made one final attempt. 'Like finding Daedalus?'

'Like finding Daedalus. But first I want to look around the villa – examine the slaves' quarters, for example.'

He fought with himself a moment, but in the end he burst out with it, the question he had been dying to ask all along. 'Citizen, an uncomfortable idea comes to me. This looks like Crassus, certainly, but without features it is hard to be sure. You do not think perhaps . . .' he nodded towards the inert form on the bed '. . . you may have found Daedalus already?'

I knew what he meant, naturally. The same thing had occurred to me; that was one reason why I wanted to see the body again. Any political conspiracy, for instance, that wanted to spirit Germanicus away, might well have sent us a dead slave in his stead. But now, of course, I was quite certain. 'No,' I said, 'that is not Daedalus.'

He was flapping his hands again. 'I should like to be certain, citizen. Crassus would never forgive me if I buried a common slave in his place. I worked for the man, yet I could not swear to it. Daedalus could impersonate him so well his own mother might confuse them. And without a face . . .'

'Exactly,' I said. 'Without a face we have only the evidence of the body. Look at those razor marks on his legs. See how the thick hairs have been shaved off close? Crassus may have shaved his legs to look as smooth as

Daedalus, but Daedalus could not grow hairs in order to resemble Crassus. Rest easy, my friend. This is not Daedalus. Daedalus did not need to shave his legs.'

Was it my imagination, as I left the room, or did Andretha look even more worried than before?

Chapter Five

I was glad to get out into the sweet air. In the bedroom, despite Andretha's efforts in burning aromatic herbs, there was still the faint, sickly aroma of mortal corruption. I left him to his ministrations with relief. Outside, Paulus was still waiting timidly. I drained the beaker he had been holding and sent him for more water to wash my hands. I am not usually fastidious, but that body was unwholesome. Not surprisingly perhaps; it had lain a long time in the heat of the stoke room – a hot furnace can take many hours to cool. It was as well the anointers were arriving soon; masking that smell is one of the more practical virtues of their oils.

Paulus was just scuttling off with the bowl when the first of the funeral party arrived. They came on an oxcart, bringing the trappings of their trade with them. Andretha came bustling out to greet them, and I watched him show them in, and cluck anxiously over the items they had brought, like a hen counting her chicks. There was a gilded litter with carrying-handles, so that the corpse could make his last journey in splendid state. Three female anointers arrived, stout, red-faced women with brawny arms – from lifting and pummelling people in heated rooms, they say. They carried whole flagons of scented oil with them now, and winding linens too, to go discreetly under the toga and prevent bits of the deceased from flopping embarrassingly at every jerk in the road.

Then the professional mourners and six musicians came in, with their pipes and long-horns, ready to start their infernal wailing whenever Andretha gave the word. The chief slave was sparing no expense on his master's behalf.

All the activity seemed to have dispelled his recent anxiety, and he fussed about happily, showing the women into the bedroom, organising the disposition of the litter, and sent one of the house-slaves scurrying to fetch water for the ritual cleansing. He would go to the source for that, to keep it sacred; draw it from the nymphaeum – the temple to the water gods – not from the stream that trickled down towards the house and under the latrine. And it was to the nymphaeum, I remembered, that the ashes would be returned after the funeral. That rather surprised me: I would have expected Crassus to choose a conspicuous spot beside the highway for his memorial, where everyone would see his memorial. But, as I say, private shrines have become the fashion and obviously Germanicus had felt he had to have one. Rather like the librarium, I thought with a smile. Perhaps I would go up to the nymphaeum later, to see what the builders had made of it.

The water-carrier had returned by this time, with his ewer of sacred water, and the rites could begin at last. When Andretha began instructing the musicians to start the lament, I decided that after all I would go up to the water shrine straight away. I have no stomach for professional keening. That dismal noise alone is enough to drive a spirit shuddering to the underworld. Perhaps that is the idea.

Walking to the spring would give me time to think, and besides it would take me as far as possible away from that demented wailing.

It was a little walk to the nymphaeum, out through the rear courtyard and inner gate and up a steep path between thick trees. At first I enjoyed my stroll, glad of the chance to clear my head after the thick air of the death room. But I had not gone many paces before I paused to listen. I could hear sounds. Small things, the crack of a twig, the scrabble of stones, a stealthy rustling. As I stopped, they stopped too. I felt the hairs on the back of my neck prickle. Someone was following me.

I turned. Nothing. I was imagining things.

I walked on, and there it was again, the unmistakable sound of footsteps on gravel. I whirled around, but there was no one to be seen. I felt my heart pounding, and I also felt conspicuously alone. After a morning when slaves had been drawing water constantly, to my knowledge, it seemed that suddenly the path to the spring was deserted.

I looked around. The path here was hidden from the villa, and with the household busy with funeral preparations, any cries for help would go unheard. And Crassus had after all been murdered. It would be ironic, I thought, to discover the murderer's identity only by becoming the next victim.

I moved swiftly, diving behind a nearby tree and waiting silently. At least I would discover who it was. I waited a long time. Nobody came. My pursuer, it seemed, had given up – or had never really existed. I emerged, feeling rather foolish, and at that moment a dark-haired figure hurried round the corner. Paulus. He looked startled to see me.

'Ah, citizen!'

'Paulus! What brings you here? You have not come for water. You have no jug, I see.' On the other hand, I noticed, he had no weapon either.

He smiled weakly. 'No, citizen. I came to look for you. Andretha said you had come this way. Aulus, the gatekeeper, wishes to see you. He has information, he says, which he forgot yesterday – and he cannot leave his post.'

Aulus. Marcus' spy. That seemed a plausible reason for coming to find me. Was it a real one or had Paulus been following me? Or, again, by coming this way himself, had he frightened away my pursuer? I did not know. I could only say, 'Very well, tell him I will come. I will go up to the spring later.'

I did not go directly to the gatehouse, however. I walked around the side of the villa, on my way, to look in at the stoke room by daylight. I was not followed this time, but one glance into the furnace room was enough to tell me that I was too late to learn anything there. The whole area had been swept and cleaned, and even the pile of fuel had been removed. There was a faint, rubbed line on the trodden earth of the floor, as if something had been dragged across it from door to furnace. I thought of the graze on the dead man's foot, but there was nothing further to be proved from that. A glance towards the back gate showed me why. Half a dozen slaves, under the supervision of Andretha, were already engaged in dragging garden sledges laden with logs from the woodpile towards the farm cart standing in the lane. For the funeral pyre no doubt. Any of the sledges might have made the mark.

It also explained how Andretha knew where to find me. He must have seen me go towards the nymphaeum. Why else would anyone seek me on that path? I gave myself a little shake. I was becoming unreasonably suspicious.

I turned away and went to find the gatekeeper.

He was sitting vacantly on a stool in his cell-like room beside the gate, watching the road through an aperture in the wall and looking even less prepossessing than yesterday. He was the right build for a country gatekeeper, I thought, tall, strong and swarthy, with lank hair to his tunic-collar, muscles like a gladiator and a stout club at his belt. A man to deter unwanted visitors, beggars, pedlars and wolves. He certainly deterred me. I eyed the club nervously.

'Libertus!' He crossed the room in three strides. 'So you got my message. Come in, come in.' He seized my arm, with an air of uncomfortably confident chumminess.

I winced. The man had the strength of a bear. Yet, yesterday, when we had interviewed him, he had seemed edgy and nervous. I was on my guard. Nervous bears are dangerous.

I gave him an encouraging smile. He released me, dropping his voice and bending his head to mine as if we were in a conspiracy. 'Have you heard from Marcus?' He smelt of onions and sour wine.

'Not yet.' I almost found myself whispering back. It must be always like that for spies, fearing the very walls are listening. I went to the window – away from the onions – and pretended to look out of it. I said, in a normal voice, 'We shall see him tomorrow at the funeral. He will come at least to hear the oration read.'

Aulus made a knowing face. 'Thank Bacchus for that. I have things to tell him. At least we won't have to trudge halfway to Glevum to see him, though naturally the pyre is in the furthest field. No doubt Andretha will have four of us slaves carrying the litter all the way – and in the darkness too. Why do funerals always take place at night?'

I shrugged sympathetically. I would have to follow the procession myself, and that was an unpleasant prospect in the cold and dark, even without the weight of Crassus on my shoulders. 'There will be torches,' I said.

Aulus scowled. It was not an encouraging sight. I attempted a joke. 'I wish the torches would shed light on my enquiries.' I was uncomfortably aware of his physical presence, large and loutish. He looked big enough to carry a funeral litter singlehanded.

He didn't smile.

'But,' I prompted, appealing to his professional pride, 'you have something to tell me, too.'

That was better. He breathed conspirational onions at me again. 'I should have told you before, my friend. You and Marcus. But I feared trouble. It concerns someone in the villa. Someone who did not stay at the procession the whole time with the others. I wanted to speak to him before I told you, but . . .' He shrugged and did not finish the sentence.

'But he would not pay?' I suggested. I tried to sound world-weary and matter-of-fact, as though taking bribes was all in a day's work to me, too. It was a risk, but even if he took it ill Aulus could not well attack me in broad daylight when I was under Marcus' protection. At least, so I told my pounding heart. Besides, I must not let him frighten me. Bullies are often cowards.

Aulus looked at his sandals and toyed with his cudgel.

I made a mental note to tell Marcus that if he wanted to choose a spy, he would be better served by one who did not fidget so openly when asked an awkward question. His uneasiness, though, gave me a little more confidence.

'So,' I hazarded, 'Paulus left?'

'Paulus?' He sounded genuinely surprised. 'Not that I know. He is a cowardly youth. I should have thought he was too frightened to have risked the lash again by leaving without permission. He is often beaten, as it is.' He gave me a knowing leer. 'They say he has joined the Druids, to seek revenge.'

Paulus was right, I thought. It had not taken long for that rumour to reach me. 'So I have heard,' I said dismissively. 'I should have thought the Druids would frighten him more than Crassus does.'

He scowled, annoyed at having his gossip forestalled. He was probably hoping to be paid for that snippet of news. He rallied, though, enough to ask, 'Why do you suspect Paulus?'

'Paulus was not present for the whole procession. He told me so himself.'

'Really? I suppose we must believe it. Did he say why he left?'

'I hoped you might tell me that. And how long he was absent.'

Aulus glowered, but he looked uncomfortable.

'Andretha said nothing about it,' I went on, conversationally, 'but you are a paid spy. I had imagined you might have noticed a thing like that?'

Aulus fidgeted again. 'The truth is, citizen,' he said shiftily, 'it is not easy to watch everyone. Once we had got to Glevum we were not necessarily together all the time. People moved to get a better view, or buy things from the street sellers. Besides, when the procession passed, everyone was looking at the marchers . . .'

'Where did you go yourself, gatekeeper? No – don't

deny it. If you had been there you would have noted Paulus' absence. You were in Glevum, I presume? You were not left behind to guard the gates?'

He shook his head. 'No, I was there. Only . . . I was following someone else. This man I told you about.'

'And who was that?'

He hesitated. Perhaps he was still hoping for money, but I had none to give him. 'It was Rufus, the lute player. I saw him slip away, and naturally I followed.'

'Where to?'

'That is the trouble, I don't know. I could not follow him for long – I had others to watch. He went out towards the South Gate, hurrying, that is all I know. I think he saw me, because he dived into a shrine. I could hardly follow him there. I thought he had gone to meet that slavegirl of his, but there was no sign of her. I waited a little and then came away.' He shrugged. 'I tried to challenge him this morning, but he would not answer me.'

So, I was not far wrong with my guesswork. Aulus had tried to extract a bribe. And probably not for the first time. I had noted the smug smirk when he mentioned the slavegirl.

'A slavegirl, you say? A secret love affair?'

'Yes, citizen. Though it was scarcely a secret. Half the villa knew about it. I think even Crassus suspected.'

Aulus had told him, I surmised, hoping to make trouble. Rufus was a slave, and a slave was not entitled to have relations with a woman without his master's consent. What is more, if the slavegirl belonged to Crassus she was his personal property, and any man who took her without permission was a kind of thief. I was surprised that Crassus had let theft go unpunished, even theft of something as trivial as a slavegirl.

Aulus was watching me. 'They used to meet,' he told me, a salacious smile touching his lips, 'whenever Crassus did not need their services. That was not often, but sometimes he did leave the villa overnight, to attend a banquet, or a gaming feast.'

'At night?' I said. 'Surely the gates are locked?'

'They are. Anyone coming to the villa would have to knock and wake me. But anyone could unlock the back gate from inside and slip out unobserved. They do not even have to pass this window to do it. But of course, on those occasions I was always awake, waiting for Crassus to come home. They did not know I saw them, but I did. They used to slip up the old lane. Going to the abandoned roundhouse, I imagine. I've seen soldiers go that way occasionally with their women, presumably for the same purpose.'

'Risky,' I said. 'It's a fair step from the villa.'

He shrugged. 'I would not choose it. The place is dangerous and it stinks. Crassus used to use it for the animals, but it is too ruined even for that. But – where else is there? It is not too far, and it is well out of sight of the villa.'

He was right about that. There is very little privacy for a slave inside a villa, though they must have risked a thrashing if Crassus suspected. I said so.

Aulus smirked. 'I think Crassus did suspect, but he found other ways to stop them. He always enjoyed that. Choosing the punishment to fit the victim. He fenced off the roundhouse and had the roof pulled in. Said there had been beggars sleeping there. And took Rufus to every banquet with him after that, as well. Though that was all. Rufus has been . . . grateful . . . for my silence.'

He looked so gloatingly pleased with himself that I felt the need to leave before I lost my temper and one of us got hurt. It would almost certainly be me.

'I think I will take a look at this roundhouse,' I said. 'It may hold the answer to our mystery. Anyone might have hidden there on the day of the feast and murdered Crassus on his return.'

Aulus sneered. 'It would be difficult. How would they get to the hypocaust? The villa gates were locked and I had the key. Anyway the aediles had the roundhouse searched, and they found nothing – except fleas. I told you – Crassus used it for the animals.'

'All the same,' I said, 'I think I will take a look.'

I went out into the lane. However much the roundhouse stank, I thought, it could not be worse than the stench of stale onions and oafish self-satisfaction.

Chapter Six

I was wrong, as I discovered when I got there. Things could smell a great deal worse.

It had taken me some time to reach the roundhouse. The lane was steep, and even when I got there I had to pick my way to the entrance. There was a path of sorts, but the old neat enclosure had fallen into disrepair, the outer ditch and wall had both collapsed and the inner compound had all but disappeared under bushes, thistles, grasses and young trees. The building itself was little more than a ruin. What nature had begun, Crassus had completed by pulling down most of the roof, so that what remained offered little protection against the wind and rain and only then if one huddled under the fallen thatch near what had been the door. The only thing still standing was the smell.

It was a strange smell, compounded of damp straw, rotting vegetation and animal droppings, and a horrible odour of corruption which I eventually traced to a pile of old fish-heads under the fallen thatch. There was an old dark patch on the earth floor besides, where some unfortunate creature had once been slaughtered bloodily, and there was a general ambience of pigs. Hardly a welcoming habitation, and although a pile of bedding straw had been raked together in the one place of shelter, it was dirty, rumpled and damp. I remembered what Aulus had said about beggars sleeping here.

And this was the only place that Rufus and his lady could find to be alone. I felt a twinge of sympathy. It was hardly a senatorial palace, even for Crassus' hogs.

Yet, ruined as it was, the building revived memories in me. I had not been in a Celtic roundhouse since they had dragged me, at sword-point, away from my own almost thirty years ago, and there was a strange bitter sweetness in visiting one again. Mine was a little bigger, of course, but otherwise no different. A Celtic chief measures his wealth, not in draughty corridors, but in the beauty and workmanship of his possessions, in music and song and the loyalty of his people. In just such a house was I born, and to such a house I brought my bride. I could picture as if it were before me the central fire, giving off its cheerful smoky heat, while something bubbled deliciously in the blackened pot. I could see the women huddled around it, weaving cloth and plaiting baskets, the dog basking by the hearth, one ear already cocked for the returning menfolk, while a lad – it might have been myself – struck music from a little harp and sang the old, sad, proud songs of my youth.

I was accustomed, now, to Roman ways: to stone walls and floors, latrines and drains and aqueducts, to braziers and fullered linen. But there was a part of me which remembered, with regret, an older, wilder, less directed life, when a man's time and land and labour were his own, without patronage or taxes, and a woman who needed an extra room could weave one out of osiers in an afternoon. Of course, there were drawbacks too, pirate raids and dirt and draughts, but all the same I felt a disagreeable tingling behind my eyes. There were so many things a man had to forget, so many compromises to make, simply to stay alive. I was proud to be a freedman now, but I had been freer, and prouder, then.

But this was no time for morbid introspection. I had come here for a purpose. I broke a stick from a tree nearby and scratched about in the straw, though not with any great hope of discovering anything. I found the fleas – or rather, they found me. I obviously represented their first square meal since the arrival of the aediles, and I wondered fleetingly what they lived on when I wasn't there. Something, obviously, since there were plenty of them. I could see nothing else, however, and was about to give up when my stick dislodged something small and metallic among the straw.

I bent forward to retrieve it.

It was a single, small piece of hammered metal, thin and worn and shaped like a fishscale with a small hole in one end. I knew what it was. A piece of scale armour, like the ones on Crassus' shirt.

Yet it had not come from Crassus' shirt. I had examined that only an hour ago and it was undamaged. Anyway, I asked myself, what would Crassus be doing here, in the resort of pigs and beggars? So, where had it come from? One of Aulus' amorous soldiers perhaps? Or from some imperial conspirator? Whatever it was, Marcus would have to be told. I slipped the piece of metal into the pouch inside my belt, and sighed. The more I saw of this business, the less I liked it.

There was nothing else to be found and I made my way back to the villa. Aulus was waiting for me.

'There you are, citizen. Did you find the ruin?'

'I did.' I wanted to avoid further intimacy with the onions, but he was ushering me into his room again. I made a bid for escape. 'I must speak to Rufus. What is he like, this man?'

'Hardly a man.' Aulus preened, relishing the opportunity to impart information. 'He is small, red-headed, young. He is the lute player. You must have seen him. Freeborn, but poor, although so proud you'd think he was of patrician blood. He was sold into slavery by his parents, for ten years.'

I nodded. It was not unknown. Parents too poor to support their children sometimes sold them into slavery for a fixed term, especially if they had a talent, like Rufus. Usually they hoped the child would get manumission at the end and citizenship with it, but Rufus had had the misfortune to be bought by Crassus.

'He will be lucky to escape when his contract ends,' I said.

'Yes,' Aulus agreed. 'At least, that was true yesterday. Now, I suppose, he will be given to Lucius. That will ensure his contract is honoured. Lucius might even free him at once – unless he has use for lute players in his hermit's cell.'

'Why Lucius?'

Aulus shrugged. 'That is an open secret. Crassus has no other family. He has sealed a will naming Lucius as his heir.' He chuckled, an unpleasant loutish sound. 'Not to enjoy the villa, though. That would be too simple for Germanicus. Lucius is to sell everything and have only the money, to build a church. It was agreed during his visit. Daedalus told me. Crassus would not wish this property to be openly owned by a Christian, it might dishonour his memory, but at the same time I suppose he will have secured prayers for his soul. Germanicus always preferred to bet on both sides of any coin.'

I was thinking about the will. 'Are there any other bequests?'

Aulus shrugged. 'Daedalus himself was to have something; and Andretha a pension and freedom, provided he could render the accounts. Apart from that it was mostly bequests to "substitute heirs". The estate will go to them if Lucius refuses to accept the money – which, being Lucius, he might do I suppose. The substitutes are people that Germanicus wanted to impress. You know what wealthy men are like, always bragging about what is in their testaments, in order to win favours while they are alive. I hear Marcus and the governor are named as substitutes. There may be others, too. Of course, we shall not know for sure until the will is opened and read publicly in the forum.'

'You realise,' I said, 'that you have just attributed to Andretha a motive for wishing his master dead? A pension and freedom.'

'Andretha?' That was a new idea, I was sure. 'He's a peculiar man. I suppose it's possible. He's got a mania about buying his freedom. He worked for a younger man before, you see, and was arranging to do it, but the youth died of a fever and Crassus bought him instead. Andretha still talks about saving his slave-price and buying his release – but now, I suppose, he will not have to. It has turned him into a hoarder, though. Crassus used to torment him by fining him for misdemeanours. Parting with a few sesterces was more painful to Andretha than the lash, I believe. Every fine delayed his freedom a little further.'

I nodded. A slave, particularly a chief slave, might hope to receive an *as* or two from departing guests – assuming that Crassus' gambling friends were more generous than he was. All the same, it would take a long time to save up those 'few sesterces'. Every fine would sting. This was presumably the 'subtle method' that Paulus had talked of. But speaking of Andretha reminded me. 'And what about Daedalus?' I said. 'What kind of man was he? He was promised freedom even without the will. Why would he run away?'

'He was a strange man, too. Oh, he was clever – knew how to flatter, how to laugh at the right time, how to find out people's weaknesses. But—' Aulus got up sharply. 'Why are you asking me this, citizen? Facts I can give you, but who knows a man's motives? I am a spy, not a soothsayer.' He towered over me.

I stood my ground. Like Daedalus, I knew how to flatter. 'You have sharp eyes, gatekeeper. I value your impressions. If I am to find Daedalus, I must know what kind of a man he was. Could he have done this murder? If Crassus had suddenly denied him freedom, say?'

Aulus took a step backwards and began looking at his sandals, with the air of a great philosopher. 'I have asked myself that. I don't know the answer, citizen. I do not believe so, murder was not his weapon. But people will stoop to almost anything, for a price.'

An interesting sentiment. 'And Daedalus had his price?' I asked.

There was a pause. 'Oh yes, he had his price.'

'And what was that? Money? Freedom?'

No answer.

I waited. At last he raised his head and looked at me. He was a big, brutish man, but he would not last a minute, I thought, in front of a hostile magistrate. No one had even threatened to torture him.

He sat down again, avoiding my eyes. 'I suppose, power. Freedom and money perhaps, but most of all power. I don't think he would murder for revenge. One can have very little power over the dead.'

'But in exchange for power?'

He looked at me then. 'He might do anything.' He leaned forward, leering excitedly. 'I see what you are thinking, citizen. Those soldiers at the gate . . .'

It was not exactly what I was thinking, but I said, 'Go on.'

'Suppose Daedalus was paid to murder Crassus? Bribed by some high official perhaps, or offered a lucrative post – that would explain everything. If Crassus was plotting against the empire, as Marcus thinks, he would have powerful enemies. Men with the money to offer Daedalus anything.' He smiled triumphantly, seizing my arm again. 'If you prove this, citizen, do not forget that it was me who reported those soldiers at the gate.'

'Or "soldier",' I said. 'One each time.'

'Yes,' Aulus agreed, 'but there might have been others behind the scenes. They were centurions, after all. They could have had a military gig, for instance, to bring the body back unseen.'

'Of course,' I said, 'such powerful men would have the means to buy your service, too.'

He got up, terrified. 'I swear, citizen . . .'

'After all,' I went on remorselessly, 'you are known to be a spy.'

'That is different, citizen! Quite different! Marcus is a state official, and besides I had no choice . . .'

'A man will stoop to anything,' I quoted softly, 'for a price. What was your price, doorkeeper? And do not lie to me, I have Marcus' ear.'

He slumped down upon his stool again. 'It was . . . it was a small thing – a theft. I swear I did not know. I saw it lying on the highway and picked it up. I did not know it was the quaestor's purse.'

'Picking up a purse on the highway? That is hardly a capital offence.'

'No.' Aulus shifted uneasily. 'Only – there was a body lying beside it.'

'The quaestor?' I had not heard of the incident.

He met my eyes. 'No, the thief. There had been a struggle, he was wounded and must have crawled away and died. And there was I, standing beside the body with the purse in my hand, when Marcus and his lictor arrived. They had been riding some way behind the quaestor and had come to investigate the trail of blood. They said I was an accomplice.'

'I see.' It was easy to imagine. Marcus had persuaded the lad that his life was in danger – banditry on the imperial highway was punishable by crucifixion. Not a risk to be run lightly. Aulus had been quietly released in return for a promise to supply information. By such means are spies recruited.

It was neat. Perhaps on reflection Marcus' choice of spy was not a bad one, even if he did seek the occasional bribe. A man terrified for his life could be relied upon to tell everything that he knew, prompted by a threat or two. Wasn't I, after all, using a similar technique?

It was effective too. Aulus was positively babbling in his desire to offer information. 'There is one other thing, citizen. Something I learned about Daedalus. It may not be important – I don't think it is – but I believe he had . . . a woman.'

It was so unexpected that I almost laughed aloud. The picture of Daedalus that Aulus had been building up – cold, clever, talented, calculating – did not allow for *women*. I said 'Love?' incredulously.

'I know,' Aulus said, 'it sounds ridiculous. But I saw him with my own eyes. Crassus had a woman here who claimed a marriage contract. He refused to see her at first, but she threatened to make a fuss. He gave her the old slavegirls' room in the villa in the end, and finally paid her off, I think, because she went off happy enough. But several times, at night, I saw Daedalus loitering outside her room, and twice afterwards, when she had gone and was supposed to be travelling home, he slipped out in the middle of the night and was gone until daybreak.'

More nocturnal adventuring, I thought. That back gate had a lot to answer for – although little seemed to escape Aulus. And no doubt Daedalus had paid for silence, too. Aloud I said, 'I thought she was Crassus' woman – or wanted to be?'

He shrugged. 'She was, once. But that was years ago, and she'd aged worse than an army horse. Looked a bit like one, too. If Crassus wouldn't have her, I think she'd have taken anyone. She was desperate, after all. Her father had just died, and left her penniless. She'd have ended begging on the roads, or selling herself into servitude, if she hadn't found out where Crassus was, suddenly, and come to look for him.'

I nodded. In that case, I thought, any man's attentions might have been welcome.

Aulus seemed to read my thoughts. 'I was awake one night, and I am sure I saw her with Daedalus. She was lying under those trees, and a man – I believe it was him – was bending over her with his arms around her. I must have made a noise. When I went out to see, they were gone. She was freeborn, of course, and Crassus would never have permitted his slave to have her, even if he did not want her himself.' A thought seemed to strike him. 'Perhaps Daedalus was offered the lady and a new life in return for killing his master. Men would murder the emperor himself, for less.' He leered, hopefully. 'If this is proved, you will tell Marcus that I thought of it, first?'

'Aulus,' I said, 'you have been most helpful. Two more questions, and that is all for now. You did see Crassus leave the villa, the day of the procession?'

'Of course.' He sounded surprised. 'He and Daedalus. They set off together. They were laughing – Daedalus was favoured in that way. Most slaves would not dare to speak in Crassus' presence, far less laugh – but with him Germanicus seemed to encourage it. I watched them walk to the end of the lane, out of sight.'

'And who,' I said, 'was the last slave to leave the villa?'

He thought for a minute. 'I believe it was Rufus,' he said, slowly. 'The cart came around from the back of the lane, and Rufus got off and went back into the villa, as if he'd forgotten something. Yes, I had to wait for him to come back before I came out and locked the gate.'

'Then I have two reasons for finding Rufus,' I said, and escaped from the gatehouse before he had time to breathe on me again.

Aulus had told me a great deal. I wondered how much of it I could trust. He had told me at least one obvious falsehood. Even by his own testimony, the last person to leave the villa was not Rufus, but Aulus himself. If anyone, going to the procession, had opened the gates or left them open for an intruder, who was more likely than the gatekeeper-spy?

Chapter Seven

I found Rufus in the slaves' quarters at the back of the house. It was a big barn-like building with a central nave, and aisles divided by columns. One side of it was screened off for the women slaves, and at the far end of the building was a partitioned room, which I guessed was for Andretha. Between the aisles were the sleeping spaces for the household slaves; the land labourers, obviously, had more rustic accommodation elsewhere.

Rufus was sitting on a bed – presumably his own – stringing his lute. He was clearly preparing to join the musicians and I had arrived just in time. I wanted to speak to him quickly, before Andretha had him in there for hours playing the lament.

I had not said so to Aulus, but I knew Rufus very slightly. He was a Silurian from the rebel tribes in the West, a slim, graceful youth, with delicate features – almost pretty, like a woman, with his blue eyes, fair skin and aureole of auburn curls. But for all his girlish looks there was an air about him, something in the stubborn jut of the jaw, the determined lift of the chin. When I had first been at the villa laying the pavement, he had come into the room one day, and admired the work.

'We are both artists,' he had said, at once, 'I in music and you in stone. We are both Celts. It is in our blood.'

I had found the sentiments rather endearing, although I should have been more impressed by his flattery if the pavement had been one of my own design, and not Junio's *Cave Canem*. Even so, I wondered that any slave cared to look.

I am too easily flattered. Aulus had just unwittingly suggested a much more likely explanation. The librarium had once been used for the slavegirls, as I knew, and Regina had been given 'the slavegirls' room'. It was not hard to deduce the rest. When Regina had gone again, Rufus had come to the room, probably hoping to find his girl. No wonder he had never returned to see the finished pavement.

He looked up now as I approached, though his hands continued to caress the lute. Long, tapering, sensitive fingers, but strong and dextrous too, from plying the strings.

'Rufus!' I said heartily, sitting down beside him uninvited. 'How fares your lady?'

He did not ask who I meant, or make any attempt to deny it. 'Faustina? She is well. And likely to be so too, now that oa— now that her master is dead.' His voice sounded passionate; he had been going to say 'that oaf', I was certain of it. I saw, too, that he had been crying.

'Then why the tears?'

He looked at me helplessly. 'It occurs to me . . . I hadn't thought before . . . even if we are not executed, when the villa is sold we may be separated, Faustina and I. Sold to different masters. You cannot imagine . . .'

Oh, but I could. I could imagine only too well. For a moment I was back in that roundhouse thirty years ago, a raider's dagger at my throat and a rope around my neck, watching helplessly as they dragged Gwellia from me, shrieking and struggling, her hands outstretched and her lovely face ugly with tears. I could imagine, perhaps better than Rufus. I had seen that scene a thousand times in my dreams.

I must be careful, I thought. Rufus was not at the procession, and he had lied to me about it. It would be too easy to let personal sympathy for his plight cloud my judgement on that fact. Still, he prided himself on a kind of Celtic honesty. I decided on a direct approach.

'You were not at the procession.' He made to protest, and I went on, 'Not all of the procession, at least.'

His cheeks turned the colour of his hair, but he met my eyes. 'So Aulus told you? I am not surprised – I refused to pay him. I have no money anyway. Yes, it's true. I couldn't see Andretha anywhere – I supposed he had slipped off to a tavern somewhere – but I forgot Aulus. He would inform on anyone for money. I suppose you paid him?'

'I did not, though he is certainly someone's spy.' I did not enlighten him further. 'Where did you go?'

'Didn't he discover that too? I am surprised.'

'He thought,' I said, choosing my words carefully, 'that you might have gone to meet Faustina.'

He seized on the words. 'And if I did, what then? It isn't easy to find five minutes alone. Yet I love her. If I had not been sold to slavery myself, I would have bought her and married her. I would have found the money somehow.'

He was freeborn, of course, Aulus had said so. Before they sold him, such a marriage would have been possible. But not now. Slaves could not legally marry anyone. Even previous marriages, like my own, were legally void for slaves.

I smiled at his simple fervour. 'Supposing that Crassus would agree to part with her.'

That sobered him. 'Yes. Though I would have waited. Ten years if necessary. He would have tired of her by then.'

'Then you still may. Is not your slave contract for ten years? And if Lucius owns you . . .'

He brightened. 'It is true, then, that Lucius will inherit? There was a rumour, but I hardly dared to hope. Faustina says—' He stopped.

'What does Faustina say?'

He looked at me anxiously. 'I should not have heard this, it was woman's talk . . .'

'All the same,' I urged.

'She seemed to think Regina would inherit some-thing, that she had some kind of hold over Germanicus. Something he did or said when he was young. Regina came here a moon or two ago, claiming to be his . . .' he glanced at me. 'Do you know about this?'

'I have heard something.'

'Faustina did her hair and helped her bathe and dress when she was here. Regina had her own slave and a *custos* – a travelling companion – but she preferred Faustina. She sent her own maid away. She really wished, I think, to marry Crassus. For his money, perhaps. Faustina could not understand it. All the money in the world would not tempt her to his bed, if she had the choice.'

But of course, as his slave, she had no choice at all. 'Did Germanicus know,' I said carefully, 'about your feelings?' I had heard Aulus' account of this, but I wondered what Rufus would say.

He surprised me. 'Yes. He must have done. He never spoke of it. But it gave him pleasure, I think, to make me witness what he did to her. If he made her dance for him at entertainments – he had a costume for her, a skirt only and a necklace of hazelnuts – he would make me play while she danced. She would have to dance closer and closer, half naked, right over him, and he would snap at the nuts with his teeth. Sometimes he bit the nuts, sometimes her breasts – savage bites – while the other guests laughed and cheered. She would be weeping sometimes, with pain and shame, while I was forced to watch it. And then he would send her off, to wait his pleasure, and when the guests were gone he would call for me, to play the lute outside the door, and listen to him with her on the bed within.'

Suddenly, I could imagine that. Crassus was like a cruel cat with his victims, not striking them outright but teasing them with careful tortures.

There were tears of anger in the boy's eyes again. 'Oh, yes,' he said bitterly. 'Crassus knew.'

'Did you kill him, Rufus?' I could almost have understood it if he had.

'I never touched him,' Rufus said. He got up. 'And now, excuse me, I am wanted at the lament. I risk a beating already.' He moved towards the door.

I called after him. 'Rufus, how well did you know Daedalus?'

He stopped, surprised. 'Better than most. We shared a love of music. He was a clever man. I liked him, although many didn't.'

'Then why,' I said, 'do you speak of him like everyone else in the villa, in the past tense? As if he were dead?'

Rufus paused at the doorway to look at me for a moment. 'Well, isn't he?' he said. 'Daedalus was an honourable man. If he was alive, he would have come back.' And then he was gone himself.

I sat for a moment gazing after him. One thing I was now completely certain of. Crassus had possessed at least one mortal enemy in his household. Two, if you counted Faustina. I have moved, with Marcus, in some exalted circles but I have rarely seen more concentrated hatred than I had just seen on Rufus' face. Whoever had done the murder, Rufus had wished Germanicus dead. 'I never touched him,' he had said, but he hadn't denied the killing.

And he had been last actually to come out of the villa and he had missed much of the procession. I noticed, too, that he had evaded my question about where he had actually been.

I got up and looked around the sleeping space.

Slaves do not have many possessions. What they do have is usually hidden somewhere away from the buildings, in some hollow tree or buried in a spot which the hider devoutly hopes is secret – there is little privacy in the slaves' quarters. Nevertheless, there are one or two places where it is always sensible to look. I knew them. I was once a slave myself.

I knelt down and buried my hand under the bed covering, among the pile of straw and reeds which was Rufus' bed. At first I could feel nothing, and I was almost about to give up, when my fingers closed on something smooth and soft, wrapped with a leather thong. I drew it out.

A woven pouch. My fingers probed the cloth, but there were no coins in it. Rufus had spoken the truth about that. That was surprising. A lute player like Rufus might expect a few small coins at least, after playing at a banquet – from the guests, if not from his master. But there was no money here. I untied the thong, and opened the pouch.

There were two packets inside it, each wrapped in a small folded piece of cloth. One held a lock of reddish hair – long, curled, and dyed. Perfumed, too. Faustina's almost certainly. The other was a surprise. There was a wisp of hair in that, too: short, dark, coarse and curly. Not more than a hair or two, and no longer than my thumbnail, but carefully wrapped as though each single strand was precious.

I squatted back on my heels and looked at it. Not a second girl, surely? Rufus was too much in love for that. A sister or mother, perhaps? No, it didn't look like a woman's hair. His father's then? But what was he doing with his father's hair hidden in his mattress? It made no sense at all.

There was a movement at the doorway, and I wrapped the pouch quickly together again and stuffed it back where I had found it. But no one came in.

I waited. Still nothing happened. I felt that prickling sensation on my scalp again.

I went to the door and looked out. Nothing. Only the distant slaves still loading the last of the logs onto the farm cart. It was unnerving.

I glanced back up the sleeping room. No, I told myself, I was imagining things. I must do the second thing I had come for – glance into Andretha's room while I was here. 'A hoarder' Aulus had called him. It would be interesting to see what he was hoarding.

I walked slowly down the room. On the way, though, my eye was caught by a small chest-cupboard beside one of the beds. It belonged to Paulus, obviously: there was the strigil and the oil still on the carrying-tray on top. I paused.

A noise. I whirled around, but too late. All I saw was the flutter of a tunic at the doorway, and the room was still again. But there was no doubt of it. I was being watched.

Well, if they came again I would be ready. I went over deliberately and opened the cupboard. It was not fastened. There was nothing of interest there, simply the tools of his trade.

I glanced behind me. The room was still empty. I knelt down quickly, intending to rummage in the bed straw, as I had done earlier further down the room.

Then something hit me hard on the back of the head. I had a confused sensation of pitching forwards, and that was that.

Chapter Eight

The next hours are a blur to me. I do dimly remember shouts and voices, being carried uncomfortably over a strong shoulder to the accompaniment of a strong smell of onions while my head ached and throbbed, and then being lowered gratefully onto a soft, welcoming bed. I seemed to spend a long time then halfway between waking and sleeping, but I preferred sleep. It hurt less. When I did awake at last, and opened an experimental eye, I found Junio bending over me with a goblet of something aromatic and steaming.

For a moment, I fancied that I was at home. I blinked myself awake, cautiously. Window-glass, a raised bed, fine coverings, spiced mead, Junio at my side and half a cohort of anxious slaves (including a pair of pretty girls) waiting at my feet – I had either been kidnapped by Bacchus or I was still in Crassus' villa.

I struggled to sit up, but a blinding pain in my head made me grimace. Not heaven, then.

'What are you doing here—?' I began, but my voice wouldn't answer my command. Junio pressed the goblet to my lips.

'Hush,' he said. 'Marcus had me sent for as soon as he saw you.'

'Marcus?' I said stupidly, trying to assemble my

scattered wits. 'Is he here too?'

Junio waited for me to sip the reviving mixture again, before he answered. 'Andretha sent for him, immediately Aulus found you. And Marcus sent for me. He will be exceedingly glad to find you recovered.'

He meant Marcus, I realised after a fleeting confusion. For a moment I thought he was still talking about the chief slave. Poor Andretha, I thought indistinctly. Another culpable lack of security. First his master's body found and now an official guest attacked. The man must be flapping like a bat. I managed a faint grin, but the pain in my head immediately reminded me that this was no smiling matter.

Junio, however, had noticed my expression and grinned too – with obvious relief. 'I confess that I have been worried myself, though I should have known you were tougher than a badger. You have had the whole villa in an uproar. Marcus was almost ready to read a second funeral oration tonight.'

Even my scrambled brains detected that something was amiss with that. 'Tonight?'

Junio took the goblet from me and somehow contrived to press my hand as he did so. 'My dear friend and master, the sun has been to bed and risen again since you were carried here yesterday.' He sounded genuinely upset. 'Andretha has had slaves burning herbs by your bedside and bathing your face with water ever since. Marcus was ready to send for the army physician, but Faustina here is skilled with herbs. She has bathed your wounds and I . . .' he released my hand and grinned again, 'I said that spiced mead would revive you, if anything could. And it did. Between us, as you see, we have robbed Charon of one passenger tonight, at least.'

This time I did manage to struggle upwards and support myself on an elbow. I had forgotten Crassus. 'And the other passenger,' I said. 'What of him?'

Junio's grin broadened. 'Germanicus, master? Much as he was,' he said, with a cheeky twinkle. 'I fear he is beyond the help even of spiced mead.'

I would have smiled at his impudence, but my head deterred me. His words, though, had given me cause to think. 'Spiced mead,' I said slowly. 'Or Faustina's herbs either.'

I turned to the slavegirls. One was slight, fair and blue-eyed, with delicate arms and a slim, shapely body. The other was rounder, older, with heavy breasts and darker features, her long, dyed red-brown hair tied back in a golden braid. 'Which of you is Faustina?'

I shouldn't have needed to ask, except that my mind was still functioning slowly.

'I am, excellence,' the darker girl said. Of course! That lock of hair in Rufus' pouch.

I summoned a smile. 'Thank you for your care.' A slavegirl, my sluggish brain was thinking, with a knowledge of herbs and a motive to detest her master. Enough to poison him, perhaps? And then put him in the furnace, to disguise the signs? 'I should like,' I said, 'to speak to you, alone.'

They misinterpreted. Even Junio threw me an astonished glance. The other slaves withdrew instantly, of course – Andretha had obviously left instructions that my every whim was to be obeyed – but I saw the looks they exchanged. They must have extraordinary illusions, I thought, about my powers of recovery.

'I am at your service, excellence.' She stepped forward, wary but resigned, in the manner of young slavegirls everywhere. 'What is your desire?'

'I wish to talk to you,' I said, 'about your master's death.'

Her relief was visible. It was hardly complimentary, perhaps, but I was secretly amused. Her whole being relaxed. 'Is that all? We can talk, of course, but there is nothing more I can tell you.'

I sat up, warily. My head swam and the blood rushed in my ears, but I felt I lacked authority, lounging awkwardly on a bed while the girl stood before me. Besides, despite that blow on my head, the last few moments had set my thoughts in unexpected directions. I needed to look directly at her face; from where I had been reclining the image of those dancing hazelnuts was too disturbingly vivid.

I dragged my gaze reluctantly to her eyes. They were dark and defensive. 'I am sure you answered all our questions, then,' I said, 'but I have discovered some new ones, since we spoke. For instance, at the feast of Mars, when Rufus left the others at the procession, did he go to meet you?'

She hesitated. 'So you know of that? I am surprised he told you.'

I forced myself to think clearly. 'He didn't. Not in so many words. To do so would have implicated you. But Rufus is a poor liar.'

'He is no liar. He is scrupulously truthful.'

'He did not tell us that he had left the parade.'

She looked at me frankly with those dark, brown eyes. 'Did you ask him that? Directly?'

'No,' I conceded. It was true. All Marcus had asked was whether Rufus had attended the procession, and come and gone with the others. All of which, presumably, he had done. When I had asked him direct questions, he had answered frankly, or skilfully evaded answering at all. 'No, I suppose not,' I said again. I was beginning to have a new respect for Rufus.

She smiled. 'There you are, then.'

I was beginning to wonder what other information I might have obtained if I had asked the right questions. 'So that, if he tells me that he did not touch his master. . . ?'

'He did not touch him. I would swear to that.'

Even then I needed to spell it out for myself. ' "Did not touch" – those were his words. Could he, do you believe, have killed by other means?'

She coloured and looked away. 'I do not understand.'

'You lie, Faustina,' I said gently. 'Even if *he* does not. You understand perfectly. There are ways of killing a man without touching him. Poison for instance.'

'Poison!' She was shocked and shaken. Whatever she had been thinking, it was not that. 'No, Rufus did not poison him. I'm sure.' She believed that passionately, if I am any judge of humankind.

'So,' I said, 'what did he do?'

She shook her head. 'Nothing. No. Not really. He did not murder Crassus. You have my life on it.'

'But he wished him dead?'

There was a pause. Then, reluctantly, 'Yes. He did. But which of us did not?'

I said gently, 'And you, Faustina. Did you wish him dead?'

She paused, then said, in a voice unsteady with anger, 'I have prayed for his death a thousand times. Rufus was not alone.'

'You had the means, Faustina,' I said. 'You are skilled with herbs, so Junio says. You learned that skill from someone. Someone in the house?'

'It is nothing, the merest rudiments. She had no time to teach me more.'

'She?' There were few females in the villa. Faustina's mother perhaps, or one of the older slaves? Surely not the other dancing girl? But 'had no time' – in the past tense? My fuddled brain made a leap of understanding. 'It was Regina,' I said, with sudden certainty. 'Regina taught you what you know? She was an expert with potions.'

I did not know that, but it seemed a likely guess. In the circumstances, I was proud of my deduction.

I had hit the mark. Faustina raised her eyes to mine. 'Well,' she said, 'what of it? Many a countrywoman is an expert in the properties of plants. Regina is famed for it. Ointments and potions, balms and salves – she can make them all. She has a whole chestful of dried herbs, and little jars and phials. Everyone came to her. She even gave Paulus a salve for his bruises. That was how she met Germanicus, she told me. He came to her to buy an infusion of herbs against the toothache. Her cures are good. She gave me berry leaves to ease the pangs of childbirth – better than all the midwife's charms and tokens. Without that brew I think I might have bent the bar they gave me to strain upon.'

It took me a moment to digest this news. 'You have a child?'

The dark face darkened. '*Had* a child.' Her voice trembled. 'Almost three moons ago. It is dead, of course. Eliminated at birth.'

I felt a pang of sympathy. Had Gwellia, I wondered, ever borne a child to some wealthy master, only to have it killed or exposed at birth? It is one aspect of the Roman law I have no stomach for, this denial that a newborn baby is human. I murmured something sympathetic.

'What would you expect?' she said bitterly. 'Germanicus would hardly take it up.'

'Take it up' literally, she meant. Even a man's own wife must present her newborn child, and the father must accept it as his by lifting it up from the ground when it is shown him. If he does not, he rejects it, denies it legal existence, and it is left to die. A slave baby is often not even accorded the dignity of a quiet death. It is the master's property already, since he owns the mother, so if it is not required as a 'pet', it is likely to be disposed of by drowning, like an unwanted puppy, or fed to the hounds.

But there was nothing unusual in this – indeed I was slightly surprised that Faustina should mourn the death of Crassus' child. Unless . . .

'Germanicus was the father?'

She turned away. 'How can I know? I hope not – or rather, I hope so, since the child is dead.'

'But it might have been Rufus'?'

She looked at me and her eyes were trembling with tears. 'Yes. Perhaps. Germanicus may have guessed. But he did not seem to care. He liked me . . . swollen. His only concern was that I should stop bleeding and be purified, so I could get back to his bed again. He had Regina make a potion for me.'

'Was it successful?'

She grimaced. 'I did not take it. I was in no haste. But I would have had to come to him soon. I could not delay much longer. No doubt it would have worked. Regina is skilled with herbs. Germanicus thought so. He was afraid of her, you know. She made a love potion for him years ago, he claimed – she is plain-featured, and thin, not how he likes his women – and he would not eat or drink while she was in the villa without Daedalus tasting first.'

Despite my throbbing head, I smiled. The idea of ugly Germanicus employing a food taster to protect him from a plain woman was laughable. 'And did she make a love potion this time?'

Faustina laughed. 'Perhaps. She was certainly confident of being married soon, she told me so. But if she made a potion, Crassus must have known a cure. He persuaded her to take money, I think. She left here without him and we have not seen her since.'

'Married?' I said. 'But to whom? To Crassus, or to Daedalus?'

She laughed again. 'You think perhaps the taster took the potion? That may be true. Daedalus liked her. Rufus would believe it, he had faith in these things. Myself, I trust her remedies for wounds and illness, not for charms. She is a healer, not a sorceress. I know, she taught me something of her art. Simple cures: ivy for burns and bruises, aconite for pains in the joints and teeth, Hercules-wort for a wound, hellebore for ulcers, and belladonna for the eyes. All the herbs of Saturn. They have great power.'

'And most of them are poisons, are they not?'

'For those with knowledge, no, or you would long be dead. I put bruised henbane and hemlock on your head, and you have sniffed the fume of them for hours – it is to soothe the swelling and reduce the ache. But the dose is vital. A man absorbs the essence through his skin. Too much of it can kill.'

I put a tentative hand to my throbbing skull. There was a tender lump on the back of my head, and when I took my hand away there was indeed a small curled leaf adhering to my finger. I picked it off and looked at it in dismay.

'Henbane?' I said. 'Hemlock?' I would have to soak my fingers in the stream.

'Parsley,' Faustina said. 'To stop the bruise from blackening. I have removed the others, though the leaves of all three are not unalike. Aconite too.'

And any of those poisons, I thought, might have dispatched Germanicus. Perhaps they had done. No wonder Crassus feared his would-be wife.

'Tell me something of Regina,' I said. 'Did you like her?'

'Very much. Too good for Crassus – yet she wanted him. She was no longer young, of course, and her family have lost their lands. The army took them, she says, and her father died leaving her with nothing. She has no dowry, otherwise Crassus might have taken her, plain or not. But, equally, without a husband she was afraid of starving. I suppose that was why she wanted to marry Crassus. It cannot have been for the charm of his company.' She spoke with fervour.

'Yes.' I understood that. When the army settled in a place, they took over the surrounding farms as a *terratorium* to feed the legions. Often the local landowners were reduced to working as labourers on the fields they once owned. But it was harder for a woman, especially an older one. Even Crassus, presumably, was better than beggary.

'She was good to me,' Faustina said. 'She tried to influence Germanicus, about the baby. Tried to persuade him to let it live. Daedalus did too. It might have been given to some childless peasant, or a Roman family who wanted a future whipping boy. But Crassus had it drowned, just the same. Without Daedalus, though, it might have been stoned for sport, or left to the dogs.'

'You could be forgiven,' I said softly, 'for feeling murderous yourself.'

'I do. I did. But I did not kill Crassus. And Rufus did not either, for anything he says.'

'He says – or rather, he implies – that he was with you,' I said. 'Where did he meet you, during the procession?'

She hesitated. 'You must ask him that.'

'I have asked him. Now I am asking you.'

I saw her waver. She was an honest woman but she would have lied, cheerfully, to protect Rufus. Perhaps in that regard she was less scrupulous than he was. But she did not know how to answer.

She was not above inventing some reply. I said, 'I should warn you, someone followed him.'

'Aulus!' she said at once. She saw a way out, and took it. 'But since you have a witness, you must know where we went! Now, citizen, you should lie back a little. You have done too much. You are turning pale.'

I could not argue. I could feel the blood draining from my face, and I felt suddenly giddy.

'Come,' she said, 'I will fetch you a linctus. Junio!'

The last words were a summons. Junio came hastening in. 'Great Jove,' he said, when he saw me, 'you are whiter than a marble tessella. And Marcus is asking to see you.'

'Then you had better show him in,' I said. It is one of the more obvious secrets of long life, not keeping the governor's representative waiting.

Chapter Nine

Marcus, of course, did not come unattended. Andretha was with him, fluttering and bowing like a courting pigeon.

I was lying back onto the bed by this time. I tried to stand when Marcus arrived, but he waved me to lean back against the cushions which Junio had found me. I was still reclining, therefore, while he sat down beside me on a gilded chair – I felt like the governor receiving homage.

Andretha flapped a hand in my direction. 'Here he is, excellence. Recovering well, as you see.' He glanced at Marcus' face and hastened to change his tone. 'But what a terrible thing. That this should happen to him, in my care! Anything that I can do to help, please name it, anything.'

'What do you need, old friend?' Marcus said affably, to me.

It was almost worth being knocked on the head for. Lying back and giving orders like the emperor himself.

'A little wine, perhaps? Some meat or soup? This cur shall fetch it for you, or I'll have him whipped.' Marcus has a vitriolic style when he chooses.

I could have had anything the villa offered, but I felt delicate. 'Water,' I said, 'and a little fruit.'

Marcus whirled on Andretha. 'Do you see what your carelessness has brought him to? Dining on fruit and water. My poor friend!' I did not tell him that in my workshop I often dined on less. He gestured to Andretha who was duly cowed. 'Fetch it – and some wine for me. And when I find who did this . . .'

The chief servant, in his desire to please, bowed himself out backwards like the lowliest of slaves.

Marcus leaned forward. 'He will be punished, too, of course,' he said, lazily. 'But that does not help the matter. This attack has laid you low and disturbed my plans. Here you are, hurt, and you have had no chance to learn anything.'

Typically patrician. He was concerned for me, of course, but equally concerned about his errand. I must have been still half dazed, for I could not resist boasting. 'I have learned a little, excellence.'

I should have known better. Had I agreed with him, and simply lain back complaining of my head, I might have spent the next ten days recovering in comfort, with Andretha and Junio tending my every need. As it was, though, Marcus brightened.

'I should have trusted you! What news, my friend?'

I told him briefly, struggling to put the facts in order. 'Four slaves, at least, were not at the procession. Paulus, the barber slave, confessed his absence himself.' I didn't tell Marcus about the Druid connection. Even in my stunned state I knew better than that. 'Rufus, the lute player, was seen to leave. Andretha was missing too, if my guess is right. He did not tell us of the other absences, which he certainly would have done if he had known. Rufus confirms it. He thought Andretha had gone to an alehouse – which might well be true.' If he had drunk the vilest brew in the taverna, I thought, his head could not ache more than mine did.

'Where did the others go?'

'I am not sure, yet. Rufus would have us think he went to meet the girl slave, Faustina.'

'A lovers' meeting?'

I shook my head, and then wished I hadn't. 'I do not think so. Aulus saw him leave, and followed him, but Rufus hid in a wayside temple. Faustina is trying to shield her lover, and is agreeing that they met, but she does not know what to say. I don't think they had time to arrange a story before Andretha summoned the boy to play the lute at the lament.'

Marcus inclined his head. 'He is there still. I have been talking to the chief musician. Rufus left once to change a broken lute-string, but apart from that none of the musicians has left the room. They are taking it in turns to play, and sleeping at the door.'

Strange, when I came to think of it. I could not hear the dirge. I said so.

Marcus smiled. 'I ordered them to mourn more quietly. I feared their wailing might disturb you while you slept. I have no wish to lose you, and be forced to mourn in earnest.'

He had paid me a compliment, and for a moment I basked in it. It was, after all, the only thing he was likely to pay me. But just for a moment. Marcus said suddenly, with the flourish of a schoolboy outguessing his master, 'So, even if she did not meet her lover, Faustina was the fourth slave missing?'

I said, 'I doubt if she ever left the procession. She implied that she went to meet Rufus, but that was to protect him. I imagine the other slaves could tell us. No, the fourth missing slave was Aulus himself. By his own admission he left the others, and we only have his testimony for exactly what he did next.'

Marcus was a little crestfallen. 'You think, then, that this was an internal affair after all – Crassus was killed by someone from the villa?'

I shrugged. 'Others do not think so. Aulus believes those soldiers had a part in it. He may be right. Andretha insists that we must find Daedalus. He has a case, too. After all Daedalus was the last person from here to be seen with Crassus, and now he has disappeared.'

'And if his freedom was refused,' Marcus supplied, 'he might have a motive. I have told the guards to watch for him, anyway. He will soon be found if he is in Glevum.'

'Have them search, too, for this Regina, Crassus' would-be wife. Ask in the nearby inns. Aulus thinks Daedalus has gone to her.'

We were interrupted by Andretha, bearing wine, water, and a platter of luscious-looking fruits. Plums, apples, medlars all of a sweetness and ripeness that my humble purse could never have commanded. Marcus handed me the water, and took out his knife absently. Most Romans carry one, in case of dining out, since few houses provide knives for guests. I devoutly wished that I had brought my own. He waved Andretha out of the room again and began to peel a plum.

'And?' he prompted.

'She – this promised wife – is an expert in poisons, and she has taught the slavegirl to be the same. Faustina and Rufus loathed Crassus. Faustina swears she did not *kill* her master, but does not say she did not touch him. She may have moved the body, for instance. Rufus did not *touch* him, but may have killed him all the same. They choose their denials with care.'

Marcus speared a piece of peeled plum with his knife.

'Perhaps, but you are forgetting one thing. When could they have done it? They may have missed the procession, but Crassus didn't. He was leading his cohort.'

I said, respectfully, 'It occurs to me, excellence, that one man in armour and a mask looks very like another.'

'You mean, it was not Crassus in the march?'

'That is possible, yes.'

He thought about that for a moment. 'So the murder may have happened during the parade? While they were missing?'

'That seems a likely explanation. It does not answer the question of how the body was brought back to the villa, or why, but it offers a beginning.'

'Perhaps Crassus did not leave the villa at all.'

'I thought of that. Aulus says he did. How reliable is Aulus? If one man can buy his services, perhaps another could, by offering a higher price.'

Marcus cut another piece of plum. 'There is no higher price. I hold his life. One word from me and the courts would have him.'

'For picking up a purse that he happened upon? That's not a crucifying offence, surely. One word from the quaestor would prove that he is innocent of the real theft?' I was surprised. Marcus can be cruel, but he is not wanton.

Marcus laughed. 'Innocent? What makes you think he was innocent? The man who died – the one who stole the purse – that was his brother! How do you think that Aulus just "happened" to be there? He was waiting, at an arranged spot, to take the money and disappear while we chased fruitlessly after the thief. It had worked before. Only they reckoned this time without the quaestor's sword. Aulus wasn't innocent. He was guilty as Tantalus.'

I felt rather foolish.

'And another thing,' Marcus went on. 'Something you have overlooked in your calculations. You have done well, certainly, but there is one thing more. Someone else from the villa who was not at the procession.'

I tried to follow his line of thought. 'Ah, yes,' I said, 'Regina.'

'Not her,' he said impatiently. 'A slave. A member of the household.'

'Who, excellence?'

'Why, Daedalus himself,' he said triumphantly. 'Your fugitive slave. You are quite right, we must find him. He is more likely than anyone to have killed Crassus.'

If Andretha was listening at the door, as I suspected, he was doubtless smiling now.

'It is essential to find him, excellence,' I agreed. 'And your sources are good.'

That pleased him. 'By the bye, I have not been idle since I saw you. I had enquiries made at the barracks. Those soldiers Aulus reported, they are not from Glevum. Everyone in the garrison was accounted for at curfew every day. Perhaps, though, if this is a household murder, it no longer matters.'

'On the contrary, excellence,' I said. 'It must be significant. A Roman soldier, twice – at dusk, at a private villa, down a country lane? And Germanicus keeping it secret? It cannot be coincidence.'

Marcus got up, preening. 'Well, I must let you rest. I have arranged transport for you to the funeral, if you are well enough to come. I am having two litters sent from Glevum, and a dozen slaves to carry them. The will was formally opened and read in the forum this afternoon, incidentally. Everything to be sold and the money to Lucius, just as you said.'

'No memorial games?' I asked. Most wealthy men left a substantial sum to endow a gladiatorial contest, to ensure that the local populace remembered them with affection.

Marcus laughed. 'Crassus did not care for good opinion, if he wasn't to profit by it. More to his taste to endow a church, and try to bribe his way into the hereafter. Now, is there anything you want?'

'I would like to see Junio,' I said. Marcus was looking so pleased with himself that I did not dare say what I truly wanted – a plum, if only he had left one! It would not do, either, to tell him that he was mistaken in his reasoning.

If Germanicus was not among the marchers, then someone else was. And there was only one obvious candidate, one man who could pass himself off as his master with ease. I had suspected something since I saw those shaven legs. The dead man in the villa was not Daedalus, but the live one in the marching veterans was.

So if Crassus was killed during the procession, Daedalus was the one man who could not possibly have killed him.

All the same, like Andretha and Marcus – though for different reasons – I was very anxious to discover where Daedalus was now.

Chapter Ten

'And what,' I said to Junio, who had come in with a grin as wide as the West Gate, 'are you so pleased with yourself about?'

He put down the beaker and the bundle he was carrying. 'Well, master,' he said, 'since you are laid abed with a headache, I have been seeking information for you. And more than information. I have things to show you. But first, Faustina sent this for you to drink.' He handed me the beaker.

I looked at the evil-smelling green fluid with dismay. 'It looks like pond water.'

'It isn't pond water,' he said, cheerfully. 'It is a decoction of herbs. To soothe the headache, she said, and clear the wits. It tastes like pond water, certainly, but it will do no harm. I can promise that.'

I sipped it doubtfully. He was right. It did taste like pond water. Or at least – since I have never knowingly drunk pond water – it certainly tasted like pond water smells. I grimaced.

'Let us hope it is as powerful as it tastes.' I sipped again. Perhaps it *was* efficacious for the brain, because a thought struck me. 'How do you know what it tastes like?'

He didn't have to answer, of course. It was self-evident. Someone in the villa was a murderer, and I had just been struck on the head.

He said it anyway. 'I couldn't allow you to drink it without making sure.' He grinned. 'Where would I find another master to teach me pavement making?'

He had tasted it for poison. While I was talking to Marcus, obviously. He knew it was a service I would never ask him to perform. It was hard to know how to thank him. He had done no more than what might have been his duty, but he had risked his life for me.

'You young rascal,' I growled. 'What did you mean by that? Suppose it had been hemlock? Where should I find another servant with your impudence?'

He smiled at me in perfect understanding. 'In any case,' he said, 'it was not a great risk. I did not think Faustina would brew a poison and openly send it to you. You were in more danger, perhaps, from that fruit and wine.'

That was true, too. It was to be hoped that Marcus did not fall down dead – although, of course, he had peeled his plums. *My* plums. 'Her potion seems to have sharpened your wits, at least,' I said.

He grinned again. 'More than you think. While I was gone I asked Andretha to show me the spot where you were found. Aulus discovered you, it seems, face down on the barber's bedding pile.'

'Aulus? What was he doing there?'

He shrugged. 'Who knows? On the way to the slaves' latrine, perhaps? Or gone hoping to beg a clean tunic from the women who wash the slave linen?' That was possible. Crassus, like most rich men, might send his own linen to the fuller, but a quick rinse in the stream would suffice for his servants' clothes. Junio laughed. 'Or maybe he was just snooping. He is a spy after all!

Andretha had sent him a relief, because he will be needed tonight to carry the bier. He has the strongest shoulders in the villa.'

I nodded. Perhaps it was the result of Faustina's herbs, but the pain was less already.

'I asked myself,' Junio said, 'what *you* were doing there. Looking for something, I guessed. So while Marcus was talking to you I went back and looked myself. It was easy to see which was the barber's bed – there was a cabinet beside it with his tools on a tray. So I investigated. It was well buried in the bedding straw, but I found this.'

He handed me something long and hard, wrapped in a piece of stained leather.

'What is it?'

'I have not looked. I had just found it when a slave came in, so I got up quickly and hid it inside my tunic. Naturally I didn't want him to see me. It was just as well. It turned out to be Paulus himself. He was obviously terrified to find me there.'

I nodded. 'Paulus spends his whole life in a state of terror. It is one of Crassus' legacies.'

'Poor fellow,' Junio said. 'Anyway, I tried to reassure him. I said I had come to see where the accident happened. Paulus fell over himself showing me the spot, but of course I knew already. I felt rather treacherous, with his secret in my pocket. I don't know how Aulus does it. I would have searched further, but Paulus said he had come out looking for me because Faustina had your potion ready. So I fetched that, and then came straight here. I haven't opened it. I thought you would prefer to do that yourself. The leather seems sticky, it has stuck to what's inside. I was afraid to damage it.'

It was sticky, the dark leather stained with darker patches. I eased it open.

'A shaving knife!' Junio exclaimed. 'Great Jupiter!'

It was indeed a novacula. A recently sharpened one, for the blade showed the marks of the whetstone. A man would not need much oil to soften his skin with a blade like that at his hair-roots. Yet it was not the sharpness of the blade which had caused Junio's startled exclamation, it was the thick red-brown substance which still lingered on the base of the blade and the handle. The same substance which – slightly diluted it seemed – had discoloured the leather in which the razor was wrapped.

I did not need to sniff my fingers, although I did so. I recognised blood when I saw it. So too did Junio.

'Is that human blood?'

'Presumably! One does not go to the trouble of concealing a blade because one has skinned a rabbit with it.'

'Could it have been used on . . . him?' He nodded in the direction of the lament which seemed to have struck up anew.

I thought for a moment before answering. 'I suppose it could,' I said. 'Since the face is burned, it is possible that the throat was cut. But there would have been so much blood.'

He looked at the knife. 'Perhaps there *was* so much blood. Someone has rinsed the edge of the blade.'

I voiced the question which was troubling me. 'What happened, do you think? Yes, someone tried to rinse the knife, in the stream perhaps, but there must have been blood on his hands besides. Look, you can see the mark of a finger here. It makes no sense. Why would he not stop to clean the handle too?'

'Perhaps he was in a hurry,' Junio said. 'Especially if there was a lot of blood. Perhaps he even had to wash the corpse. Was there blood on the body?'

'No,' I said. 'None on the body or the arms. A little dried blood on the legs – they had not been washed. And none on the armour.'

'Then perhaps it was his own blood, whoever he was. Certainly it has cut through flesh. This knife is sharp enough. If only fingermarks and blood were like hairs, so that one could start to match them with their owners! That would give us some help.'

'There is a hair here,' I said, removing it carefully from the leather cover. It was short, dark and curled. It reminded me of the lock of hair I had found in Rufus' mattress.

'It looks like Crassus' own,' Junio said. 'That does not assist us much. If this razor was used to shave him, that hair might have been there since full moon.'

I had to agree.

'So,' Junio sounded disappointed, 'my discovery hasn't been a great help, after all.'

'I don't know,' I said. 'We could try asking Paulus. He hated his master. This novacula was found in his bed. He is the barber slave. Presumably he put it there.'

Looking back on it, I must have been more dazed from that blow than I thought. If I had had a quarter of my wits I should have seen the fallacy in that. Obviously, whoever used the knife, it wasn't Paulus who hid it in the bed. The reasoning didn't occur to me then, however, and I was feeling quite triumphant as I said, 'Let's have Paulus in here, and see what he has to say.'

Chapter Eleven

Paulus, however, was nowhere to be found.

Junio came back apologetic. 'I am sorry, master, I cannot find him anywhere. And why are you not on the bed, resting?'

I was asking myself the same question. While he was out of the room, I had clambered unsteadily out of bed. My head spun and my legs were strangely reluctant to hold me. They seemed to have turned into river eels. Nevertheless, years of slave life had taught me harsh habits. If I could stand up, I preferred to do so. One is less vulnerable on one's feet.

'You can thank Faustina's herbs,' I said, as cheerfully as I could manage. 'I think they are working.' There was some truth in that. I *was* feeling better. Groggy, but better. 'Anyway, Marcus expects me to attend this funeral; I should like to practise walking and standing a little first. A little fresh air perhaps? A short stroll up to the nymphaeum?' I did not mention my previous venture in that direction, or the mysterious footsteps which had followed me. Junio would have deduced that the footsteps belonged to my attacker and, fearing another attack, prevented me from going – or rather (since he was a servant and couldn't personally prevent me from doing anything) he would have told Marcus, which came to the same thing.

So I kept my counsel and went to the water temple, glad of the fresh air against my face. Junio accompanied me, grumbling all the while.

'If you should fall, now, what would become of you? And what would Marcus say if he heard that I'd brought you out here and you collapsed? He'd have me whipped.'

'I shall have you whipped myself,' I growled, 'if you don't stop jabbering. Look down there and tell me what you see.' I felt feeble enough, without his dwelling on it.

We had reached the nymphaeum by this time, a small semi-circular temple on pillars, enclosing a clear pool. The back wall was of natural stone, and from its base the water bubbled up, fresh from the spring, under the gaze of a slightly ferocious stone deity on a plinth. Beside the statue I could see the funeral niche, ready prepared, with room inside it for the urn and the feeding amphora – though putting food and drink into that on the anniversary of death was likely to be a damp business, given the position of the spring. There was also a space, I noticed, for a large carved stone over the niche. No doubt Crassus had left instructions for the inscription.

'I can see the little side gate, and the lane,' Junio said, making me jump. I had forgotten asking the question. 'And the villa – at least, the back and side of it. There is nobody there, only the slaves – eight, nine, ten of them.'

'What are they doing?'

'The usual things – fetching wood, sweeping the court, two of them tending the gardens, a couple of kitchen slaves with a chicken, someone coming this way with a jug, Andretha looking important . . . you can see all this for yourself; why do you ask?'

'I was thinking,' I said. 'The path which leads up here is invisible from the house. I noticed that yesterday.

That is interesting. It is difficult for a man – especially a rich man – to be alone and unobserved in a villa. Nobody there, you said – and yet there are ten of them.'

'Eleven now,' he said. 'There is Paulus, at last.'

'Then you can help me back to the house,' I said, 'and go and fetch him to me.' I would be glad, in fact, to sit down again. Faustina's herbs were good, but they were not magical. And I had seen all I wanted to see. I had examined the path carefully coming up, and I did the same going down, but there was no hint of my pursuer of the day before: no tell-tale little pieces of cloth or unexplained footprints. I didn't really expect there to be. Slaves must have been coming and going for water all day. The lad with the ewer, for instance, arrived again as we were leaving.

It took me longer than I expected to get back to the villa, even on Junio's arm, and I tried to divert his attention from my difficulties by telling him everything I had learned about the household. Then when, at last, I was lying back on my cushions again, he went off to find Paulus. He was back in a trice.

'I found him just outside the door, master,' Junio said, ushering in the barber. 'He says Andretha posted him there, ready to serve you.'

'You were not there a little while ago,' I said, though I remembered that at other times Paulus seemed to make a habit of being close outside my door.

Paulus smiled weakly. 'I have just come from the lament, citizen. Andretha arranged a roster. It was my turn to wail.' Ironic, I thought, to be obliged to mourn a man that you hated. 'When I had finished, I was to wait outside your room again in case you wanted anything. Of course you have your own slave now, but those were my orders.'

'Very well,' I said, feeling very clever and devious. 'I do want something. Marcus wants me to attend this funeral this evening, and I have not trimmed my hair or had a shave for two days. I am in danger of looking like Hadrian.' That wily old emperor had sported a beard, and set a brief fashion, years ago. 'You are a barber. You can do it for me.'

Junio shot me an astonished glance. I do occasionally visit a barber shop in Glevum – it is almost as good as the public baths for hearing the town's gossip – but on the whole I prefer to avoid their nose-hair tweezers and their bear-fat-and-ashes treatments for thinning hair. A simple piece of Roman pumice and a dab of oil suffices me, or for special occasions, a painful scrape with a sharpened blade from Junio himself.

He had enough wit, however, to say nothing.

I watched Paulus carefully. Would he betray anxiety? Make excuses? Go and rummage for the knife?

For a moment it seemed promising. Paulus clearly was both flattered and terrified. 'Yes, citizen. At once. I need only to collect my tools . . .'

I produced my masterstroke. 'Go with him, Junio. Help him to carry them.'

Junio nodded. I did not need to tell him what I wanted – someone to watch Paulus.

The barber looked startled. 'I have a carrying-tray, citizen. There is no need . . .'

'All the same,' I said. 'I would prefer that he went with you.' I was improvising wildly. 'Someone hit me on the head yesterday, close to your bed. If Junio looks carefully he may discover something which will tell us who or why.'

'Citizen, there will be nothing there. I can promise that. The sleeping spaces are cleaned and swept daily.

Andretha insists on it. Truly, there is nothing to be found. In any case, Junio has examined the place already. I found him there earlier.'

'I will come with you anyway,' Junio put in quickly. 'I can tell you which oils my master prefers – and I have this drinking-cup to return to Faustina. But I will see that Marcus leaves a guard posted outside this door this time. The citizen keeps ordering me away but he does not require another blow on the head.'

Faustina's brew, I thought, had improved my head – but not enough. I should have thought of that danger myself. I should have thought of others, too. Was it safe, for instance, to let Junio go to the slave quarters with Paulus?

It was too late now. The two young slaves had gone.

Now I did come to think of it, I felt in no real danger myself, especially with one of Marcus' guards at the door. That blow on the head had been hard, deliberately hard, but it had not been meant to kill. Surely a killer would have struck again? I had been helpless. A second blow could have finished me, but it was never given.

Suppose the attacker had intended to strike again, but was prevented? Because he was surprised in the act, perhaps? Or because spending too long at that time and place would have betrayed him? Andretha was outside, supervising the loading of the logs. He would have noticed anyone coming to the building.

Who had hit me? Aulus had 'found me' lying there. Was that because he himself had laid me low? A sharp tap with that cudgel would be an effective sleeping draught. Or Rufus? Marcus had mentioned, now I came to consider it, that Rufus had left the mourners to restring his lute. Had he found a handy weapon some-where and seized the moment? Or wasn't it a 'he' at all?

If my attacker was a woman that might explain why the blow had not been mortal.

Or was it never intended to do more than stun? To prevent me searching? I did not know. My addled brain refused to reason clearly. I could only wait on events. I was very interested in what Paulus, for instance, would do now.

And then, of course, the obvious occurred to me. Of course Paulus would not hunt for the novacula. It made no sense. Why should a barber hide a razor in his bedding, when all he had to do was place it on his tray, where it would excite no interest whatever? He might have hidden it, certainly, if it were bloodstained and he had no time to clean it – but Paulus had prepared a tray of toilet accessories for me only yesterday, and the blood on the handle was older than that. It would have been simplicity itself to clean the knife. Besides, I was found face downwards on his bed, obviously I had been search-ing his bedding. Anyone might wonder what I was looking for – as Junio had. A man with a guilty secret would not leave it there.

I took out the novacula from inside my tunic, where I had hidden it during the walk, and unwrapped it carefully. It was a wicked blade. Paulus had not hidden it, I was sure of that, but had he used it? That was a different question. I folded it back into its leather covering, and placed it carefully among my cushions. Just in time.

The two servants came hurrying in. Paulus had his carrying-tray, which he set down, and he began spread-ing out his tools with an air of professionally preoccupied detachment. Junio caught my eye and shook his head slightly. No, he meant, the other man had not looked for the shaving knife. It didn't surprise me, now.

Paulus seemed timidly eager to oblige, busily polishing and laying out his scissors, phials and ear-scoops. I could see a knife, too, very like the bloodstained one that was already lying under my pillow. I thought of the cuts on the lifeless legs and shuddered.

'Before you begin,' I said, 'I should like to see what you have there.'

He looked surprised, but showed me the tools of his trade readily enough. Combs and rough scissors. Strigils and pumice stones. Tweezers to pluck the hairs and oil to soften them. Powdered antimony to colour the eyebrows. Oil and earthworm ashes to combat greyness. Some sort of greyish powder in a pottery phial, and a sinister bottle of spiders' webs and vinegar – both preparations which were excellent for staunching bleeding, he informed me reassuringly. And, last of all, the shaving knife.

'A novacula,' I said. 'Let me see.'

He handed it over, unwillingly.

I examined the edge. 'This knife is blunt,' I said. 'It would pull the beard savagely. No wonder your master beat you.'

'There is another,' he said, apologetically. 'Much sharper than this, and new. I have not had it above two moons, and Crassus had it fresh-honed since then. It is almost too sharp; when my hand shook the day before the festival, I cut him badly with it. But I cannot find it now. I could not find it yesterday, when I came to serve you. I had to bring this one. I hoped you would not ask.' He was almost trembling. I realised he was half-expecting a blow.

I had a blow for him, but not of that kind. I slipped my hand under the cushion. 'Is this it?'

I was waiting for his reaction. I was expecting

something – fear, suspicion, anxiety. What I had not been prepared for was his evident relief.

'Where did you find it? Be careful how you hold it, it is very sharp. That is why I always keep it wrapped, so.' He was startled into candour. He even put out his hand for the package, and then he stopped doubtfully. 'This has been wet,' he said. He sounded puzzled. 'It should be dried or it will spoil the blade.' He seemed to recollect himself. 'Your pardon, citizen. I was amazed. Where did you get it from?'

'Where did you leave it?'

His pale face flushed. 'Where I should leave it, citizen? With my equipment, in my sleeping space. I have a cupboard there. It was there, the morning of the feast of Mars. I was prepared to shave Crassus but he did not call me.'

'Were you surprised?'

'I was relieved. I had shaved him only the night before, for a banquet he attended, and had earned myself a beating for it. He was in a hurry that morning – and he had the mask, I suppose.'

And, if his place was taken by Daedalus, the shave did not matter, I thought.

'The knife was there that morning,' Paulus went on, anxiously. 'I could swear to it. Before a priest if need be.'

A Druid priest. That was no idle boast. I said, 'But you did not use the knife?'

'Not then.'

'Someone did. Open it and see.'

He did so and, seeing the blade, almost dropped it in horror. 'Dear gods! Was Crassus stabbed with this? We shall all be executed!' There had been no fear before, only anxiety, but he was terrified now.

'Germanicus was not stabbed, that I could see,' I said. 'But this was used for something. Look at the blade and tell me what you learn.'

He looked at it gingerly. 'Yes, it has been used. Used badly, see the edge? A novacula needs an expert hand. And the blade has not been properly cleaned – just roughly rinsed and not dried. Only a fool would put the knife away without cleaning it. See, it will rust. And the blood on the handle – ugh! What was it used for? There must have been a scalp wound to have bled so much.'

'A scalp wound, possibly,' I agreed, 'or perhaps a deep wound – to the neck for instance. If someone was trying to sever the head, perhaps?'

'With a novacula? Impossible! A determined man might cut through the neck of a child, or a feeble woman, if he used great force. But a strong man who resisted, never! Not to sever the head.'

'You know that, Paulus? How can you be so sure?'

He had answered as an expert, thinking only of the blade, but suddenly he understood the implications of his answer. He gulped but said nothing, and I went on, conversationally, 'There have been rumours – I cannot swear to the truth of them – that Druid circles still sever human heads occasionally, to hang them in their sacred groves and use the blood for sacrifice.'

Paulus was turning whiter and whiter. 'Crassus' head was not severed,' he managed at last. 'And as for the rumours, I do not believe them. Those groves are dreadful, but they are not Druid – as I understand the matter, that is. I do not know personally, of course.'

'Of course.' He was right about one thing. The groves were dreadful. I have seen one myself, an evil, silent thicket of a place, the trees smeared with dried blood and with half-rotted human skulls grinning from the branches. It was a place to haunt your nightmares, so horrible that the very birds refused to sing there. Furthermore, although the place was 'disused' according to the law, the blood in that grove had been newly spilt.

Paulus – so I guessed from his words and the greyish pallor of his skin – had also seen such a grove.

'So, you did not cut your master's throat with this? Or anything else?'

'You would not ask that, citizen, if you had seen Crassus shaved. He was a big man, strong. The first hint of trouble and he would knock me senseless. Besides, how could I cut him when he was not here?' Paulus was earnest with terror.

'You could have cut him later,' Junio put in, 'when he was already dead. To take his blood for one of your rituals – to curse him, perhaps.'

I looked at Junio sharply That was an interesting thought.

'If he was dead he would not bleed,' Paulus said simply, although there was a catch in his voice. I noticed that he did not deny the rituals, this time.

'How do you know that, Paulus?' I said. 'Do you often cut the dead?'

He was shaking now, but he tried to answer with dignity. 'No. But I did shave a corpse once, when Regina was here. It was her *custos* – her travelling companion. He died suddenly, of a fever, just before she left. He was only a slave, but Regina had him shaved and cleansed, and buried with a coin in his mouth and a flask of wine at his feet. Rufus and Daedalus helped me – we did not dare tell Crassus.' He sniffed, trying to disguise the tears.

'About the death?' I was deliberately gentle.

He looked at me gratefully. 'About the funeral. He

116

would have been furious at the expense. Though Regina swore he gave permission for it.' He gave me a watery smile. 'Perhaps he did. He was afraid of her – you heard he had Daedalus acting as food taster? He would not have crossed her openly. But he did not attend the burial.'

I smiled encouragement. 'Which was where?'

'Out in the top field, where the pyre will be tonight. That's where Crassus buried all his slaves – though not usually with such ceremony.'

I could believe that. Wrap them up as they were and drop them in a hole, that was Crassus' style.

'I thought that pit was where I would end, more than once,' Paulus went on. 'Now, I suppose, Lucius will have me sold. He has a beard, like most hermits, so he won't want a barber himself.' He took a visible grip on himself. 'But you, citizen, you wish to have a shave?'

I shook my head, smiling. 'With a blunt novacula? No thanks. And I would prefer, I think, not to be shaved with that other one either.'

'I could wash it, citizen. It could be washed spotless, given a little time. Even the handle, although the blade is sharp. And you need not fear bleeding – there's a snakeweed powder here Regina gave me. Even Crassus could not complain of that. Or I could pluck your chin. I have good tweezers and an ointment here to loosen the beard. Bats' blood and hedgehog ashes. It is very effective.'

I imagined this procedure, and winced. Enduring such things uncomplaining was a mark of manhood in the barber's shop, but it was doubtless different in private. Small wonder Crassus sometimes struck him – Germanicus was not a long-suffering man. 'No,' I said, 'you can use your scissors, and then Junio can wield his pumice. I have no wish to attend the funeral looking like a plucked pigeon. Besides, I think that Marcus should see that knife.'

Paulus said nothing for a long time, although his hand trembled on the scissors as he worked. At last he said, 'Citizen, that knife. When Marcus sees it covered with blood, he will jump to judgement. It was my knife and my master is dead. He will have me locked up and flogged, if not thrown to the beasts. Speak for me, citizen, I beg of you. You know I did not have that razor in my possession.'

'Yes,' I said. 'I can speak for you. Crassus was not murdered with a knife. I am sure of that.'

'So, you will tell him that blade had nothing to do with it?'

'I did not say that. A bloodstained knife is not an accident. But my opinion should spare you execution and a flogging at least. As to locking you up, however, Marcus may still do that if he hears where Junio found the knife.'

'And where was that?' He sounded wary.

'In your bedding, Paulus.'

It was my own fault. I knew that he was unaware of that fact. I should have waited till he had finished my haircut, but I could not resist the dramatic gesture. He let out a cry and his scissors faltered. I was obliged to attend the funeral feast with one section of my fringe cut peculiarly short.

Chapter Twelve

I was not looking forward to the funeral. Formal Roman funerals are not warm, undisciplined, tumultuous events like the Celtic ones, where the mead and tears and tales flow copiously far into the night, and which always end with a magical quality in the telling of old myths in the firelight. Roman rites are organised, tedious, demanding affairs, even when one has genuine affection for the deceased and has not recently been knocked on the head.

What with lengthy torchlight processions, long graveside speeches and elaborate religious observances – all in the cold and dark – it is a wonder that more of those attending do not have funerals of their own shortly afterwards. With a cremation these problems are magnified. The ashes must be reverently collected into the funerary urn and laid to rest, and that can hardly be done with dignity until the deceased has cooled a little. It seemed likely to be a very long night.

There was to be a funeral banquet first, it appeared, for the living. It is not always arranged that way, of course. More often the feast is held after the ritual, and many a man has been laid to rest without a single morsel being consumed at his expense. But Crassus had dictated 'preliminary refreshments' in his will – perhaps to ensure that he had a decent retinue of mourners for the occasion – and Andretha was interpreting this liberally.

He was expecting at least thirty. Crassus was wealthy enough to have his own *clientes*, the local hangers-on who court and flatter any man of substance, and he had always been careful to flatter and court the more powerful in his turn – as he had courted Marcus, for instance. Most of these were doubtless the 'substitute heirs' named in his will, and it would have been unseemly for them not to attend the funeral, even if they were a long way down the list of substitutes and therefore unlikely to see a single denarius of his money. Especially unseemly if a dinner was provided. So, for a man who must have had few friends in life, it promised to be quite a party.

The slaves, who had been working non-stop preparing for the funeral, or taking their turn at the lament, now turned their attention to arranging the feast. The smell of boiled meats and cooking spices from the kitchen mingled with the aromatic herbs from the death room: whatever delights the dead man was taking with him for the afterlife were likely to be served also at the banquet. There was no point in cooking twice. Slaves were already hard at work in the public rooms, sweeping floors, arranging greenery and trimming the wicks of lamps and candles.

I put on my toga again and went into the atrium, attended by Junio. I had already obtained a little barley stew for him, like the other slaves attending the funeral, otherwise he would not have been fed until after the feast. I wanted him beside me at the cremation. Marcus was nowhere to be seen but Andretha was already in the main lobby, fussing over arrangements.

'Ah, citizen.' He bobbed over as soon as he saw me,

full of agitation as ever. 'You are a friend of Marcus, you can advise me. Would it be proper, do you think, to ask him to make the oblations? There is no member of the family to do it.'

I could see his dilemma. According to strict Roman custom a libation should be offered daily at the household shrine to placate the god of household accounts and the spirits of the store cupboards, and to honour the *genius paterfamilias*. That little figurine is always accorded particular reverence, representing as it does both the householder's own personal guardian spirit and the emperor himself, in his role as protector of his citizens. Whenever a formal meal is served, a sample of the food and wine is always offered to these gods first. I recall Crassus making the oblations before that banquet of his, and showing the utmost devotion to his *genius*, in particular. Only, of course, Crassus was not here to make the offering, and his brother would certainly refuse to do it, even if he consented to be present.

'It has not been a problem before,' Andretha fretted. 'There has been no proper meal served since the festival, and since Lucius is presumably the head of household now, I was not especially concerned. I thought he would have all the Roman statues and shrines destroyed. I kept the Vestal fires burning – I think the other slaves would have panicked otherwise – but I did not concern myself with the lararia. But now Marcus' messenger has returned from Lucius at last, telling us that he will not attend, but that we should continue to honour Crassus' wishes until the house is sold. My master would have wished to sacrifice to all the proper gods, especially at his funeral.'

I smiled inwardly. Of course he would. Germanicus almost certainly did not believe in any of it, but he would observe the rituals, just in case. I am no expert in Roman rites, although I observe the required public rituals. I have more faith in the ancient spirits of woods and rivers than in squabbling deities and stone statues. But I thought I knew the answer. To Andretha I said, 'I can see no difficulty. Marcus is named as a substitute heir; surely he can take Lucius' place quite properly? Indeed, it seems the duty falls on him.'

Andretha looked relieved, but there was something else to worry him. 'My thanks, citizen. I should put the statue of the *genius paterfamilias* on the shrine, you think? Between the *lar familiaris* and the *penates* as usual? Ordinarily, when the master dies, the new *genius* should take its place, but Lucius, being a Christian, will not have his own figurine.'

It was awkward, I could see that, making offerings to a man's spirit when he was lying dead in the next room. On the other hand if ever there was a man whose spirit I should wish to placate, it was Germanicus. I said doubtfully, 'It should be there, I suppose. After all it represents not only Crassus, but the spirit of the emperor too.'

'I am glad of your guidance, citizen. I did not know what to do. I even thought of taking one from Germanicus' stone store – he collected one or two from the more Romanised rebellious tribes, as trophies of war, and took particular delight in having them broken up for use on the estate. I thought it would represent the emperor at least. But Crassus was particularly superstitious about his *genius*. He and his brother had an argument about it. Lucius said it had become a kind of idol to him, and should be destroyed; Crassus said that Lucius could think what he liked, he personally was taking no chances. That statue was to stay with him always. That is why I ordered it to be placed on the funeral bier.'

'Is that where it is now?'

'Yes. I sent Rufus to fetch it when he went for his lute string.'

So, I thought, when Rufus went to the sleeping room he might have been carrying a heavy statue. That was interesting. I had dismissed the idea of Rufus as my assailant because he had no weapon; he could hardly have laid me out with his lute. But with a lump of carved stone? I was interested in this statue.

'Could I see it?'

'If you wish.' Andretha shrugged. 'It is on the normal pattern. A figurine of a man with his toga over his head to ward off evil. Crassus had it made, I think, when he bought the villa, and it was of no great value, but he was very superstitious about it. But if I am to reinstate it on the shrine, of course you may see it. It will have to be fetched.'

I turned to Junio, but Andretha forestalled me.

'I had better fetch it myself, citizen. To enter the room now will be to disturb the lament, and it is better I do it than a stranger. Unless, of course, you wish to take part in the dirge yourself?'

I excused myself hastily. Here in the atrium the sounds of mournful wailing were audible enough, and I knew the banquet would be interspersed with doleful music and speeches in praise of Germanicus. Possibly even an ode, if one of his *clientes* was feeling inspired, and we were very unlucky. I was going to do all the honouring of Crassus that I could possibly desire.

'I must have seen this statue,' I said to Junio, when Andretha had gone, 'at the banquet with Marcus at least. I remember Crassus making an oblation, but I paid no attention to the figure. I had not even noticed it was missing, now, though I have just walked past the shrine. Of course it is in the corner, where it is dark, and one does not tend to look closely in the normal way.'

Junio laughed. 'Especially not to look at Crassus' soul! But it proves what Andretha said, the statue has no artistic merit. I wonder who told him that, by the way? Yet it must be true. If it was fine work you would have noticed it, however shadowy the corner. It would have attracted your artist's eye.'

I grinned at him. Junio has a way, sometimes, of being very flattering. And he sees the obvious, which others overlook. He was right, for instance, about Andretha. The man had not one scruple of artistic taste. I was about to say so when Andretha himself came hurrying in. If he had been anxious before, he seemed desperate now.

'It is not there, citizen. I have searched the bier and the grave-goods, discreetly – it was unseemly, in the circumstance, interrupting the lament – but there is no sign of the statue. The anointing women have gone, back to Glevum.' He was clasping and unclasping his hands in distress. 'Perhaps they have taken it. I must send after them at once. Would Marcus lend us a messenger? We need a horse and we have only the cart animal. If only Crassus had not given his mount to his brother!'

'Germanicus had his own steed?' I had not known that, though I might have expected it, since the villa was some distance from the town.

'A steed, no. Crassus was no horseman. If he wanted transport he usually hired a carriage from Glevum. He had a mule, though, which he rode sometimes, and even that may be quicker than a man on foot. If only we had it now!' he wailed. 'But when Lucius left he was so weighed down with gifts that Crassus gave him the animal to transport it all.'

'Crassus was generous.'

Andretha was concerned with other things. He said, abstractedly, 'Perhaps.'

'You think not?' He looked impatient, so I added, 'This is important, Andretha. It may have a bearing on your master's death.'

'I should not speak ill of my master,' Andretha said.

'But . . . ?' I prompted. That sort of remark is usually the preface to doing so.

Andretha sighed. 'But the day after Lucius left, half a dozen high officials came here for a gambling party. It was arranged beforehand, for Lucius' benefit, but of course he no longer dices. Crassus was as jumpy as water on a griddle, wanting his brother safely away from here. He thought Lucius was likely to march into the party, deliver a sermon on the subject and urge them all to repent.'

I grinned. 'That would be embarrassing, with a houseful of important Romans.'

'Yes,' Andretha agreed. 'Crassus would probably have given him twice as much to ensure that he was safely gone. But it was more than just embarrassment; the supper would have begun with a sacrifice, like tonight's feast, and he knew that Lucius would refuse to take part in that.'

So, we were back to that statue again. For the *lar* and *penates* it might not have mattered – the Romans are tolerant about household gods – but if Lucius refused to honour the *genius paterfamilias* there would have been trouble. Obviously, since it represents the emperor as well as the head of household. Refusal to honour that could have meant wild animals in the arena for both of the brothers.

'Crassus bundled him out of the house the day before,' Andretha went on, 'with so many gifts for his new church that he needed a mule to carry them. Lucius was delighted, and surprised. I don't think he guessed the reason.'

'And now the statue has disappeared?'

I should not have reminded him. He began to twist his hands again. 'I cannot understand it. Who would steal such a thing? It was here yesterday. It must have been the women. There is no other explanation.'

I was not so sure of that. 'Have you asked Rufus? He was in the room when you went to search, surely?'

'Rufus? He has gone to prepare for the procession – food, ablutions, latrine. We cannot offer baths to our banquet guests tonight, it would be disrespectful to light the furnace in the circumstances, but at least our slaves can be clean. You think I should speak to Rufus? He is in the kitchen.'

'I think I should speak to him myself.'

I went out to the kitchen, following Andretha. It was in a separate building at the end of the wing, isolated from the house: Germanicus, of course, had built in the latest fashion and this arrangement was supposed to prevent fires. Certainly it prevented the food being very hot when it was served, as I knew from that supper I had shared with Marcus, and the banquet I had attended.

It was hot enough in the kitchen, however, and crowded, too. Slaves hurried about with charcoal for the baking oven and platters for the table, while cooks stirred at bubbling cauldrons suspended on hooks, sliced vegetables with wicked knives, pounded spices in *mortaria,* or carried bubbling pans from the hot griddles on the hearth. Amidst all this Rufus, standing at the table, was gulping hot stew from an unglazed bowl.

My toga provoked an instant consternation. Cooks stopped in mid-stir and stood staring, their ladles suspended and dripping. Boys ceased to stoke the fires, and the lad setting the baked bread on the serving discus dropped his platter with a crash. Rufus gaped.

I remembered what had been said about his truthfulness. 'The statue,' I said cheerfully. 'The *genius pater-familias.* What did you do with it?'

He stood like a statue himself. 'I . . . nothing.'

'I asked you to take it in to the anointers,' Andretha said, bristling with self-importance.

'It wasn't there,' Rufus said, finding his tongue again. 'I went to look for it as soon as I got my string – but it wasn't there. I presumed you had sent someone else for it, while I was stringing the lute.'

'You didn't mention that it wasn't there?' I asked.

Rufus looked at me. 'I was frightened. I supposed someone else had fetched it – that I had not responded fast enough and that I risked a beating. I hoped that having so much to do, with the funeral preparations, perhaps Andretha had forgotten my failure. I didn't remind him.' He swallowed. 'I didn't break it.'

'Break it?' I said. 'I didn't suppose you broke it. The statue is missing.'

'Missing?' Rufus paled. 'I didn't take it, either.'

One of the slaves with the platters chimed in. I had almost forgotten their presence. 'It wasn't there yesterday morning, citizen. I noticed when I was cleaning. But it *was* broken. I saw it the day before. The head had been chipped off. We were talking about it, we younger ones. We . . .' He paused, embarrassed. 'We thought it was taken down because the master was dead. That Lucius had ordered it to be destroyed. But it was not our place to ask.'

I turned to Andretha. 'Did you know of this?'

He didn't. 'No one,' he said, flapping like an outraged hawk, 'would dare do such a thing.'

'Well then,' I said, ironically, 'perhaps it was an act of the gods.'

I wasn't prepared for the effect on Rufus. He licked his lips nervously and turned deathly white. 'All right,' he said. 'I admit it. It was on the feast of Mars. When we had come back to the villa and were waiting for Crassus to come back, I was sent to tend the brazier in the atrium and I happened to look at the shrine. The *genius* was on the floor – it seemed to have been knocked over. I replaced it and stood it upright. It was damaged; the statue was chipped in several places and the head was broken off.'

My mind was racing. Could this be true, or had Rufus for once invented a story to explain his own actions? Could being used to deliver a blow to a human head, for instance, damage a small stone statue?

I said, 'You told no one about this?'

'No. I was afraid. I knew I would be blamed if I reported it, and when Crassus' body was found, I was even more worried. That statue was virtually his talisman. I did not even look at the niche again, in case I drew attention to it. When I was sent to fetch the statue and it was not there, I was relieved. I thought someone else had taken it to the anointers.'

And someone else would get the blame, I thought, but I did not say so. A slave's life is difficult enough. I took a different tack. 'So, first the figure is mysteriously broken, then it still more mysteriously disappears. And each time it seems that you were there.' That was not quite fair; the younger slaves had noticed its disappearance before today. But I didn't say that either. 'Does not that seem very strange to you?'

He was pale but he shook his head. 'Strange, yes. But not impossible.'

'Because you have an explanation?'

His words startled me. 'I thought . . .' he said slowly, 'I thought it was a sign.'

Chapter Thirteen

A stunned silence greeted this announcement. I saw the kitchen-slaves exchange glances and one of the charcoal bearers sniggered.

Andretha was the first to speak, high-pitched and anguished like an old crone shouting after apple-stealers. 'What a pack of lies, you ignorant whelp! How dare you invent such tales! Break the statue, did you, and hide the pieces to escape suspicion? Well, don't suppose you will escape with merely a whipping. You will be fined for this – every penny of the replacement. I am responsible for presenting the accounts. I shall not be answerable for the cost of this.'

Of course, I remembered, Andretha's freedom and a pension depended on his balancing the books. The terms of a man's will are taken very seriously. All the same . . .

'Come,' I said. 'This is harsh. You have no proof that Rufus broke it.' That was a poor plea, admittedly. A chief steward does not need proof of misdemeanour before he disciplines a slave. 'Besides, you yourself were going to have it burned on the pyre,' I added.

Andretha's face had flushed a sullen red. 'Thank you for your advice, citizen, but this is not part of your enquiry,' he snapped. 'This is a household matter.'

Rufus set his bowl down on the table. 'It makes no

difference,' he said, the girlish face set with determination. 'It happened as I said. And Andretha can flog me all he chooses. I have no money. I cannot pay what I do not have.'

The answer seemed to infuriate Andretha still more. 'That is not true, lute player. I have seen guests give you gifts of money when you have played for them. Recently, at that dice party, when the quaestor was flushed with wine and winnings, I saw him give you two coins then.' He turned to two of the kitchen-slaves. 'Take him to the librarium and lock him up. We'll see if imprisonment will loosen his purse strings.'

I had noticed when I laid the pavement that the librarium door had been fitted with a lock. Now I knew why, I thought. To keep the slavegirls secure. To keep Rufus out. Ironic that it should now be used to keep him in. At least he would have an attractive floor in his prison. Though surely he would be wanted among the musicians tonight? 'But the funeral . . .' I began.

We were interrupted by a slave hurrying in from the gatehouse. 'A message from the gatekeeper, steward,' he said breathlessly. 'The first guests are arriving, and Marcus Aurelius Septimus already awaits you in the atrium.'

Andretha's face was a portrait of agonised hopelessness.

'Perhaps,' I murmured to him, 'it would be wise to consult Marcus on this? And Rufus could, I think, be spared for the funeral procession. The guards are armed, it would be hard for him to escape during the ceremony.' I made a calculated guess. 'Besides, if he plays at tonight's banquet, someone might toss him a coin or two. He could at least begin to pay.'

Andretha wavered visibly. 'Perhaps . . . ?'

I took him to one side, further out of earshot, and murmured, 'Andretha, you are a man of the world. You will have to make some sort of shift this evening, for the funeral. It is impossible to replace the statuette tonight, but if you have to account for the figurine by having one walled into the funeral niche, it is not necessary to purchase an expensive one. No one will ever see it. And any statue consecrated to Crassus would serve to appease his spirit. You cannot use one of his war trophies, they are already dedicated to someone else, but the cruder models can be obtained anywhere in Glevum for a few sesterces.'

If I reasoned aright, Andretha was more interested in obtaining money than justice. Those all-important household accounts, I suspected, did not altogether balance. That would explain, among other things, the extravagance of the funeral preparations; no one would question the cost of an additional bottle of spikenard for anointing, for instance, or the price of an extra dormouse or two for the feast. On such small adjustments to the accounting can a man's freedom rest.

Andretha looked at me. He raised his hands helplessly. 'I do not know what you are suggesting, citizen. But perhaps you are right about the funeral.' He turned to the lute player. 'Rufus, you should be grateful to the citizen. You owe him your freedom, for tonight at least. But I shall alert the guards. Once the rites are over, we shall have our reckoning! Come!' He hustled out of the kitchen.

Rufus followed him, throwing me a grateful glance.

I followed too, more slowly, taking a stroll with Junio around the inner garden first. If Marcus had been kept cooling his heels by Andretha, I did not wish to be visibly associated with the delay. By the time we arrived in the atrium most of the guests were assembled and Andretha was flitting amongst them like an agitated moth, overseeing the distribution of napkins and the provision of knives to those not carrying their own.

Rufus stood forward, striking up the lute, and the room fell silent. (His left cheek, I noticed, was reddening – in the distinct shape of four fingers. My intervention had not entirely saved him from Andretha's wrath.)

Marcus led the way into the triclinium where, taking a goblet of wine from a young cupbearer, he poured out a few drops on the shrine before the *lar* and the *penates* in turn. Then he took a morsel of sweet cake and set it in front of the plinth between them, on which a seal of Crassus and a small bust of Commodus had been reverently laid. He intoned the usual invocations, scattered a pinch of salt upon the Vestal flame, and the feast began.

There were too many mourners to seat. Important people like Marcus were shown to the five couches by the low tables on the dais; we lesser mortals sat on chairs and stools, or simply stood against the wall, at the other end of the room.

'Neatly handled,' I muttered to Rufus as I took my place against the farthest wall. 'Using the seal.'

'Marcus' suggestion,' he returned. 'The emperor bust is from his own travelling shrine.' Then he was gone, to sit cross-legged on the patterned pavement, playing solemn music while the feasters ate.

There were quails' eggs and speeches, shellfish and more speeches, the stuffed dormice were followed by yet more speeches and when, after the boiled lamb with plums (spoiled, as usual, by the inevitable fish sauce), a solemn-faced young man began: 'O warrior and companion soul, farewell . . .' I could scarcely restrain a groan.

The man beside me must have felt the same. He gave a stifled sigh. I glanced at him. Grizzled hair, leathery skin, hands toughened with weathering and the livid scar of an old wound visible on one wrist. He wore a civilian tunic now, but this was an ex-auxiliary soldier if I ever saw one. He caught my eye and I flashed him a smile.

'You were a friend of Crassus?' I murmured, when the interminable ode was over and it was possible to speak again.

'Not a friend, no. I served under him. I was a tesserarius in his century.'

'But you knew him?' I was interested. I remembered those rumours about Crassus' promotion – and those soldiers in the lane.

He looked at me suspiciously.

'I am a pavement maker,' I explained. 'He commissioned work from me, that is why I am here. I hardly knew him. But he has not paid me, and you know how these things work. I must seek his heirs.'

His face cleared. 'Ah! They will be hard men, if they are like him. A brave soldier, they say, but the most brutal centurion north of the Tiber.'

'Ambitious, too,' I prompted. Hinting that a superior is ambitious is enough to make the average soldier gossip like a woman.

This one was no exception. 'Ambitious? Great Mars, I should say so! Always on the look out for a ransom or a bribe, and it was always Crassus who profited, not the company. He didn't care about his men. It was rumoured once that he killed his own commander to gain the promotion.'

I pricked up my ears, but I was disappointed.

'It can't be true,' the soldier said. 'Treachery in the field is a capital offence. But he was ruthless enough. Some said he would betray the emperor himself if the bribe was high enough.'

I thought of Aulus, and that soldier in the dusk. Every man has his price.

'You think he might have?'

He laughed. 'He was planning something. Some wager he had laid. He was boasting about it at the Mars procession.'

The words stopped me, honeyed date to mouth. 'You were at the procession?'

'Yes, I told you. I was in his century. I marched behind him. He was late. He didn't reach the column until the signifer arrived. Too busy talking to another centurion. He had to put his mask on as he came.'

'I see.' So that was how Daedalus had managed it, I thought. He would have needed to see the standard to know which column to join. 'And afterwards? Did you see him leave?'

'Oh yes, he rushed off as quickly as he came. He was in high spirits. Someone asked him to join us in the feasting, but he would not come. He said he had just won an important wager, and hurried off towards the West Gate.'

'Strange!'

He laughed again. 'Yes, very strange. Usually Crassus loved a feast. It must have been a substantial sum. He seemed very pleased about it.'

'Did he unmask?'

The man gazed at me. 'Now you mention it, I don't think he did. He was pulling his mask off as he went away. But it was Crassus, I would know him anywhere. I recognised his voice.'

'And this centurion he was talking to? Did you know him too?'

'No,' the tesserarius said. 'He was not from our legion. He was clearly a stranger. I assumed Crassus knew him from somewhere. It was not surprising. There were hundreds of visiting veterans in Glevum that day, in the procession and out of it. Most soldiers honour the feast of Mars.'

'But it was a centurion,' I insisted, 'you are sure of that?'

'I saw the crest,' he replied, irritated. The transverse crest of the centurion is the badge of office. 'And the baton.'

'It could not, for instance, have been a disguise?' I asked. 'This is important. That may have been the last time Crassus was seen alive.'

'And you think the centurion might have killed him? Over this wager perhaps? It is possible. But a disguise? I shouldn't think so. A centurion's uniform is heavy, and the helmet awkward, with the plume going round the head, instead of front to back. A man has to be accustomed to it to wear it well. One can often tell a new centurion from the way he holds his head.'

I had time to murmur 'Thank you' before there was a ripple of tambours. Marcus got to his feet and the feast was over.

What followed was a long and tedious business. The body was brought out, on its bier, and carried in procession, preceded by torches and by the professional mourners and musicians, playing, singing dolefully and dancing. Then Rufus with his lute, more mourners, wailing, and after them the guests. The household slaves walked beside them, carrying lights or braziers, while

the women followed at the back. I was glad of Marcus'
litter, though it lurched appallingly. There had been
little wine at the feast – a mark of austerity – but my
head was buzzing, as if to remind me that I had recently
been hurt. I had much to think about, too.

We followed up the cart track to the hill, a strange,
flickering procession in the torchlight. Some of the
house-slaves had already brought fire and the back of
the pyre was alight; the additional braziers would not be
necessary. They were a useful precaution, however.
Nothing is more embarrassing than a cremation pyre
that does not burn.

The bier was lifted reverently onto it, with some of
the grave-goods, and the fire raked around it. The
director of ceremonies, one of the funeral guild,
sprinkled something over the body – wine and oil
perhaps – and the flames leapt higher. The oration
began. There were the usual cremation smells: burning
cloth, burning wood, burning flesh, mingling with
the perfume of the sprinkled oils. I was grateful for
the pyre, the night was cold. How the slaves must have
felt in their thin tunics I shuddered, literally, to
remember.

Then at last it was over. The pyre had burned down
very fast. Someone sprinkled wine over the ashes, and
the slaves bent forward to scoop them into the urn. It
was carried on a special salver, as if it was still warm,
back to the nymphaeum. A long, last speech, an offering
to the gods, the urn was placed into the niche and the
remaining grave-goods with it – charcoal, food and the
feeding jar, into whose neck the yearly offerings would
be poured. Who would do that, I wondered, when the
villa was sold?

A stone was placed in front of the urn, shaped to

leave the jar-neck visible. A simple epitaph – probably it would be replaced by an elaborate one later: *Crassus Claudius Germanicus, builder of this place.*

Chapter Fourteen

I woke late, with a headache. Anyone who did not know me better might have supposed that I had drunk too much Roman wine – the last funeral guests had left at daybreak in their hired carriage – but the painful place on the base of my skull reminded me of the truth. I sat up cautiously.

Junio, who had been sleeping on the floor at the foot of the bed, roused himself instantly. 'You are awake, master?'

'Almost,' I groaned. 'Go and get yourself something to eat, and then you can come back and help me strigil and dress – and fetch me some bread and fruit from the kitchens too. And some water, my head aches abominably.'

Junio grinned. 'Then I shall find Faustina and ask her to send a draught for you. Her "pond-water" did you good yesterday.'

I grimaced. 'Perhaps. But be quick about it. I learned some important facts last night. I must speak to Marcus and go back to Glevum. I have some news that might help us to find Daedalus.'

'So you have finished here?'

'There are some things I want to ask Aulus, first.'

'Then . . .' He hesitated. 'Before we go, might I visit

the librarium? I should like to see the pavement.'

I was sorry that I hadn't thought of it. Of course Junio was interested. 'I wouldn't mind seeing it, myself,' I said, and he went off, satisfied.

I sat on the edge of the bed-frame, thinking. So, if my theory was right, Crassus sent Daedalus to Glevum, to take his place under cover of the mask. Why? Because he himself wished to disappear and not be missed? What pressing business had he to attend to, which must be kept a secret from the world? Was he plotting the downfall of the emperor as Marcus feared? And if so, was he friend or foe of Marcus' governor?

And why did Daedalus, if it was Daedalus, go off towards the West Gate when the sacrifices were over? He was not going home, the villa lay in the opposite direction. Presumably then, it was to meet Crassus undetected. That would make sense. That tesserarius at the funeral had spoken of a 'wager' and I was beginning to guess what that might be. Daedalus had wagered that he could successfully take Crassus' place at the procession. Presumably he had offered something as a stake, and he was to have his freedom if he won. That would explain why he was boasting at the villa that he would soon be free, and why he had left after the procession saying that he had won 'an important wager'. He had just gambled for his liberty.

Why had Crassus consented, I wondered. If Daedalus had failed he might well have been arrested for impersonating a citizen. Either way, Crassus lost a good slave. But then I laughed aloud. Of course! Being Crassus, he had probably placed a huge stake with one of his gambling cronies, betting that Daedalus would succeed. That way, whatever the outcome, Germanicus would win, though he was obviously confident of his slave's ability.

No doubt they had arranged to meet later to settle the debt, somewhere away from the public eye. But if the murder had already taken place, Crassus could not come as arranged. So what became of Daedalus, lurking in the seedy suburbs by the river, dressed in a borrowed uniform to which he was not entitled? Knocked on the head and robbed? That would not be impossible. He had not been arrested, as one might suppose, or Marcus would have heard of it. He had not returned to the villa, either. There was only one thing to do – go to the West Gate myself and try to retrace his footsteps.

I had other reasons, too, for wanting to go in that direction. I could reassure myself that my workshop had not burned down in my absence.

My reverie was interrupted by Junio, carrying my breakfast. Apples, I noticed, but no plums. I was secretly glad, though, to have Junio fetch my food. Eating from a communal platter at the funeral was one thing, but eating alone was another. I had not forgotten that there was still a murderer abroad, probably a poisoner, and that someone had already rapped me on the head.

'Faustina will bring you a potion later,' Junio said cheerfully. 'Now, do you wish to eat first, or wash and dress yourself before Paulus comes to do it? If he has been instructed to attend you, he may not welcome my intrusion.' He grinned. 'I managed to avoid him when I went for the food and water.'

I let him strigil me and help me dress, then turned my attention to the apples. I was about to instruct Junio to go to Marcus and seek an audience for me, when Andretha interrupted us, flurried as ever.

'Marcus Aurelius Septimus sends his greetings and

asks that you will attend him at lunch. In the meantime he instructs me to provide you with anything you need.'

At lunch! That gave me a long wait, but there was nothing I could do about it. Marcus, presumably, was feeling the effects of the wine. I was on the point of saying that I needed nothing, but Junio interposed. 'I believe you said, master, that you wished to speak to Aulus. It would be convenient if he could come to you, since you are awaiting your headache cure.'

Andretha made a slight bow. Since I had been attacked he had been almost wearing in his willingness to please. I knew why, of course. My headache was officially due to his negligence, and he wanted as much of my favour as possible. 'Aulus shall be sent to you at once.' And he hastened off.

I rounded on Junio. 'Impudent pup! Sending the chief slave to fetch Aulus, as if he were your messenger boy. I wonder you did not ask him to bring the library pavement too.'

Junio grinned. 'Ah, but I should not have seen it in position then.'

Sometimes I fear I am too lenient with that boy.

'Anyway,' he went on, 'I was right about your headache cure. Here is Faustina with the potion now.'

She came in with it, ready poured in a goblet. It was darker green this time and looked even worse than the last one.

'This was quickly made,' I said. I eyed it doubtfully. She had put henbane on my head yesterday. What was she preparing for me now?

'The herbs were close at hand, citizen. Wild cress, succory and house leeks. It took little to crush and heat them.' She smiled. 'Regina would have been quicker yet. She had phials of potions ready. And she would have had rose-flower juice, which is the best of cures.'

I looked at the liquid again. Somehow it looked a little less vile when you knew what it was. Or thought you did. 'Nonetheless . . .' I began.

'You don't trust me?' Faustina said. 'See. I will lead the way.' She lifted the goblet and took a deep draught. 'The taste is rather strange and peppery, but it does clear the head.'

I took the drinking cup and drained it. Peppery it wasn't. As for strange – there are times when even Roman fish sauce would improve a flavour! Faustina was right about one thing though. It did seem to clear my head.

'You hesitated. Did you fear poison?' Junio said, when she had gone, and I was sipping a cup of cool water to dispel the taste. 'I would have tested it for you. But surely she would not poison you so openly? Marcus might grant a general pardon over Crassus, if a single killer was discovered, but poisoning you would lead to certain death.'

He looked at me for confirmation. I raised an eyebrow. I have been trying to encourage Junio in other skills, as well as pavement making.

He said slowly, 'Though I suppose she might do it to protect Rufus.' He frowned. 'But that would mean that he killed Crassus. Or that she suspected him, at least.'

'I think she does. She knows he was missing from the procession. He denies "touching" Crassus, but she knows that poison was used.'

'It was?'

'I am sure of it. There may have been damage to the face, perhaps, but nothing that could have been fatal. The back of the neck is untouched, and there is no sign of strangling. There were no marks on the rest of the body, and poison would explain so many things. I think Crassus, for instance, came back here of his own accord.' I outlined my theory of Daedalus and the mask. 'No doubt he had arranged to meet someone.'

'But,' Junio said excitedly, 'he didn't necessarily meet anybody. It may not be important who else was missing from the procession. Suppose he had arranged to wait for someone, in the stoke room perhaps? If he were tricked into taking poison, disguised in wine for instance, he might have died alone. No one would go there, with the fires down. The killer could have come back later and put the head into the furnace.'

I thought about this. 'Why should anyone do that?'

'To disguise the signs? Burning him does not hide that he is dead, of course, but it deflects the thoughts from poison.' He stopped. 'I see your reasoning. It might equally deflect the thoughts from people who know about poison – prevent them from being immediately suspected. No wonder you were hesitant about drinking that remedy.'

I raised an eyebrow, approvingly.

Another thought seemed to strike him. 'And of course, she would not poison you outright. A little poison in each drink – not too much – the thing is simply done. You have received a head wound too, so that if you become confused and ill, it is easy to account for. And all the while, it would seem as if she was trying to cure you. I am sorry, master. You were right. I should not doubt your judgement.'

I grinned at him. 'Then let us hope my judgement is correct. I drank her potion. Otherwise, you reason much as I did. Except that I am fairly convinced that Crassus was not here alone. Someone must have put the head into the furnace early, while the fires were still hot, or the face would not have been so burned. Later, after the procession, the fires would have died. But enough of that. Here is Aulus, sent to answer your summons!'

I took care that the gatekeeper did not hear that, of course. It would not have pleased him to think he had been summoned by a mere slave, and he looked even more menacingly large in my bedchamber than he had seemed in his own. I had no wish to displease him. He was already scowling nervously.

'Aulus,' I said heartily, as if this was a social call of his own desiring, 'how good of you to come. I need your talents. You found me, I hear, after I was attacked?'

The scowl lifted slightly, and he gave me a conspiratorial nudge. 'You were lying face down on Paulus' bed. I didn't see who did it. If I had . . .' He fingered the cudgel at his belt.

You would have knocked him on the head? I thought, but I did not say so. He was unlikely to see the irony, but I was taking no chances. Instead I said, 'Thank you for saving me. It is lucky you came to be there, at that hour.' What were you doing there, is what I meant.

He understood. 'Andretha sent me, to collect a clean tunic for the procession. You can ask him. I was not in the sleeping quarters more than half a minute. He saw me go in, and as soon as I found you I went out and fetched him.' Aulus was so anxious to defend himself that he was not even angry at the inquisition.

'Very well,' I said, glad to move off dangerous ground. 'Now, tell me about these meetings that you saw – when Crassus met this soldier at the gate.'

That pleased him. He seemed to take reference to his spying as a professional compliment. 'Two meetings, citizen, at twilight. And both times Crassus tried to order me away.'

'And the soldier,' I said. 'Would you recognise him again?'

He shook his head. 'No, citizen. With cheekplates, it is hard to identify a face, even when you are looking in broad daylight. In poor light it is impossible. It was a centurion both times, that is all I know; he had one of those sideways crests on his helmet.'

'And you don't know if it was the same man each time?'

'I could not tell. I was too far away. I do not think it was. There was something about the second one – he seemed bigger, more confident. More of a swaggering air, like Crassus himself. But I could not swear that they were different.'

'And from which direction did the soldier come?'

Aulus looked startled. 'I am not sure. But he must have come down the lane from the military road. There is nothing in the other direction but a few peasant farms. The track goes further, but it is a woeful one. Dangerous, too. There are wolves in the forest.'

'And towards the high road?'

'You have seen it, citizen. Nothing at all on the main lane, and not much more on the old road, except the ruined roundhouse. He would hardly go there.' He gave me a suggestive leer. 'Mind you, that has been used by one or two other people, for different purposes. Several people, apart from Rufus and his girl. I could tell you a few stories . . . at a price.'

'Related to this matter?' I said, severely. Sexual tittle-tattle was not to my taste.

He shook his head, looking disappointed. I imagine that for Aulus this kind of salacious gossip was quite a

148

profitable sideline. He brightened again. 'I do have something for you, citizen. Something I found out on the kitchen pile.'

Only a spy would search the kitchen pile – the heap of refuse and scraps which were thrown from the window, often rendered even more aromatic by the addition of leftovers from the slaughterblock.

I managed a smile. 'And what is that?'

I do not know what I expected. Incriminating love-messages perhaps, scratched on a wax tablet. Something like that. I was not at all prepared for what he offered me.

It was a small, glass, stoppered phial, no longer than my finger, and threaded with a leather thong through a small loop near the neck. It was empty. I knew what it was. I had seen one very like it recently – on Paulus' tray. One of Regina's phials. I thought of the potions I had drunk, and paled.

'I don't know,' Aulus was saying, in a whisper that today smelt of boiled cabbage, 'if that is helpful, citizen?'

I managed to say, 'Most helpful. Thank you.'

He smirked hopefully. 'Shall I be . . . rewarded?'

'I will speak to Marcus,' I said. If I started to pay for information like this I should soon be begging myself. 'I am to see him later. In the meantime, if Junio will give me his arm we will peep in at the librarium pavement. I am still a little unsteady on my feet.'

I didn't say so to Aulus but I also had another expedition in mind. Remembering that piece of scale-armour, I was not at all sure that he was right about Crassus not going to the roundhouse.

I wanted to have another look.

Chapter Fifteen

But first I had promised Junio the librarium.

Visiting it, however, was not as easy as it sounded. All of the other main rooms of the villa had been designed as such, and were either interconnecting or led off the handsome verandah-corridor across the front of the house; spacious rooms with handsome plastered walls and latticed glass in the windows. The librarium had, of course, begun as an ante-room for the slavegirls, and although its situation was surprisingly pleasant, given its purpose, it was not a convenient room to reach.

It led directly off the back left-hand side of the courtyard garden, reached by a colonnaded walk between the draughty flowerbeds, arbours and statues. While most of the walls bordering the garden were whitewashed and decorated with optimistic designs of colourful flowers and birds, the librarium's façade, half-obscured by a bush, was dominated by a heavy door. This, being an outer door, was a wooden one and (unlike most in the villa) secured with a key.

It was locked, though presumably not now to save the slavegirls from unwanted attentions. Junio looked at me helplessly.

'Andretha should have the key,' I said. 'Wherever he

is. In the kitchen, I would judge, arranging refreshments for Marcus' breakfast.'

Junio scampered off to ask, while I admired the murals and counted the drooping herbs in the borders: rosemary, sage, leeks, parsley, thyme. Germanicus had planned his garden less for his eyes than for his stomach. I was just gazing at the statue of Minerva which stood in an arbour, when Junio returned.

'He went to the slaves' quarters,' he reported, breathlessly. 'He's looking for Paulus, Marcus is calling for a shave.'

And the barber was missing again, I thought sympathetically. He would pay for that, especially if the chief slave had to search for him in person. Andretha was already smarting from being sent to fetch Aulus. Senior slaves do not expect to have to chase after menials.

I had no such difficulties myself. 'We'll go to him, then,' I said and led the way out of the courtyard to the slaves' quarters at the rear.

I had not been in the building since I was attacked, and I was uncomfortably aware of a little shiver of nervousness as I went in. However, this time I had Junio with me, I reminded myself, and I strode down the aisled centre with a fair imitation of boldness, glancing from side to side into the sleeping areas as I went. There was no sign of Andretha, until we came to the partitioned room at the end. I called his name.

There was no answer, but I thought I heard a faint scrabbling sound within. I pulled back the screen, and there was the chief slave, kneeling on the floor, in the act of pushing a wooden chest hastily under the mattress. He abandoned it immediately as I came in and scrambled to his feet, in a parody of agitation and self-abasement.

'Citizen! I did not hear you call.' How then, did he

'You meant to steal some of his gold, in fact?'

He did not deny it. 'But I did not do it, citizen.' He raised his head, and lifted his hands like a Vestal Virgin making sacrifice. 'I could not find the key. Imaginary theft is not a crime. But who would believe me?'

'You have the chest now,' I said. 'What were you doing? Prising it open?'

He sighed, defeated. 'It would do me no good, citizen, if I tried. The chest is empty. It is still locked, but you have only to shake it to know that. That is why I moved the chest from his bedroom. I thought if it was discovered there, with nothing in it, suspicion would fall on me at once.'

I confess, I had not expected this. 'But you do not have the key?' I said. 'Or know where it is?'

He looked at me, and I saw that ferocious despair in his face again, but not directed against me this time. I have seen that look before, in the arena; the furious terror of a man who has staked his life and lost.

'I think I know where it is,' he said at last. 'I have been foolish, citizen. Foolish and tricked. Daedalus must have it. Find Daedalus and you will find the key.' He hunched his shoulders hopelessly. 'I suppose you will take me before Marcus now?'

'I should,' I said. 'You say imagined theft is not a crime, but this is not imagined theft. There is a shortfall in the accounts. You have been stealing from your master for some time, haven't you? I suspected as much, earlier.'

He havered. 'No, citizen, I . . . Yes. Yes, it is true. I wanted my slave price. A man in my position acquires, you know, an *as* or two here and there, sometimes as much as a sestercius. I was saving them. Tradition has it that a slave may keep such gifts, and even buy his freedom, if he can. But Crassus—'

'Fined you,' I supplied, remembering what Aulus had said, 'each time you almost had the price?'

He nodded. 'It was as if he knew. He always found something to fine me for – an insolent slave, a meal not to his satisfaction, a broken goblet. I was responsible, you see, for everything. I have even thought he did things purposely; there was a fine Samian dish once, I swear it was not cracked when I took it to him. It cost almost as much as I do, that one dish alone.'

Junio was looking at him, appalled. That kind of cruelty is outside his experience.

'So,' I said, 'you started stealing from him? To take back what he owed you, was that it?'

'It was not much, citizen. I did not dare. A few sesterces, no more. An extra *as* for hobnails, or to the pottery seller. I did not think it would be missed.'

'It wouldn't,' I returned. These were trifling amounts, and easy to disguise. Hardly a shortfall in the books. 'One extra dormouse invoiced for a feast – it would be impossible to trace.'

He blushed. 'You are right, citizen. That was how I had intended it. And as I say, he had effectively stolen it from me. But . . .' He stopped.

'It proved too easy? The temptation was too great?'

'No, citizen. Not that!' He was almost weeping now. 'But Daedalus discovered it. I don't know how. He threatened to tell Germanicus, to have me handed to the public torturers, unless – unless I stole for him as well. He wanted money, real money. A hundred denarii – and for the feast of Mars. He was to be freed, he said, if he won a wager. He would not tell me what it was, but he was confident. But he needed to raise the money as a stake. He was a personal slave, he never worked for others, and Crassus never gave gratuities. He had

156

no money. Without me, that is.'

'So you struck a bargain? The money in return for his silence. You trusted him?'

'Not really, but what had I to lose? The torturer can only execute you once. Crassus would have had me killed just the same, whether I stole a hundred denarii or two. It is not as though a man can execute his own slave, now – Germanicus would have delighted in exacting "fitting" punishment, but one job is like another to the executioners. Besides, Daedalus promised that when he was free, he would try to buy me from Germanicus. It would mean changing one master for another, but Daedalus could not be worse than Crassus. He would let me earn my freedom honestly, he said.'

'And you believed him?'

'Daedalus has been good to others in the household. He tried to plead for Regina, and for Faustina's child. It did no good, but at the least he tried. I thought he might have kept his word. But I was wrong, it seems. Daedalus has won his freedom and escaped, taking all my money with him.'

No wonder Andretha had been so anxious to find Daedalus. I shook my head. 'He could not claim his freedom, if Crassus was dead.'

'He did not need to,' Andretha pointed out. 'He has it anyway. Crassus gave him freedom in his will. Daedalus is a free man – as I would be, if I could render the accounts. I wish I had not stolen anything!'

'At least,' I said, 'you have escaped with your life. Lucius surely will not have you killed. You will be sold, at worst.'

'I will be sold,' Andretha said, helplessly. 'Lucius will show mercy, but he would not condone a theft. I will not gain my freedom. All the world will know the contents of that will, they will know I could not render the accounts – and who will buy me then? I will be worthless. I, who have been chief steward to a big estate, shall be lucky now to scrub the chamber pots or empty the vomitoria of some sick poverty-stricken master – until I catch his fever and die myself.'

There was truth in this. A dishonest slave is worse than a cracked cooking pot – useless to any buyer, and likely to be reserved for the basest tasks.

'I thought that if I told you the truth about the chest,' Andretha said bitterly, 'I might have spared myself. But since you guessed about the stealing, I suppose you will hand me to Marcus just the same.'

I shook my head. 'I am here to investigate a killing,' I said. 'Not thefts from Crassus. The shortfall in the accounts will come to light of its own accord. I see no reason to involve Marcus for the moment, unless the two things prove to be connected. Where, for instance, did you go during the procession? You were not there, or you would have noticed other people missing.'

He sighed. 'You know about that too? Well, there is no point in denying it now. I went to the moneylenders.' That was possible, there were dozens of them in the forum, and on public occasions they could do a roaring trade. 'I was in their hands,' he wailed helplessly. 'Crassus fined me for the Samian dish and I had given Daedalus all the money that I had. Without him, how shall I ever pay them back?' He plucked at my sleeve. 'There is still hope, if you find Daedalus. Try to find him for me, citizen.'

'I intend to,' I said. 'And you had best find Paulus, in your turn, if you wish to escape punishment. Marcus is still waiting for his shave.'

Chapter Sixteen

'What now?' Junio said, as Andretha scuttled off in search of the barber.

'I want to go and look at this roundhouse I told you about,' I said. 'We have time to do so. Lunch will not be served early. Marcus has not breakfasted yet, if he is still awaiting his shave.'

Junio grinned. 'He may regret having a shave, with a blunt novacula.'

'All the same, it gives us an opportunity,' I said. 'We will try taking that little rear path to the lane, from the nymphaeum. I am interested to avoid Aulus, if I can.'

It seemed we had succeeded. The path down from the spring was more difficult than I had anticipated – steep, uneven and overgrown. It was obviously not much used, although from the broken twigs and grasses it appeared that someone else *had* used it, and very lately. At the bottom it was particularly treacherous, half-blocked by broken branches, as if they had been deliberately placed there. I needed Junio's assistance to clamber over them. The path did, however, bring us down into the lane.

There was no sign of Aulus. Part of my intention was to see how easily a man could escape his attention, so, motioning to Junio to follow, I slipped into the trees on the opposite side of the lane, and made my way among them until I was sure we had safely passed the gates and were out of view down the main lane. There was no real path here. It was treacherous ground, damp and muddy, and we were forced to struggle among thick branches, roots and clawing undergrowth. I was thankful I was not wearing a toga. In full armour, I thought, this would be impossible. Another promising theory had to be abandoned.

A little further on, though, we crossed the lane and struck out again in the direction of the old road, up to the roundhouse. There were signs that someone else had been this way – and recently. Branches were broken, bracken trodden, and there was a faint parting of the grasses as if they had been bent aside as someone struggled through. Someone small and light, I thought. Even a girl perhaps.

'I have been thinking,' Junio said, rather breathlessly, when we had fought our way back on to the old lane again, 'do you suppose that Andretha had a hand in this killing, after all? He is more scheming than I thought, and he had a lot to gain from Crassus' death. At least he may have thought he did.'

I looked at Junio, thoughtfully. 'Go on.'

'Suppose he had a plan with Daedalus? Daedalus is to imitate Crassus in the procession. Crassus agrees, for a wager – the missing stake money may have been arranged between them – but during the march Andretha takes his master away and poisons him. He doesn't visit the moneylenders at all. Maybe he met his master by appointment; Crassus would have to hide somewhere during the march. Once Crassus was dead, both slaves would have their freedom, provided that it was clearly impossible for anyone in the household to have killed him.'

'And how did the body get to the villa?'

'I have thought of that. We know no horses were hired after the procession, but during the procession – no one has asked about that. On a horse a man would have time to return here, hide the body in the hypocaust and get back to Glevum before the rites were over. But suppose Daedalus cheated him, or simply took fright and ran? That leaves Andretha with a hundred denarii missing, and no chance of his own freedom. Andretha cannot do more than report a missing slave; that would draw too much suspicion to himself. But certainly he is anxious to find Daedalus.'

I nodded. 'That is possible,' I said. 'Yes, certainly it is possible.'

'But . . . ?' Junio said, looking crestfallen.

'It might be a little conspicuous, galloping across the country with a dead centurion across your saddle,' I pointed out.

'Then perhaps they both came here alive, but only Crassus rode. That would make sense. If Andretha walked here and rode the horse back, he would not have to pay for the hire, either. Crassus would have done it.' He stopped. 'Though I suppose there would be scarcely time, especially if he had to return the horse. He had to be there in time to shepherd the others onto the cart.'

He sounded so disappointed that I felt moved to say, 'All the same, you reason well. That is why I wanted you to look at this roundhouse. Here it is.' I added the last words as we turned the corner and Junio saw it for the first time.

It looked more ruinous than ever. I saw it suddenly through Junio's eyes: a collapsing, pathetic old straw hut, hardly more than a hovel. No wonder Crassus had kept his pigs in it.

Junio looked at it thoughtfully. 'That was someone's home,' he said.

There are times when I recognise why I love that boy.

I told him all I knew about the place, and showed him the piece of scale-armour from my pouch. 'I found this here,' I said.

He took it from me and turned it between his fingers. 'It must have come from Crassus' shirt. See how the hole has broken away where it was sewn or riveted to the cloth? That proves that Crassus came in here before he died.' He caught my eye and amended himself. 'It proves that Crassus came in here. Or at any rate that his armour did.' He grinned. 'Is that better reasoning?'

'Somebody's armour did, at any rate,' I said, and his grin broadened.

'What other soldier would it be?' he said, playfully. 'You don't believe in Aulus' conspiracy, do you? Although he did say that the roundhouse was used for "other purposes". Shall we look inside? We may find something else.'

He led the way, turning up his nose at the fish heads. The stink seemed to have become worse than ever. He looked at the bloodstain and the fleas, but apart from that we found nothing, although we spent a long time searching.

At last he kicked over the little pile of rotting bedding. 'That piece of scale-armour must have come from Crassus. I wonder what he was doing here? Checking on his property perhaps. I don't believe what Aulus said. Rufus and Faustina might have come here "for other purposes", but I can't imagine that any soldier ever did. How would they know about the roundhouse?

They wouldn't go up and down this lane, when there is a perfectly good gravelled one not a mile away.'

I did not have time to answer. With the perfect timing of a spectacle in the amphitheatre there was the sound of hooves passing in the lane. More than one horse, too, and moving at a fair pace. Junio shot me a startled look and hurried to look out of the door-space. A slow, reluctant smile spread across his face.

'Well?' I said, straightening up painfully. I had been examining the bedding.

'Soldiers,' he admitted. 'I don't know how many, I only saw the last one before he turned the corner. But several. Cavalry.' He grinned again. 'If I didn't know you better, I would think you had arranged it, simply to prove me wrong.'

'I wonder what they *are* doing here,' I said. 'I am sure Marcus would have mentioned it if he was expecting them. Perhaps we should go back to the villa. He will have had his shave by now, and there is nothing more to be discovered here. I found this.' I showed him a hairpin which I had picked up from the floor.

Junio grinned. 'So there has been a woman here!' He examined it for a moment. 'Fine metal – too fine for a slave. No, it isn't Faustina's after all. Very well, I admit it. Aulus was right. So now we know what our soldier was doing in the straw!' He looked at me thoughtfully. 'Regina's, do you think?'

'It could well be.' I too had been struck by the workmanship. 'I think it is.'

Encouraged by my find, we resumed our search with fresh enthusiasm, but we discovered nothing.

'Poor woman, whoever she was,' I said at last, swatting at a biting flea. 'This can't have been a pleasant love-nest. Unless the fleas came here later, on the pigs.

163

Perhaps they did. We don't know if Crassus kept his hogs here before or after Regina left.'

'I keep forgetting about Regina,' Junio said. 'I wonder where she is? She is an expert on poisons, too, of course. Listen! What's that?'

He hardly needed to ask. It was the sound of hooves. From the other direction this time, and only a single horse. I looked at Junio. He looked at me. The horse stopped, there was the sound of dismounting armour, and footfalls at the door.

We stood facing it together, like a pair of naughty schoolboys awaiting the paedagogus. The cavalry-man seemed to fill the narrow doorspace. He ignored Junio and spoke directly to me. 'You are Libertus, the pavement maker?'

I gulped. If Marcus had sent for me, there would have been a formal message, greetings, repeated verbatim. I did not like the sound of this. A thousand petty misdemeanours floated across my memory. The time I had helped myself to a couple of carrots from an army supply cart on the road, the night I lied my way past the sentry at Glevum after the gates were shut. Had my favourite joke against the garrison commander somehow come to his ears, or (I felt my heart sink through my sandals at the thought) had Governor Pertinax suddenly fallen from Imperial favour? If he fell, Marcus fell, and then I too could expect to be hauled off to Glevum in disgrace. Or had Marcus simply finished his shave and become impatient of waiting? I found my voice. 'I am Libertus.'

'Citizen. You must return to the villa at once. There is something which they think you should see.'

Better, but not good. Who were 'they'? If the man had meant Marcus he would certainly have said so.

Being messenger for the great confers status of its own, as I knew myself.

'Very well,' I said. 'I am coming. Help me to the path, Junio.' Under cover of leaning on his arm, I slipped the armour scale and the hairpin into his hand. If there was trouble, I preferred to have my evidence in safe keeping. It was much quicker returning down the lane, and it seemed a very short time before we were back at the villa gates.

There were five soldiers in all; the other four were waiting with their horses just beyond the gate. I was about to speak when Aulus came hurrying out to meet me, wearing an air of conspiracy even more over-powering than he was.

'A word, citizen.' He drew me aside, away from my escorting cavalryman.

I allowed myself to be shepherded to a verge under the trees, where Aulus bent forward, towering over me, and whispered urgently into my ear. The smell of sweat and stale beer was staggering. 'I hope that I did right, citizen, in telling them where you were. I know you meant to be alone.'

I braved the odours to look him in the face. 'How did you know where I was?'

'I saw you come down the back path, earlier, and go into the trees. I thought at first you were looking for Paulus. When you didn't come back, I guessed you had gone to the roundhouse.'

That answered my question at least. It was not easy to get past Aulus.

He gripped my arm. 'Then the soldiers came, asking for Marcus. They had orders to report in person, but I said that you were working for him, and he would be angry if you were not informed at once. He knows they are waiting – he will be here himself in a moment – but he doesn't know what they have brought. Better that he learns it for himself, and I thought you should see it first.'

'See what?' I said, although I had a sinking feeling that I knew.

Aulus gestured towards the waiting men, and I saw for the first time that there was an extra horse. It was tethered to a tree, with something long and heavy strapped across the saddle, something roughly wrapped in hessian but still dripping from either end.

I strode towards it, trying to look as much like Marcus' agent as I could, dressed as I was in a simple tunic, with dirty straw in my hair. 'Let me see it,' I said, imperiously. 'I am a citizen.'

The soldiers looked at one another doubtfully.

'On Marcus' orders,' I said. That worked. The soldier who had escorted me stepped forward and pulled away the wet, coarse cloth.

It was a man, or it had been a man, once. The head and hands dangled gracelessly downwards, the legs hung limp and awkward in death.

'Found him in the river,' the soldier said, grasping the short, curly hair and lifting the head upwards to reveal the face. 'The armour would have pulled him down anyway, but the cloak was weighted with stones. We would not have found him if we had not been ordered to search. I don't know if it is the man you want – the rats have been at him as it is.'

The water-swollen face was too gnawed to recognise, but I moved forward and, slipping my hand under the arming-doublet and the scaled tunic, I found what I sought. I brought out the chain, and read aloud the inscription on the tag. ' "If found, return to Crassus

Claudius Germanicus, for this is a fugitive slave." This is the man.'

'I am sorry, pavement maker,' the soldier said. 'We did not look for name-fetters. He seemed to be a soldier, not a slave. He has no helmet, though he might have worn one once. The currents there are fierce. No weapon either.'

'There was a dagger at least,' I said. 'In his back.' It did not need me to say so; the dreadful bloodied rents told their own story. This man had been stabbed in the back, several times from the look of it, and thrown into the river afterwards.

'He was robbed, too,' the soldier said. 'See where the purse has been cut from the thong? Strange, it seems to have been a civilian pouch, slung underneath the scale-shirt. That is awkward to manage. A soldier usually wears his purse under the wristpad on his arm.'

Junio was beside me, and he looked at me, his eyes shining. 'So,' he said, 'that is why Daedalus did not return. It might be, then, as I suggested.'

I silenced him with an eyebrow. 'We shall see. But look, here comes Marcus now, and Andretha with him. And still unshaved. That will not please him.'

But Marcus was, in fact, looking extremely pleased with himself. 'Ah, Libertus, my old friend. There you are. I have been hoping to speak with you.'

I had kept him waiting. He was in good humour, but it was not wise. I said, hastily, 'Humblest apologies, excellence. I was delayed about your business. These men have made an important discovery. They have found Daedalus.'

Andretha, who had been bobbing like a salmon in his wake, followed my gaze and let out a stifled sound. 'Dead?'

'And robbed,' I said, and watched his face turn whiter. Junio did well, I thought, to suspect Andretha, but the steward had not known that Daedalus was dead, I was sure of that.

I do not know what I was expecting Marcus to do. Thank the soldiers, perhaps. Be surprised. Be interested at least.

In fact he gave a cursory glance at the lifeless bundle. 'They have done well,' he said, 'but it hardly matters now. The man was only a slave. As well for him he was not found alive, impersonating a soldier. But since he is dead already, he is beyond our power.'

'But excellence,' I said, 'the question of Germanicus . . .'

He interrupted me, holding up his hand with an air of lofty indulgence. 'Ah, yes, the murder of Germanicus,' he said. 'You have done your best for me, as usual. But this time, it seems, my methods are superior to yours. The matter is resolved.'

'Resolved?'

'Indeed.' Marcus tried, and failed, to keep the triumph from his smile. 'While you were out this morning. Rufus has confessed.'

Chapter Seventeen

'Rufus?' I must have sounded as startled as I felt. Rufus, the scrupulously truthful! It was the last thing I was expecting.

Marcus looked smug. 'I had Andretha announce this morning that if anyone named the culprit I would grant unconditional pardon to the rest of the household. I thought it might sharpen Andretha's memory, but I need not have worried. Rufus came to me almost immediately and confessed. I had him locked in the librarium.'

'The librarium?' I echoed, and heard Marcus sigh. I was beginning to sound like a schoolboy practising rhetorical intonation. I resolved to stop repeating everything he said, and tried to look more intelligent than I felt.

There was a punishment cell, elsewhere, Marcus explained, but he had ordered this as a temporary measure. Rufus was to be taken back to Glevum in chains. 'Crassus was a veteran and a citizen, after all,' Marcus said, almost gleefully, 'and there is always a shortage of convicted criminals for the entertainments.'

It would be a pity to waste the opportunity for winning popular acclaim, he meant, by simply bringing in the torturer to flog Rufus to death. There would doubtless be a hearing, of sorts, before he was thrown to the wolves and bears.

I nodded. 'May I talk to him?'

Marcus looked reluctant. 'Is that necessary, now? The matter is settled, and I am anxious to get back to Glevum,' he said fretfully. 'There is the matter of the sale of the villa to be negotiated. I may offer for it myself, and Lucius will have to be consulted.'

The question of the murder was settled to *his* satisfaction, perhaps. I was not so sure. I thought quickly. 'Surely, excellence, he should be consulted about Rufus, too? After all he is the owner of him now. He should at least be informed.'

Marcus frowned. I was afraid for a moment that I had overstepped myself, but he gave a rueful smile. 'True!' he said, smacking his palm with his baton in that characteristic way which showed his irritation. 'Oh, Mercury! I had overlooked that fact. Though Lucius is a Christian; they have these sympathetic ideals. He will be unlikely to object to my amnesty. As the nearest relative he might even apply to deal with the boy himself, flog him and have him sent to the mines, perhaps, or trained up as a gladiator instead of going straight to the arena. All right, Libertus, you speak to Rufus. Persuade him not to appeal to his new master. Persuade him that the bears would be a better fate.'

It might even be true, I thought. The beasts were savage, but they were quick. A sentence to the mines would mean a lingering brutal death, especially for a lightly built musician of Rufus' sensibility. Even with the gladiators there might also, given Rufus' girlish good looks, be humiliations of a more intimate kind. It occurred to me, for the first time, that Rufus might already have suffered something similar at Crassus'

hands. Or not his hands, perhaps. What a man did with
his slaves was his own affair, but it would help explain
why Rufus hated his master enough to murder him.
Presumably he had murdered him, since he had confessed. But when, and how, and what about Daedalus?

I didn't like it at all.

I put on my toga to conduct the interview. They had
left Rufus in the dark, and when they opened the
librarium door for me the sudden light blinded him for
a moment. He was sitting huddled on the mosaic floor,
his chained neck roped to his shackled hands, and his
hands to his ankles, so that he could not attempt to
stand, or even raise his head at my approach. I felt a
pang of sympathy.

I had worn such bonds myself, they were of the kind
commonly used in the slave market, and although it was
more than twenty years since I had been captured,
chained and sold, I remembered only too vividly how
painful they could be. The single rope that links each
set of shackles is drawn uncomfortably taut, so that the
captive can only sit in one position and the slightest
movement tightens them. I knew from experience how
cruelly the iron chafes with every least attempt to ease
the limbs, and how swiftly agonising cramp sets in. I
wondered vaguely where Marcus had obtained the
fetters, and then realised that Crassus probably always
kept unpleasant chains of that kind somewhere in the
villa.

I left Junio to wait outside and heard the door lock
behind me. I set my candle on the wall-spike, but even
so without a window-space the room was very dark.
Rufus looked up at me, pale but defiant in the candlelight. Someone, I noted, had given him a thrashing
already. There were weals on his arms, and a thin stripe

of blood coloured the shoulder of his tunic. Andretha, I guessed, furious at his own close brush with execution.

I squatted on the pavement beside him, glad of my toga to moderate the chill on my own extremities. 'So,' I said, conversationally, 'you murdered Crassus, did you? Did you do that alone, or with Faustina?'

The effect was much as I had hoped. A bright spot of red flared on each pale cheek. He tried to lift his chin defiantly, but the cruel chain constricted him. He said, in a strangled voice, 'Faustina had nothing to do with it. Nothing. She knew nothing about it.'

'So,' I continued, in the same casual tone, 'you administered the poison and put him in the hypocaust unaided?'

That flush again. 'I did not say that.'

'Ah,' I said. 'So you did have help? Which part did you perform? It was clever of you, in so little time. Aulus saw you at the South Gate halfway through the festival.'

He lifted his head and almost choked himself again. It was cruel, I thought, to question him like this, but I had to learn the truth before there was another innocent killed. 'I did not do it with my own hands,' he said. 'But I brought about the killing. I paid to have him dead. That is enough.'

'You paid?' That explained why Rufus had no money, despite the fact that Andretha had seen him given coins. 'Whom did you pay? Someone in the villa?'

He tried to shake his head and winced with pain. 'I cannot tell you that. I have sworn an oath, before the gods.' He looked at the long pale hands shackled at the wrists. 'I did not expect that his death would be so quick. I –' His voice broke. 'I thought that it would answer everything. But it has not. It has made things worse. Faustina and I would have been separated, perhaps for ever – you cannot know how that feels.'

I thought of Gwellia, but I held my tongue.

'Marcus told us you had made progress with your investigation. I could not stand by and watch Paulus blamed. It was not his fault. If he used a poisoned razor, he was forced to do it.' He managed to turn his head and look at me. 'He told me, you see, about the novacula – that you had found it covered with blood, and that you suspected him.'

'You think the blade was poisoned?' I doubted it myself. Given Crassus' appetite, I guessed the fatal dose had been disguised as food or drink, and probably swallowed eagerly as a result.

'If the blade was poisoned, it was not Paulus' fault. He was a tool, no more. An instrument of stronger forces. He had no choice.'

I thought about that, turning a hundred theories in my brain. One thing, though, I was certain of. 'That may be,' I said. 'All the same, you did not confess to protect Paulus. You are a brave young man, but you are not quite a fool. I am an old man, but I am no fool either. There is only one person for whom you would willingly give your life. What has Faustina done, that you suspect her so?'

He glowered in the candlelight, but did not answer.

'Well.' I got to my feet. 'There are ways of discovering.'

That did it. 'No – ahh!' (as he pulled his neck). 'No. I told you, she knew nothing of my plan.'

'Then you believe she had a plan of her own? Or, she had the poison.'

That moved him. 'Libertus, you must believe me. You must protect her. She did not do it, I know she didn't. She could not have done it, she didn't leave the procession. But . . . Crassus was poisoned. I believe it was aconite – it had all the signs. One quick dose, and the man is dead.'

'And Faustina had aconite? How does one persuade a man to eat a poisoned herb? Disguised in a meal, yes. But there was no sign of that.'

He looked at me hopelessly. 'When Regina was here, she had a chest of herbs. She made decoctions from them, dried them, made them into philtres. She gave some to Faustina.'

'I know,' I said. 'Berry leaves for child-pangs, something else to stop the flux. Faustina told me.'

'She did not tell you everything,' Rufus replied. 'She did not take the second medicine. I do not believe it was for the flux at all. Regina came to the slaves' quarters one day, from the furnace room. She had been drying aconite. Too dangerous, she said, to use the kitchen fire; one bunch of that in place of cooking herbs would kill us all. She was decocting it into a phial. "In the right hands and the right dose," she said, "this can do miracles. Has done and will again. We shall see if Crassus refuses to marry me now." And then she laughed. Laughed.' He paused, as if the memory were painful to him.

'You think Regina poisoned Germanicus because he refused her?'

He looked away. 'Not personally, no.'

'You think Faustina administered the poison for her?'

He could not answer that. 'I know Regina gave her a tiny phial of something. Faustina wore it hidden on a thong around her neck. I thought nothing of it, at the time. I thought it was for the flux, as she said.'

'But now you do not think so? When did you change your mind?'

'This morning. I had not seen her alone since Crassus died. You know how it is between us, so I will not pretend. We had only a few moments. She slipped off her tunic – and the phial was gone.'

I nodded. A phial threaded on a leather thong. I had a good idea where that phial was now – under my pillows, where I put it when Aulus gave it to me. I didn't say that to Rufus.

He was still explaining. 'I asked her about it, and she laughed. A strange laugh. I knew there was something wrong. She told me she had used the potion for my benefit. Now Germanicus was gone we could rejoice, she said. Whoever killed him deserved our heartfelt thanks. She was talking wildly. If anyone had heard her utter such sedition it would have been certain death, but she did not seem to care. It frightened me. When I pressed her, she turned on me. She denied poisoning Crassus.' His voice trembled. 'She accused me of plotting his death myself.'

'Of which you are completely innocent?' I said. 'Notwithstanding your confession?'

He sank back into a huddled heap again. 'What does it matter now? Libertus, she did not kill him. She would not lie to me.'

'If you believed that, young man,' I said, 'you would not be sitting here in chains.'

He set his face. 'I brought his death about. I am as guilty as if I poisoned him myself. I paid. I knew that Germanicus would die – I did not know how, I swear to that. I did not dream that it might endanger Faustina. I did not pay enough, I suppose. A richer man might have made a better bargain. If I delay, she will be suspected. She is an expert with herbs, and if I noticed that the phial was gone, others might do so too. I could not have her accused. You have your culprit – let it go at that.'

'And what about Daedalus,' I said. 'Did you pay to have him killed?'

'Daedalus?' He was so surprised he almost hanged himself. 'Of course not.'

'Then perhaps you can explain how you knew that he was dead, three days before his body was discovered in the river?'

There was no mistaking the genuineness of his reaction. He said sadly, 'You have found Daedalus?'

'The guard found him,' I said. 'He had been stabbed and robbed.'

'A cut-throat, then? Poor Daedalus. I knew he was carrying money. Yes, I feared the worst. He was no coward. He would not have run away, and if Crassus had freed him as he promised, I would have heard. Daedalus promised to go to Lucius and beg him to buy us.' He looked at me, as fully as his bonds would allow. 'We had high hopes. Crassus would have promised his brother anything to keep him away from here – he didn't want the world to know there was a Christian in the family. Daedalus was a friend. When I didn't hear from him I knew that he was either imprisoned or dead.'

I looked at him, a small, pathetic, manacled scrap in the candlelight. His childlike faith in friendship was rather touching; an echo of the old Celtic ways. 'Yes, he is dead,' I said softly. 'Now, are you going to tell me where you went during the procession, and whom you paid to have Crassus killed? You know Marcus could have you tortured?'

A little moan of terror escaped him, but he stiffened himself. 'I cannot tell you, citizen. I cannot. Marcus will have to do his worst. I will be killed, I know that. But if

I am certainly to die, I dare not also die cursed. I have sworn an oath of silence to the gods. And the gods repay. See how Crassus perished!'

I thought of all the legends of my people – the warrior hero with his lute refusing to stoop to cowardice. I wished that I could promise this brave, misguided youth that I could spare him additional lashes at least, but I knew that I could not. I had made my own compromises long ago. It was the price of survival. I said, 'Then I must leave you. Faustina loves you. Do not despair.'

It was not much in the way of reassurance, but it was the best I could do. When I came out into the colonnade, the sunlight must have hurt my eyes. I found that they were smarting.

Chapter Eighteen

Marcus was waiting impatiently. He was not, in any case, in the sweetest of moods by this time. All efforts to find Paulus had failed, and he had been obliged to submit to the attentions of a less experienced slave. The experience had not improved his temper. Nor his beauty, I was bound to admit.

'Very well, Libertus. Now that you have condescended to come, perhaps we can get back to Glevum.'

Under the circumstances it did not seem an auspicious moment to argue. I had only wanted to return to Glevum to search for Daedalus, but when Marcus motioned me into the gig with him I obeyed, even though it meant leaving Junio to follow us on foot, and prevented me from any closer examination of Daedalus' body.

It had been stripped by now and was being thrown onto a cart for disposal in the communal grave on the hill. Since he was a dead slave, and not a runaway, he would be accorded a household funeral. There would, with luck, be a cursory prayer mumbled over him, a piece of coarse bread and a little water stuffed down the pipe which 'fed' the souls, and a solitary *as* coin in his mouth, as he was tumbled in on top of the other rotting bones exposed by the digging. The passing of an unregarded slave is different from his master's.

The armour, however, was travelling with us in the gig. It rattled and lurched alarmingly at every bump but I was able to confirm two things I had suspected. First, there were several segments of the scale-armour missing. That solved the problem of the piece I had found in the roundhouse. Secondly, the pattern of the whole was, as near as I could recall it, exactly like that which Andretha had taken from the body before the funeral. I wished that I had taken the opportunity to examine Germanicus' accoutrements again, but that was not possible now. Marcus, always a model of efficiency, had sent the whole uniform back to the armourer with the returning funeral contingent, on the grounds that all Germanicus' effects were to be sold.

'At least,' I said to Marcus, as we settled into the gig and let the driver bounce us at an uncomfortable trot up the main lane to the Glevum road, 'I now know what happened to Crassus' old armour.'

He was unimpressed. 'Hardly a major matter. It will not fetch a great deal. It has not been improved, either, by spending several days in the water.' He glanced at it disdainfully. 'Though why Daedalus was wearing it illegally I cannot see. I don't suppose we shall ever know, now the slave is dead.'

'I think,' I hazarded, 'that he was wearing it at his master's command.' I outlined my theory about the substitution at the festival.

Marcus was only vaguely listening. As far as he was concerned the murder was now solved and anything else was of academic interest. 'A dangerous trick,' he said, casually.

'Daedalus was a skilled mimic. I believe he was gambling for his life – his freedom if he was successfully undetected.'

Marcus, to my surprise, threw back his head and laughed. 'Dangerous, but typical of Crassus – he would bet on two slugs if he saw profit in it. No wonder that pouch was worth the stealing, Crassus would never accept a wager unless there was a good prize if he won. I suppose Daedalus was carrying his stake money in the pouch?'

I nodded. 'That is my guess.'

I waited for Marcus to ask where a mere slave had obtained that kind of money, but he didn't. Instead he began a lengthy complaint about the rigours of spending a night in the countryside, the current lack of hot water at the villa and the impossibility of obtaining a shave. 'I had thought,' he said, 'of simplifying the procedure with Lucius by buying the villa myself. My apartments in Glevum are pleasant enough, but they are merely rented, and I have no country property at present. The farm seems profitable, I was talking to the bailiff this morning. But I am beginning to change my mind. The place is wretchedly remote and inconvenient. And there is no decent barber's shop for miles.'

I had to smile. A good many 'urban' Romans wanted a country property; a sort of dream retreat where they could go at the end of a busy few days in the town to enjoy a sculptured prospect of trees and streams and forget about business and politics for a little. The practical aspects of such an arrangement – travel and damp and inconvenience – often did not occur to them; and they were in any case carefully shielded from the ruder realities such as the presence of mud and the smell of pigs. Marcus, it seemed, was no exception.

'Part of it will come to you anyway, if Lucius declines to inherit.' I tried to sound like a man of the world, but my words came out in little breathy bounces as the gig dashed along. We had reached the high road by now and were setting a handsome pace while I clung to the side for dear life. Marcus was used to this sort of headlong transport, I was not.

'I think I will send to him tomorrow, anyway,' Marcus said. 'His seal is required, in any case, to show he accepts the inheritance. I think he will, since the money will fund a church. Perhaps I will offer for the villa, after all. He may be glad of a quick sale.'

Marcus would make a low offer, I suspected. One could not expect a hermit to be a man of business.

We were approaching the *colonia* by now, driving through the rows of monuments, graves and vaults which lined the road, some of them so large and imposing that the cemetery area looked almost like a town itself. Then we were among the straggling buildings of the outskirts, and finally under the wall itself.

'Well,' Marcus said, as we bowled through the gate, under the triumphal arch, and down the wide paved street towards the forum, 'thank you for your help in this. I am sure that you would have preferred to solve the mystery unaided, but probably Rufus would not have confessed without your investigations. I am not displeased.'

He was looking delighted, in fact. Of course Rufus' confession pleased him; not only did it 'solve' the murder where I had failed to do so, but it proved that the killing was a non-political matter. That was Marcus' primary concern.

I got down from the gig at the statue of Jupiter, in the middle of the square. Marcus was going to his apartment, and then to the baths. 'A massage and a proper shave,' he said, with relish. 'That is what I need, now this matter is dealt with. My thanks once more, Libertus.

And I shall call on you again if I need your services, never fear.'

'You are sending to Lucius tomorrow?' I said. That was daring of me. I had received my dismissal.

Marcus tapped his palm with his cane. 'I am considering it, certainly. Why do you enquire?'

Careful, I told myself. That answer had been brusque. I hitched my toga more comfortably over my shoulder (a discreet reminder of my status) and produced my most disarming smile. 'It is foolish of me,' I suggested meekly, 'but I am curious to see this brother of Crassus. It was for his approval, after all, that the librarium pavement was ordered. I wondered if I might accompany you?' I did not add that I was looking for a reliable witness to give me the answer to some unresolved problems.

I had judged correctly. Marcus gave me an indulgent smile. 'A question of professional pride?' he said. 'I understand. Then of course you may come – although I shall send a messenger, I think, rather than go myself. Do not be disappointed, my old friend, if Lucius does not even recall your famous pavement. So much else has happened since.' He signalled to his driver, and was gone.

I walked slowly away, avoiding the moneylenders, letter writers and pimps who always loiter around the forum, out into the busy streets again. Under the shadow of the basilica I stopped to buy a pigmeat pie and a pot of foaming ale – what a pleasure to eat honest food again – and then, instead of going straight home, made my way towards the South Gate.

I had no idea what I was looking for.

'A shrine' Aulus had said. There were temples enough. Not only big temples – the central civic one to Jupiter,

Juno and Minerva, and the shrine of Mars where the
festival took place – but dozens of little buildings
dedicated to minor deities including, here and there,
altars to the local gods. The Romans have always
tolerated lesser religions, provided that they do not
interfere with the proper running of the state and
worship of the emperor. And many native people, like
myself, do not greatly care what name you give the gods
provided that you reverence them somehow. So these
smaller temples do a roaring trade, with all kinds of
little stalls at the doors selling incense, fire-sticks and
offerings to the faithful.

So at what shrine had Rufus shrugged off his follower?
And where did he go thereafter? There was not a great
deal beyond the South Gate except centuriated fields –
great areas of rectangular enclosures (mostly owned by
retired veterans) growing crops to feed the army – and
a rather unsavoury inn for any unwary traveller who
failed to reach the Glevum gates before sundown.

I glanced into one or two of the shrines, under the
watchful eye of the temple slaves. All were dedicated to
different gods, but apart from the nature of the statues
and the quality of the floors, they were all largely the
same. They were built on the Roman pattern: smallish,
dark, enclosed areas beyond a pillared portico, the stone
altars and carvings made more mysterious by the
flickering of candles or oil lamps. They all had the same
smell too, characteristic of temples everywhere: the
smell of smoke and offerings, singed pigeons, burning
herbs and incense, strewn flowers and libated wine, and
– seeping everywhere like the dark stain at the altar –
the odour of sacrificial blood.

I did not visit the Mithraic temple, nor the Vestal one;
the rites there were too complex to permit a casual

passer-by. Nor, I was sure, would Rufus have strayed into one, even by accident. Then, suddenly, I struck gold.

It was more primitive than most of the others. The same pillared entry, the same dim and smoky interior. But the statue in this temple was of an older, wilder god, beardless, but with his long hair streaming and the carved eyes full of power. I knew him even before I saw the attendant images of dogs, their tongues extended to lick and heal, or the models of diseased limbs and hands petitioning a cure. Nodens, god of the river, the healer and the justice-giver. He was overtaken now, by Roman gods, but he had once been much honoured hereabouts. He still had his adherents, and there was a huge temple to him a few miles downstream. Even here the pool of water at his feet was full of votive offerings – amulets, plaques and figurines. Lead tablets too: even the devotees of Nodens had taken to the Roman habit of inscribing their petitions, as if the god would somehow prefer to read their prayers than hear them.

Of course. Of course. Suddenly I understood. Rufus was a Silurian. This was where he had come – not, as Aulus had thought, because he was hiding from his pursuer, but because this was his destination. I went to the pool and leaned over to read the lead tablets. 'All thanks to Nodens for healing my boils.' 'A curse on Cenacus who has stolen my ox.'

It would be sacrilege to take them from the water – already the attendant slave was eyeing me suspiciously – but somewhere among them, I was sure, there would be another inscription. Very likely a long and sonorous one. 'May Nodens chill the blood of the man who injured my beloved and feed his carcass to the worms.' Something like that. Probably Rufus would not have dared to name names, not even his own, for fear the curse might be traced back to him – especially with Aulus watching. Many humble people wrote oblique curses of that kind, for much the same reasons, so even if I found a likely plaque, proving that it was Rufus would be difficult. But he *had* offered a curse-tablet here, I was certain of it.

I wondered how much it had cost him. A votive offering inscribed even with a general curse did not come cheaply, especially to a slave. Little wonder he had no money left. It was useless to ask Rufus about it, either. He had sworn an oath of silence to the gods and made a votive offering for Crassus' death. The outcome had not been exactly what he hoped – he should have paid more, he said – but he believed that Nodens had done his part. Rufus would fulfil his bargain to the grave.

I parted with five *as* coins for a votive candle, to the satisfaction of the attendant, and lighting it from the altar flame, stuck it on a spike near the image. Not as a prayer – I am not a follower of Nodens – but as a kind of homage from one old Briton to another. The stony old deity had been a god in this island before Caesar was ever heard of.

Then I went back into the street, and hurried home through the grey light of a cloudy afternoon. The workshop was still standing, and by the time I got there Junio was waiting for me.

Chapter Nineteen

I have no access to water-clocks or hour-candles, but it was nothing like the second hour, if I am any judge. It was still early morning. I was sitting back on my folding stool in tunic and bare feet, luxuriating in a homely breakfast of boiled oats which Junio had prepared for me (we have a fire, and I can never come to love the Roman habit of buying everything ready cooked from the street stalls), but I had barely had time to take my first lingering mouthful before a messenger arrived from Marcus. His excellence had decided to send an envoy to Lucius straight away, and invited me to present myself at his apartments as soon as possible.

'As soon as possible' in this context meant immediately, of course, if not sooner. I abandoned my breakfast, wound myself into toga and sandal straps and followed the messenger back into the town and down the streets towards the forum, where we found Marcus' official envoy waiting for us.

He was a patrician-looking youth with a supercilious expression, and though he was dressed as befitted a messenger, he was clearly a very important person, not least in his own estimation. He wore an immaculate, fine woollen tunic with embroidered borders, soft red leather sandals and a wonderful scarlet cloak fixed with a huge golden brooch. He looked at my dilapidated toga with disdain. Better an exclusive servant, his glance said, than an impoverished citizen like me. He strode ahead, leading the way, and giving off a faint aroma of expensive oils.

The carriage was waiting at the West Gate. Not a gig, this time, but a closed imperial carriage, with gilded doors and leather-cushioned bench seats. It was an imposing sight. Marcus was clearly intending to create a stir. He would never normally have sent mere messengers in this. Yet there was obvious method in it. If a man in expensive livery arrives in an imperial carriage to make you an offer for a house, you are unlikely to wait for a better offer – and in any case refusal is likely to prove dangerous to your health. Especially if you are already a member of a questionable religion.

Secretly I had no complaint. I remembered Andretha saying that Lucius lived 'a long way off'. A closed carriage offered considerably more comfort than a gig, especially since the wind was cold.

There was more than wind to endure, as it happened. It began to rain, heavily at first and then settling into a damp, dismal drizzle which slowed our progress even on the military road. On an ordinary track it would have been a nightmare of mud-bogged wheels, slithering horses and broken axles. Even the envoy was driven into speech – he had been preserving a well-bred silence all the way from Glevum.

He had affected his master's habits, too, and was beating a little tattoo of impatience on his palm with his baton, as he said irritably, 'What a dreary little island this is. Water everywhere but in the bathhouse. We shall scarcely make the posting house in two hours, even on this road. Thanks be to Mercury for Roman engineering.' He turned away and gazed at the passing scenery, in case I should be tempted to an answer.

I was looking at the scenery myself. We were well over the river and out on the Isca road now where it was less frequented. Marcus had obtained directions from the messengers who went to Lucius after his brother's death. 'A foul journey' they had called it, and so it was, out past the cultivated lands and into the forbidding forest.

There were always legends about such places; apart from the obvious risks from bears and brigands, there were hair-curling stories about the road at night. Spectral legions who marched in eerie silence at your side, and when the moon rose, vanished. Eyeless wanderers who approached unwary horsemen begging for a drink, and whose faces, when they raised their heads, were so hideous that all who saw them perished at the sight (though how anyone could live to describe this horror, in that case, it was difficult to explain).

I have never personally met a phantom and do not (on the whole) expect to do so, but, creeping along a strange road through a dim, dark, forbidding forest wraithed with mist, nothing would altogether have surprised me. Brigands, though, were a more tangible possibility. Our driver was armed, of course, but I had nothing except my eating knife. I wished the envoy carried a better weapon than a ceremonial baton, though if it came to a fight he would probably refuse to get his tunic creased. I need not have worried, as it happened. All we saw were a couple of drenched messengers and a man with a depressed donkey lumbering towards Glevum with a little cart full of sheepskins.

But it was dreary. How I wished that I was making my way to Corinium instead, looking for news of

Gwellia. For that, I would have fought off brigands barehanded.

We reached the staging post, where Marcus' imperial warrant immediately produced fresh horses for the carriage and a simple refreshment for ourselves. Then we set off again, and shortly afterwards turned down the side lane as we had been directed.

It was a surprisingly good road, although it was not a Roman one and it twisted and turned fearsomely. The landowner, whoever he was, had learned lessons from the military road-builders and built his track with a raised centre so that the rain and mud drained off it, and up here where the ground was higher and free from the huge overhanging trees, the going was easier than I had feared.

We were looking for a homestead, Marcus had said, belonging to one of the Dubonnai, the local tribe. A shrewd man, clearly, since he appeared to have held onto his land while at the same time avoiding execution, dispossession, relocation or even the ruinously expensive public office which often disposed of wealthy local princes.

We found the place at last. Heard it first – the bark of dogs, the whinny of a horse – and then smoke from the cooking-fire stung our eyes and throats. My companion was beginning to look distinctly uneasy. And when, breasting the fold of a hill, we saw it, he let out an uncomfortable sigh.

To me, it was a sight to make my old heart leap. A proper old-fashioned Celtic farm, its snug little timber-and-daub roundhouses nestling inside their protective circular bank and ditch, the thatched roofs layered and golden like so many neat conical haircuts. And inside the compound the familiar, cheerfully casual noisy chaos

– haystacks, grainstores, pigsties, osier-piles, goats, grandmothers, dogs, beehives, farm tools, children and chickens. I had not seen so homely a scene since I lived in a roundhouse myself.

'At least there are a few stone barns up on the hill. The place is not entirely without civilisation,' the envoy said disapprovingly. 'But no sign of a hermit. I suppose he will be somewhere even more disagreeable.' He banged on the roof for the driver to stop, and dismounted grandly from the carriage. I followed him to the gate. A cacophony of barking dogs and hissing geese greeted us from behind the woven barrier and half a dozen grimy urchins gazed at us in wide-eyed wonder.

The envoy hesitated, and then called, in his most imperious voice, 'Who is in charge here?'

A youth in a coarse blue woven wool jerkin and britches uncurled himself from the pile of osiers he had been splitting and rose to meet us, smiling, balancing his heavy axe in his hand. With his tousled hair, wild beard, broad shoulders and air of effortless athleticism he looked, I thought, more than a match even for the brutish Aulus.

Beside me, I felt my companion stiffen.

'Citizens?' The lad spoke Latin haltingly. He glanced at the attendant on the carriage behind us and then at the envoy's embroidered tunic, staff and seal. It seemed to tell him something. He ran a tongue around his lips and amended himself hastily, making a swift obeisance. 'Excellence?'

It was a mistake, of course, but he could not have done better. The envoy was visibly flattered.

'On his excellence's business. We are looking for Lucius,' he said, and then, seeing the boy's look of bafflement, 'Lu-ci-us, the Chri-st-i-an. On a matter of ur-gent im-port-ance.' He spoke unnaturally loudly, as if by shouting he would somehow make the language easier to understand.

I murmured an explanation in Celtic, and the boy looked at me gratefully.

'There is a cave up in the hills there where he has a retreat. For a long time he did not have even the simplest luxuries, but recently my mother has prevailed on him to accept a few comforts, and gifts of food now and then. Apparently his brother, too, has given him a wealth of things, though he has already sold some of them to give food to the poor.' His dialect was not quite my own, but it was more comprehensible than his Latin. It must have been a secluded rural life indeed which had screened him so effectively from the official tongue.

I answered in my own tongue. 'Your mother seems to know a lot about him.'

He grinned, reminding me of Junio. 'You know what women are when it comes to holy men. Since he cured my brother, she never stops talking about him.'

I have a suspicious mind. 'He cured your brother, you say. Does he heal with herbs?'

The boy shook his head. 'With herbs, no. Not that I know. The only herbs I have seen him with are those he gathers to eat. No, my brother fell into the brook, and hit his head. The hermit jumped in, at the risk of his own life, and pulled him out. Elwun was given up for drowned until the hermit stretched out over him, and breathed his own breath into his nostrils. Even after he brought the boy home, he stayed here a day and night praying over him. It was all my family could do to persuade him to accept dry clothing. When Elwun recovered, it almost persuaded my mother to join the Christians.'

I was trying to imagine a relative of Crassus who would risk his life to save another. I failed. 'A brave man,' I murmured.

'He is famous in the district,' the boy said. 'Everyone comes to him. But he isn't one of your "I-am-better-than-you-poor-sinners" types. He lived a sinful youth, he told my mother, and is trying to atone for it.'

'Forgive me,' the envoy said acidly, cutting across our words in crystal accents. 'When you have quite finished your private conversation, perhaps you would favour me with a translation?'

I explained.

'If you know where this hermit is,' the envoy said, ignoring me, 'kindly send for him at once. We have a long journey ahead of us. We shall be lucky to get home before the town gates shut, as it is.'

The boy looked uncomfortable.

'Well, what are you waiting for?'

The boy looked at me, and then stumbled, in poor Latin, 'He is in mourning, excellence. The death of his brother has affected him sorely. He has not left his cell since, except to pray. He has been fasting, shaved his head and put on sackcloth and ashes. He may not wish to come.'

The envoy looked flabbergasted, rather as Jove might look if someone asked him to put down his thunderbolts. 'Not wish to come?'

'I am not sure that the boy has understood,' I said quickly. 'Perhaps if I were to speak to Lucius . . . ?'

He looked at me in surprise (it was the first time I had ventured a word to him, unbidden) and then said sulkily, 'Perhaps that would be best. Is there anywhere to sit in comfort in this cow byre?'

I translated this, politely, although from the flush on

the boy's face I imagined that he understood more Latin than he spoke. The trappings of power, however, carried their privileges even in this remote spot. One of the small boys was dispatched to alert 'Mother', and we were ushered into the biggest roundhouse.

It was such a dear, familiar scene that it quite brought a lump to my throat. There was the central hearth, filling the room with smoke, warmth and the smell of cooking. There were the chickens, pecking at the earth floor, and a great dog lying beside the fire, as my own dog had once used to do. There were the females of the household; the weaving frame, and an old woman working at it, while a child spun thread at her feet. It was a scene from my childhood. Only the faces were different.

When we came in, a young girl in a plaid dress was raking hot stones from the fire and dropping them into a heavy pot where there was already water and a joint of meat. In an hour or two, I knew, the lamb would be gently cooked and deliciously tender. Another woman was lifting hot oatcakes from an iron griddle laid on the hearth, and the sweet smell of baking almost made my mouth water. She wrapped three of the small loaves in a cloth and turned to greet us.

'If you are to visit the hermit,' she said, in her own dialect, 'take him some of these. I am worried about that man. We have hardly seen him since his brother's death.'

'Lucius healed your son?' I said.

It was like unleashing a mudslide. I was instantly regaled with a dozen tales of Lucius' holiness. How he had prayed over a sick cow. How he had fasted for a whole week when a member of the family had a fever. How for a long time he had not even permitted himself a proper bed or a servant. How he had given his own breakfast to a beggar.

The osier-cutter looked at me apologetically. 'The citizen may see for himself, Mother.'

She thrust the oatcakes into his hands. 'My son will show you the way. We speak little Latin here, and Lucius does not know our tongue.'

I explained this to my companion, and one of the children fetched him a low carved wooden stool. He looked uncomfortable and out of place, sitting there beside the hearth in smoky and disapproving state, while the youngsters peered at him around the doorpost, and the old woman nodded and smiled toothlessly. As I left, he was being plied with hot oatcakes and warm ale, both of which he was regarding with undisguised mistrust. I was glad to get outside to hide a smile.

What would he do, I wondered, if Lucius did refuse to come down and see him? From what I heard of Lucius, threats would not sway him, and if he had sworn an oath he would be immovable. Marcus would not be pleased if his messenger went back empty-handed. Perhaps Lucius did not care – Christians are said actively to welcome martyrdom. It was not a fate, however, that I was keen to experience myself. I would have to do something.

The youth led the way up the path at a speed which had me panting. 'When we get there,' he said, 'I will go in and tell him you have come. He has buried himself in his cave since his brother died, and scarcely comes out.' He looked at the packet of oatcakes. 'I hope he will accept these, or my mother will blame me. You have seen what she is like about him. She worries that he is not eating, and is shutting himself off too much. I think this loss has grieved him more than you would believe.

He hoped to save his brother's soul, Mother says, and thought he had nearly done it.'

'Nearly converted Crassus?' I must have sounded as scornful as I felt.

'She may have been mistaken. Her Latin is not good.' He grinned. 'Even worse than mine. She said his brother had promised to endow a church.'

'And has done so,' I said, 'through his will.'

'Well, perhaps she was right after all!' he said. 'Now, we are almost there. There is the cave, and there the barn. I will go in ahead. He has withdrawn from strangers more or less completely, though people still come to him to ask his prayers.'

I had never met Lucius, but of one thing I could be sure, I thought. If the reactions of these people were anything to go by, he was nothing at all like his brother.

Chapter Twenty

He was, in fact, remarkably like Crassus in many ways.
I could see that even in the dim light of the cave. The
same slightly protuberant grey eyes, the same stocky
build, even the same bristling look – the head and face
had been recently shorn but the thick grizzled hair and
beard were already growing irrepressibly back. This was
a humbler, quieter Crassus, not expensively togaed and
bejewelled, but eclipsed in a coarse grey hood and robe,
with the marks of penitential ashes still on his forehead.
Where Crassus strutted and strode, this man's movements were slow and considered; and his voice when he
spoke was almost a whisper, unexpected after
Germanicus' booming roar.

It was a large cave, rather than the poky cell I had
imagined. It was dark and shadowy in the light of two
flickering candles, although it was surprisingly warm
and dry. There was a crude stone altar at one end, on
which one of the candles was burning. The nearer part
of the cave was the living area, and someone – probably
the woman – had done their best to make it comfortable.
There was a rush mat on the floor, a straw mattress, a
cupboard and a stool, and someone had provided a tiny
brazier to lift the chill. There were evidences too, of
Crassus' gifts – a fine bowl with a few humble fruits in

it, a Samian drinking vessel, a rich woollen blanket folded on the stone bench and a fine worked knife on the clumsy table. There, beside a feeble taper in a candleholder, a crust of bread, an end of cheese and a bunch of dandelion leaves and dried parsley suggested a frugal meal. I remembered what Paulus had said about Lucius loving food. The oatcakes, I thought, would be a welcome gift.

The boy put them down on the bench, picked up a leather pitcher and hurried off. 'I will fetch water from the spring,' he said, 'and leave you to your business.'

'Greetings upon you.' The hermit had left the altar and was coming towards me, extending a hand in vague blessing. I could see why the woman was concerned for his health. The chi-rho ring which he wore hung loose upon the finger, although I noted a mark in the flesh which showed clearly where the tightness of the band had been. He was not a slim man now, far from it, but the rough garment hung awkwardly away from him in folds, making him look diminished, as sick men some-times do, as if he had lost the will to fill out his own clothes. 'You come from Marcus?'

I wondered fleetingly how he had known that, but I followed his glance and saw the view through the cave entrance down to the valley, where the imperial carriage still gleamed – small enough at this distance, but even more remarkable here than it had seemed at Glevum. This Lucius was not too unworldly to have sharp and observant eyes.

'I do,' I said, and was slightly discomfited to find that the penetrating gaze was now fixed on me.

He waved me to the stool. 'You would like wine?' he said, in that whispering voice of his. 'Or water? I have little to give you. The boy comes here in the mornings:

he fetches me food. Or there are these . . .' He turned to the package on the bench, and opened it.

The smell of warm oatcakes was so delicious that I could not refuse, although I knew that these few loaves might well be all his meal. Christians, I reminded myself, were famous for their generosity, and I was representing Marcus – he would have considered it impolite to decline hospitality. Besides, they smelt wonderful.

I accepted.

He fetched water from a second pitcher, broke one of the loaves into pieces and laid the simple food on the table for us to share.

'Now,' he murmured, reclining himself on the mattress – there was nowhere else to sit, 'you come from Marcus, you say?' He picked up a piece of oatcake as he spoke, for all the world like a Roman magnate discussing deals at a banquet.

I explained the purpose of the visit, beginning with Marcus' wish to buy the villa. I named the figure Marcus had authorised and saw a shrewd look cross the bearded face. 'He makes a poor offer,' he said. 'The villa is worth twice as much. But I have no choice. One cannot refuse a powerful man like Marcus. Tell him that I accept, provided that the sale is quick. Have him prepare a contract and I will seal it.' He dipped his oatcake in water and smiled, a slightly tight smile. 'I suppose it is useless to remind him that the money is to endow a church? He would prefer that it went to the games, no doubt, or to some Roman god?'

In fact, my patron probably had no strong views on that matter. Beyond a few propitiatory sacrifices and the obligatory public rituals, Marcus ignored the gods, and doubtless trusted that they would do the same for him. 'He might give money to the games, perhaps,' I said. 'They are useful in buying popularity. Crassus did not leave money for memorial games.'

That disconcerting smile again. 'When it concerned money, Crassus was no fool. For instance, he would have understood perfectly that Marcus was cheating me. But, as I say, I have no choice. Tell him that I accept his offer – for the villa. All the furniture and chattels come to me.' I must have looked startled at his bargaining, because he smiled again. 'I should get a good price for them. There is a table, for instance. It alone would pay for a fine building.'

I nodded. When it came to money, this man was no fool either.

'Speaking of chattels,' I said, 'what about the slaves? Marcus promised that if one of them confessed, he would pardon the others. As a holy man, I imagine that will please you. Now that Rufus has confessed, do you wish the others sold?'

He looked horrified. 'Rufus has confessed?'

'Yes, the little lute player. You were once good to him, I believe.'

He had turned paler than ever. 'Poor Rufus. Yes. But, Rufus confessed? You do surprise me. If it had been the gatekeeper, now! I always suspected that the man was up to no good.' He seemed to take control of himself. 'But yes, yes. Have the others sold. And Daedalus, I understand, is being sought as a runaway. Let him go. My brother was to free him anyway, after the festival. He may already have done so. There was some sort of wager, I believe. Crassus told me of it.' He waved the hand again. 'I do not approve of wagers, but my brother had given a promise. Daedalus shall have his freedom.'

'Daedalus has been found,' I told him. 'He is dead.'

'You have found him?' Lucius looked grave. He said

unsteadily, 'Poor fellow, then his manumission cost him dear.'

'There was no manumission,' I said. 'He had no certificate of freedom, and he still wore his neckchain, identifying him as Crassus' slave. If he had been manumitted his first act would have been to remove that. Do you know what the wager was?'

'Crassus did not tell me. He knew I disliked his gambling. In fact, it would be true to say that Crassus told me very little. We had – how shall I put it – grown apart.' The grey eyes seemed secretly amused.

'Then he did not tell you, either,' I said, dropping my voice instinctively, 'of any plots concerning the army? There are rumours that he was seen talking to a soldier, more than once, in secret and at dusk.'

'He was?' Lucius seemed genuinely alarmed. 'That could be serious. Who saw him? Aulus, I suppose.'

'Yes. There are rumours of a possible army rebellion, or even an imperial plot. That could be serious, certainly. Serious enough to cause your brother's death, if he were involved and one of the rival factions found out. Marcus was sure that was the explanation, until Rufus confessed. You knew your brother. What do you think?'

He thought about that. 'But surely Marcus is right? If Rufus has confessed, it was no military murder. No, Rufus should be executed and the others sold. That would be best.' He must have sounded harsh, even in his own ears, because he smiled. 'It saves innocent lives, besides.'

'And if Rufus did not kill your brother? You yourself do not believe he did.'

He paused at that, and then said, 'No, I don't altogether believe it. But if he confessed, perhaps it is true. Rufus prided himself on truthfulness. And the boy is offering himself as a sacrifice. You cannot expect me to condemn that.'

'He genuinely believes he had a hand in Crassus' death,' I said. 'I think he went to a temple and put a curse on his master.'

That startled Lucius into momentary sharpness. 'Did he? Perhaps then he brought this on himself. I do not hold with worshipping false gods, that is sin enough, but calling down curses is an evil business.' He seemed to reflect and his face and tone softened. 'Although his sacrifice is a fine gesture; I will offer prayers for him.'

'And what about the chief slave, Andretha? I believe Crassus bequeathed him freedom too. Should he have it?'

Lucius gave me a shrewd smile. 'Only if he can balance the accounts. Crassus suspected the man was cheating the estate.'

'You might effect a pardon,' I put in. 'As the nearest relative – and a Christian.'

He looked at me. 'You would condone his stealing?'

That was an awkward question. 'I might show mercy,' I ventured finally.

He smiled. 'You answer well. You might show mercy. So indeed might I. I might for instance, save that little concubine of Rufus' . . . what is her name?'

'Faustina?'

'Faustina, yes. I might spare her the slave market, find her a private owner who will treat her well. And I will not denounce that little Druid to the authorities. That will save his life, too. If Aulus has not denounced him already, that is. He would sell his own father for a handful of copper coins.' He smiled. 'Very well. Tell Marcus I agree to all his terms. The sale of the villa, and a pardon for the other slaves, since Rufus has confessed.

And now, if there is nothing more that I can do for you, it is the hour of prayer.' He dusted the crumbs from his fingers and rose to his feet.

I stood up too. 'There is just one thing more,' I hazarded. 'This woman, Regina; did you know her well?'

He looked astonished. 'Regina? Yes, I knew her slightly. What of her? She was my brother's camp-follower when he was young. She claimed marriage with him.'

'Yes. There was talk she had some kind of secret hold on him – something she knew about him. Do you know what it was?'

He shrugged, a dismissive gesture. 'It might have been a hundred things. She was – persistent. Perhaps he did promise to wed her.'

'Much more than that, I think. She was a herbalist. Crassus' senior officer died unexpectedly. You do not think she helped her lover to promotion?'

There was a silence. Then he said, 'You think she poisoned the centurion?'

'Or gave the drug to Crassus to do so. Was he capable of that? Of committing treachery to serve himself?'

Lucius turned away. When he turned back, I saw that he was gripped by emotion. 'Well,' he said, 'Crassus is dead. I suppose it cannot hurt him now. But if I tell you – swear that you will tell no one else.' He looked around wildly, as if seeking for something on which to seal the oath, and then offered me his ringed finger.

'I am not a Christian,' I demurred.

He rummaged in the cupboard and produced a figurine. 'Then swear on this. It represents the emperor, among other things.' He saw my surprised look, and hastened to explain. 'One of Crassus' gifts. He meant to mock me, but I could not throw it away, that would be blasphemy and treason too. And so I hide it here. But now, it has its use.'

I swore, on the emperor's life. Poor old Commodus, I thought. Judging by the whispers of conspiracy, that life was not worth a great deal.

It seemed to satisfy Lucius, however.

'Then,' he said, 'I will tell you the truth. I think that Crassus did poison his officer – tricked someone into putting a fatal dose into the centurion's wine. It was a clever move. He had a dozen witnesses to swear that he himself was miles away gambling. He used to boast to me of that.'

'Regina knew this?'

'You would have to ask her that.'

'That is what I wished to ask you. Do you know where she is?'

He looked at me, startled, for a long moment. Then he said, 'You think she killed my brother?'

My turn to shrug. 'She had the means, and motive too. Killing an officer is a capital offence. If she provided the poison, she was a conspirator herself. Perhaps she even administered the fatal dose; a man will take a poisoned cup more trustingly from a woman's hands. She risked her life for Crassus – and he rejected her. That would be hard to forgive.'

Lucius nodded. 'I see. You may be right. Perhaps she came back and poisoned him. Crassus might arrange to meet her, secretly, if he thought to pay her off.'

'There would have been food and wine, just like this,' I said, biting into the soft flesh of an oatcake. It was as delicious as it smelt.

Lucius absently ate another. He was engrossed in his imaginings. 'But Regina knew how to make a fatal infusion; she could slip it into his cup, and it would be easy to wash the containers in the stream and hide the traces afterwards.' He was becoming animated as he spoke. 'You must find her, Libertus. There is no time to lose. Proving this would reprieve young Rufus, too. Her home, though, is far away. Near Eboracum, where Crassus was serving when he met with her. Go now, take my message to Marcus, and find her, before it is too late. But there, your guide has come. I must to my prayers.'

I turned and saw the Dubonnai boy standing in the doorway, a pitcher of water in his hands, gazing at us with astonished eyes.

Chapter Twenty-one

'Lucius was pleased to see you,' the boy said, as we wound our way down the hill again. 'I thought when you first arrived that he seemed unwilling to speak to you. But you have revived him. Since the feast of Mars he has turned away visitors, and "cloaked himself in prayer and solitude" as my mother says. And he had almost ceased to eat. There was a time that he was always out on the hills, picking berries and mushrooms or collecting eggs and herbs to eat, but since his brother's death he seemed to have lost all interest in food. But there he was talking earnestly to you, and breaking bread with you besides. Our neighbours will be pleased to hear it, they have been wanting him to come and pray for their sick daughter. I told you how he saved my brother's life?'

I had to listen to the story all over again.

When we got back to the roundhouse, I found the envoy in a less communicative mood than ever. He had made himself queasy on unaccustomed ale and hot cakes and, having exhausted the family's knowledge of Latin very quickly, had been obliged to endure a long afternoon of sitting silently like a statue, being peered and giggled at by the infants while the grandmother grinned gummily nearby. To crown it all, the smoke of

the fire had made smuts on his tunic, and my intervention with Lucius had made his presence on this
whole venture a complete waste of time. Having de-
livered himself, curtly, of this information he preserved
a huffy silence all the way home.

I left him at the forum to make his report to Marcus
– at least he would get the credit for the sale of the villa
– and made my way home, quickly, before darkness fell
and the streets became too dangerous for law-abiding
citizens to walk alone. I had no money to hire myself a
carrying-chair or a protective slave.

I arrived home, without interruption from marauding
youths or drunken soldiery, to find Junio waiting for
me. He had bought some cooked meat, and roasted a
turnip for us in the embers of the fire. I stretched out on
my stool, glad of my simple pleasures.

'Cassius Didio was here to see you,' Junio said, when
he judged that I had relaxed sufficiently to receive this
news.

I groaned. 'Complaining about his pavement, I
suppose. What did you tell him?'

Junio grinned. 'That you had been called away by
Marcus. Didio was most impressed, especially when I
told him it was all a deadly secret, and I was forbidden
to tell him more.'

I ran a weary hand through what was left of my hair.
'Why did you tell him that? The story will be all over
Glevum tomorrow.'

'I know, master. But it stopped him being angry over
his pavement, and your name will be on everyone's lips.
Linked with Marcus, too. Anyone who wants a mosaic
will be agog for your services.'

I could not help smiling at his reasoning. He was
probably right about the gossip too. Curiosity draws

customers as surely as oxen drag the plough. I picked up my spiced mead.

'Marcus was not with me,' I said. 'I had a much more exquisite companion.' I told Junio about my day.

He appeared fascinated, asking endless questions about the roundhouse until I realised he was humouring me. I moved the subject swiftly to Lucius.

'So, will you go to Eboracum?' he asked when I had finished.

I shook my head. 'I could not afford such a trip, even if Marcus would pay for the travel, which he will not. And Didio is waiting for his mosaic border. It would be too late to save Rufus, in any case, even supposing I could find Regina there.'

'Which you doubt?'

'Which I doubt. Anyway, I do not believe she poisoned him. If she had come back to the villa someone would have seen her. And she didn't stay at an inn. You remember the aediles asked at all the inns, after the murder, and there were no unexplained strangers in the vicinity. And a woman travelling alone would be very noteworthy.'

'She had a male slave travelling with her, and a maid.'

'No. She dismissed the girl, and Paulus told us that the custos died. He shaved the corpse before they buried it.'

'You think Regina poisoned her custos too?'

'She might have done.' I took a gulp of mead. 'But what about Daedalus? Surely she could not have murdered him?'

'Perhaps that was unconnected, a simple robbery. That seems likely. Daedalus was waiting for Crassus by the river, but he would have had a long wait. Germanicus was already dead. It is dangerous by the river after dark, particularly to a slave impersonating a soldier. He would very likely have hidden in dark places.' Junio looked at me, seeking approval for his reasoning powers. 'One lurking thief, one sharp stab, that is all it takes. Daedalus loses his purse and he is dumped in the water.'

'Then why not take his armour? His helmet at least? It is worth many denarii, even now.'

Junio shrugged. 'It is hard to smuggle such things within the city, unless you come prepared. No, I am sure Lucius is right. The answer lies with tracing Regina. A pity we cannot go to her home town, but it is a long way – days and days of travelling.'

He said 'we' I noticed, as though he and I were working as a team.

'Perhaps,' I said.

He looked at me intently. 'There is something else?' It is impossible to hide anything from Junio.

I sighed. 'There is something that escapes me, I don't know what. Something I half-noticed at the time. I feel there is some important information I have missed. Something that Lucius said or did.'

'Something he told you about Regina?'

'No,' I said, trying to capture that elusive thought. 'I feel it was something about oatcakes.'

Junio laughed. 'You and your oatcakes! You are obsessed with Celtic food. I am sorry I did not buy some for you from the market.'

I thought of that delicious childhood taste. 'No market oatcakes ever tasted like these,' I said. 'And it does not take a Celt to think so. Lucius enjoyed them too.'

'What sort of man is Lucius? I never met Crassus, but from what you say the two men were as different as charcoal and cheese.'

I tried to describe the man. 'Shrewd, serious, solitary and very softly spoken,' I finished, rather proud of my oratorical flourish.

'A hermit,' Junio said, 'living a humble life. Not at all the sort of person to be impressed with my poor librarium mosaic. I wonder why Crassus bothered.'

'Crassus did not know that his brother had changed so much,' I said. 'He was disappointed. He had hoped for all kinds of orgies and entertainments, so Paulus says.'

Junio laughed. 'Poor old Crassus. That is the first time I ever felt sorry for him. Although you would have thought that in that case Lucius was even less likely to be impressed by a librarium.'

I took a sip of my delicious mead, and then stopped, my drinking cup still in my hand. 'What did you say?'

He goggled at me. 'I said, "I wonder that Germanicus hoped to impress his brother with a pavement." Why are you staring at me like that?'

I put down my beaker carefully. 'Because,' I said, 'I should have asked myself the same question. When Lucius loved feasts and orgies he did not care for libraria – he would think the money better spent on women and wine. Once he converted to the new religion, he did not care for mortal show. So, if it was not for his brother as he said it was, why did Crassus want the mosaic in such a hurry?'

Junio said nothing.

'I do not believe he wanted the pavement because of his librarium at all,' I said, excitedly. 'I believe he created the librarium as an excuse to have a pavement. People said that he bought manuscripts without caring what they were. "Laundry lists on vellum" would have served the purpose as well as any poet. Perhaps that was true. He sincerely did not care.'

'He wanted a pavement,' Junio was visibly working through the argument, 'because he had buried something under it.' He looked at me. 'What do you think it is? Treasure? You said that Crassus' treasure chest was bare.'

'There is only one way to find out. We must go back to the villa,' I said, 'at once.' It was my turn to say 'we', but Junio looked subdued.

'We cannot go tonight,' he protested. 'It is dark and dangerous, and it has rained all day.'

'Tomorrow then,' I conceded. 'At first light. See you wake me early. And while I am dressing you can go to the market and get some oatcakes for us to eat on the way. It is a fair walk to the villa, and Marcus will not provide his gig this time.'

'Very well, master.' It was not like Junio. I had tried to be breezy but he seemed cast down.

Suddenly I realised what he was thinking. I reached out a clumsy hand to pat his arm. 'I'm sorry about your pavement.'

I was right. He grinned at me ruefully. 'So am I,' he said.

Chapter Twenty-two

We did set out early. It was a damp, cold morning and I was glad of my woollen cloak and hood to keep me warm. I had opted to leave my toga at home this time. Pavements, I decided, were a professional affair. With Junio beside me, very similarly clad, we looked like a pair of local peasants heading to market to buy cows.

Perhaps that was why a galloping imperial messenger ordered us curtly off the main roadway, and we were obliged to trudge for several miles on the miry track at the side. By the time we came to the back road to Crassus' villa, we were both heartily glad to take it.

There was little on the road at this hour. A flock of sheep and goats impeded our progress for a while; an old man, bent double under a stack of firewood, shuffled out of our way, and two men struggled past us with a wooden barrow laden with watercress – to sell in the stalls of Glevum, I assumed. Apart from that the countryside was empty; only the drip of the trees and the occasional scuffle of an animal broke the silence. Even the birds were hushed.

The deserted roundhouse seemed more melancholy than ever. I kept a wary eye out for wolves and I noticed that Junio, too, kept one hand on his knife hilt.

As we descended the hill, though, we caught the sounds of man. Somewhere, there was the rhythmic thud of an axe, an unseen cart rattled noisily over the stony track, and a distant labourer grunted as he worked. We reached the gravel farm track with relief and made our way along to the gate of the villa.

Already there was a different air abroad. Marcus had left a guard, a pair of armed soldiers who stood, pikes at the ready, flanking the doorway. Aulus, peering through his aperture, seemed almost friendly in comparison. The guards, though, scarcely afforded us a glance. They were not there to prevent people entering the villa, they were there to prevent people leaving it. Without a master some slave might be tempted to run away – and that would be a serious loss of revenue.

Aulus swaggered out to meet us, squaring his shoulders and trying to look suitably belligerent. He seemed to fill the whole gateway. When I pushed back my hood, however, and he saw who it was, he almost fell over his cudgel in his anxiety to let us in.

'I did not recognise you, citizen. I shall send for Andretha at once.' He motioned to a slave who was crossing the courtyard, and sent him scuttling, then bent towards me confidentially. 'You have heard the news? Paulus is still missing, and Marcus has sent us those' – he nodded towards the armoured guards – 'to make sure no one follows his example.' He smiled, leaning close to my face and exposing his discoloured teeth. He had been eating boiled cabbage again. There were times when I felt that I preferred Aulus in less friendly mood.

I murmured something.

'It was uncalled for,' Aulus complained, gesturing

towards the guards. 'I could have done the job just as well.'

'Perhaps,' I said, 'Marcus was afraid you would escape yourself.'

Aulus gave me a reproachful glance, and moved away. I had insulted him, but at least it removed the cabbage fragments from my immediate vicinity.

There was no time to say more. The little slave appeared again, with Andretha at his heels.

'Citizen!' Andretha looked at my tunic and cloak in dismay. 'What brings you here? I thought your business at the villa was concluded. We are hardly in a condition to receive you. Rufus has been taken to Glevum in chains and the furniture is being prepared for removal and loaded onto the cart. Marcus sent us word last evening, and the slaves have worked all night.'

'Rufus has been moved?' I said, trying to adopt a businesslike tone. 'Excellent, in that case I can work in the librarium. I wish to remove the pavement. I shall need help.'

'Remove the pavement?' He sounded incredulous. Then he added, piteously, 'Oh, great Minerva! Does Marcus know of this?'

I did not dare to answer him. Aulus was listening, for one thing, and I have always been a clumsy liar. Instead I favoured him with a pitying look. 'Really, Andretha, do you need to ask? You know that I am working on Marcus' behalf.'

He was not convinced, I saw it, but he was in a quandary. If he guessed wrong, whichever choice he made, there was likely to be trouble. And Andretha was in enough trouble already. Even if Rufus was thrown to the bears, it was not certain that Andretha would escape execution. There was still that question of household negligence. To say nothing of shortfalls in the accounts.

In the end he chose the lesser of two evils. 'I suppose, since you come from Marcus, you must be allowed to do as you please. But let it be on your own head if Marcus is displeased.' His hands fluttered like butterflies.

I nodded. It would be on my own head, with a vengeance, I thought, if we dug up the pavement and found nothing there. However, this was not a time to vacillate.

'Let me have Aulus,' I said, briskly. 'He is strong. And two or three of the garden slaves. I need men who are handy with a spade.'

Andretha rounded up the slaves and followed me to the librarium, the lump in his thin throat moving up and down so nervously that he reminded me of a gulping frog. Though if anyone had cause to be nervous, I reflected, it was me. Marcus was buying the villa, and he would be less than delighted to find his librarium mosaic dug up and spoiled before he had even taken possession.

The door had been left unlocked after Rufus' departure, and as I walked into the gloomy little room, my confidence returned. Why had it not occurred to me before? Without the door open, there was hardly enough light to see the mosaic, and with the door ajar the room was surely too chilly to sit in. No one, surely, would choose to have a pavement laid in a poky back room like this.

I gave the sign to Aulus, and he lifted his adze. I saw Junio flinch.

'First we spend a day digging the floor over to make it even, and then another bringing in barrows of earth to lay a good foundation for the pavement, and no sooner is it finished than we start digging it all up again,' one of the land-slaves grumbled, under his breath. 'What does he hope to find?'

I did not answer him. If I was right, he would discover soon enough,

In fact, the mosaic was easier to lift than I had feared. It had been laid on smooth cement-plaster, stuck to a piece of coarse linen, and because it had been in place only a few weeks, once the plaster was lifted it came away in large pieces, instead of our having to move it tile by tile. After an hour or two the waiting barrows in the courtyard were full of jagged sections of pavement, and the trodden earth floor was once again revealed.

Even then we managed to start at the wrong end of the room. It was not until we had dug it over more than halfway, and I was beginning to fear that I had been mistaken, that Aulus' spade suddenly hit something solid, but soft.

He bent forward casually to see what he had struck, turned pale and rushed out into the courtyard, where I could see him making a sudden and unintentional libation before the little god by the sundial. A very personal oblation, with cabbage in it, I fancy.

What he had glimpsed was not a pleasant sight, admittedly, even to those well acquainted with death. It had been a woman, we found when we disinterred it further. A tallish woman in a russet gown, that much was still clear, with her hands bound and her throat slit, almost severing her head from her body. She had been dead for weeks.

It was Andretha who first recognised the ring. We slid it off the decomposing finger and I took it to the women's quarters. Faustina, red-eyed and pale, glanced at it without interest.

'I don't know,' she said dully, when I asked her whose it was. 'I think it was Regina's. Where did you find it?'

'She was wearing it,' I said softly. 'We have found her, I think, under the librarium pavement.' I was afraid I would distress her further, but Faustina had no tears left to shed for Crassus' unhappy wife.

'Have you seen Rufus?' she implored.

I shook my head.

'What will become of him?'

She did not really expect me to reply. She knew the answer better than I did. In her dreams she had witnessed him being fed to the wild animals a dozen times already.

'Is there any hope?'

'Only,' I said gently, 'if I can find some connection with this earlier murder. Rufus has not confessed to that.'

She dropped her head into her hands. 'Then we are back where we began. We are all under suspicion. We shall all die.'

'Not if I can find the killer. Are you willing to come and look? Tell me if this was Regina? You knew her better than anyone in the villa. I warn you, it will be an ordeal – especially if you were attached to the lady.'

She looked up. 'I was attached to her. Regina was kind to me.'

'She has been dead a long time.'

Faustina swallowed hard. 'Poisoned?'

I shook my head. 'Her throat is cut.'

She gulped. 'Poor lady. That is a brutal death. I hope she did not suffer long. Aconite is quick, at least. She used to say it was the way to die. "A feeling of giddiness and heat, a dryness in the mouth, slurred speech – almost like being drunk. If you are unlucky, vomiting

218

and bleeding from the mouth. But often, little time for pain. There are worse deaths." Poor, poor Regina. She found a worse one, certainly.'

'And a worse one to see,' I said.

She sighed. 'I will come, all the same, for Rufus' sake. At least you gave me a choice.' She got to her feet and gave me a wan smile. 'Willing or not, I would have had to come, if Crassus ordered me.' She followed me resolutely out of the building, and back into the courtyard.

They had moved the body by this time. I will spare you unnecessary horrors – the maggots, the smell, the decomposing flesh. Faustina, however, was spared none of them. I led her around to windward and she looked down at the corpse.

'I don't know,' she said, with a shudder. 'It might be Regina. Might have been Regina. It is hard to tell. That is rather like her hair. Yes, look – there is a comb, I put it into her hair myself. I do not recognise the veil, it seems to have been russet – like a bride's.' And then at last, she began to weep, and Andretha led her away.

' "She went away triumphant" ,' I quoted softly. ' "We have not seen her since." But you did see her, Aulus. That night when you looked out of the gatehouse, and saw her in a man's arms. Only he was not embracing her. She was already dead. He was carrying her here, to bury her secretly, where the slaves would cover her with earth and she would be safely hidden by the pavement. While you were opening the gate, he carried her up the other path, to the nymphaeum, and brought her in through the back of the house. It was a risk, but he had to take it. Hard work, but he was strong.'

'Daedalus killed her?' Junio said. 'Why would he do that?'

'Perhaps he tired of her,' Aulus suggested, 'and she threatened to betray their courtship to Germanicus. She could be persistent, as we know, in seeking a husband. If Daedalus was seeing her without his master's permission, there would be an end of his manumission. A free woman, and his master's lady once! So, you think he killed her?'

'If it was Daedalus you saw that night. You are sure it was?'

'I am sure it was Daedalus who went out earlier, and he took her food and gifts at other times. I am sure of that.'

'And now Daedalus himself is dead,' Andretha said. 'We buried him in the slave pit two days ago.' He gave a helpless sob, raising his arms like a praying priest. 'I thought this business was over when Rufus confessed. I even thought I might have been reprieved. But now we have another murder here. Only a woman, but she was freeborn. I have lost Crassus' treasure . . .' He saw the startled faces. 'Yes – that has disappeared. And now I've lost Paulus. It goes from bad to worse. I will be put to the sword, I know it.'

'To the sword at least!' Aulus said, with gloomy satisfaction. I remembered that Andretha had often been responsible for punishing him.

I said, 'I think Marcus should know what we have discovered here. And we must find Paulus, before it is too late.'

'It may already be too late,' Andretha wailed. 'He has been gone for days. He could have travelled miles in that time. Marcus set a watch for him, but he has not been found.'

'Where would he go?' Junio said. His face was still the colour of marble from what he had seen. He made a feeble attempt at levity. 'I hope he isn't going to turn up under another pavement.'

Aulus sidled close to me, and whispered in my ear. There are smells which are even worse than cabbage. 'As to that, citizen,' he hissed, 'I might have something to tell you. If I might have a word, in private.'

Chapter Twenty-three

'I thought,' Aulus wheedled ingratiatingly, 'that this might be important. I will just find it for you, citizen.'

He had led the way to the latrine beside the bathhouse and was grovelling about, removing a loose board from one of the three holes in the wooden seat set at the end of the building over the stream. I squatted on the neighbouring seat and watched him, while Junio, standing at the doorway, looked about him in wonder.

It was an impressive place. A fine stone-paved floor, with a water channel let into it, and a bucket with a sponge-stick in it nearby, so that users could have running water to cleanse themselves without moving from their perch. I thought of my own wretched arrangements, which had to be thrown out of the window daily. Crassus certainly knew how to live in style.

'Ah,' Aulus said, freeing his piece of wood at last. 'Here it is. There is a space in the wall.' He groped through the hole to produce a small, almost spherical object wrapped in a piece of hide. 'Naturally when I found this, I hid it to show to you.'

The man was lying, obviously. Until I arrived at the villa that morning, Aulus could not have had any idea that he would ever see me again. However, this was not the moment to argue. He unwrapped the object and held it out to me. I took it gingerly. It seemed clean enough, but I did not altogether care for its hiding place.

The object appeared at first sight to be a ball, a slightly lopsided pipe clay ball, but when I turned it over, the truth was obvious.

It was a head. A rather crudely carved and hooded head, smeared with dried blood, and with a jagged edge as if it had been broken from its modelled body by a savage blow.

I turned it in my fingers. 'You know what it is?' I said to Aulus.

He shrugged. 'It is hard to say. I thought perhaps . . . from the lararium?'

'A *genius paterfamilias*,' I said. 'Yes.'

Junio came over, drawn by curiosity. 'If that is supposed to be Crassus it is not a good likeness, at least from what I have heard of him. In fact, the face is so featureless it could be anyone.'

'They always are. At least the inexpensive ones. They are symbolic representations, nothing more.' I turned to Aulus. 'Where did you find it? Not in the latrine?'

He shook his head. 'No. There is a hollow place in a tree beside the roundhouse. A big oak, hung with mistletoe. He often hid things there. He did not know that I had discovered his hiding place.'

'He often hid things there?' Who did? Surely not Crassus? Aulus seemed to suppose that I knew already. Perhaps he had explained to Marcus. That was tricky. If I let him sense my ignorance, he would guess that I had not spoken to my patron about this visit.

I searched my brain, and made an association. Mistletoe. It was revered by Druids; they were even said to have a special ceremony where they cut it with a golden scythe. And an oak. Oaks were sacred too. I said, as though I had known it all along, 'You mean Paulus put it there? You are sure of that?'

Aulus shrugged. 'I did not see him do it. But who else would it be? He was always hiding things in that tree – coins, bits of food, even those herbs Regina gave him for his bruises. I reported it to Marcus long ago, but he wasn't interested. Anyway, the morning before Crassus' funeral, I saw Paulus go there, and he came away looking horribly guilty.'

I nodded. I myself had looked for the barber for some time in vain that morning.

'It wasn't easy to get away and search,' Aulus said. 'I could not be found missing from my post. In the end I had to slip up there the morning after the funeral, when everyone else was asleep. That was what I found.'

'You did not tell me at the time.'

'I tried to tell you, citizen, but you were not interested. I told Marcus that I had found something, but he said it was unimportant because Rufus had confessed.'

I remembered. Aulus had hinted that he could tell me 'stories' at a price. I had supposed he was offering scurrilous gossip. Marcus had obviously thought something similar, since he also refused to buy the information. Now, of course, everything was changed. If Daedalus had killed Regina, as Aulus believed, the whole household of slaves was under threat again. He was only too anxious to turn informer.

'I took it away and hid it in the latrine, just in case.'

In case Paulus could be blackmailed, presumably, but he didn't say that. I said, 'And?'

He shrugged, regretfully. 'Paulus disappeared after that and did not return.'

The regret was genuine. He must have been hoping for a substantial bribe. A suspected Druid in possession of the bloodstained head – even the stone head – of a murdered man would have some serious explaining to do. Merely to be a Druid was an offence against the state, as was being involved in anything that smacked of Druid practices. Paulus would no doubt have been willing to pay a high price for silence. That much, at any rate, made sense.

We were interrupted by Andretha hurrying into the latrine.

'I was looking for you, citizen. May I come in?'

It was daring, while I was there. Some villa owners, like my own one-time master, permitted household slaves to use the house latrine – although never at times when any citizen might require it, naturally. I doubted that Crassus was so generous. There was probably a servants' open latrine or cesspit somewhere, which would be emptied occasionally to provide fertiliser for the estate.

On the other hand, I told myself, Lucius was the official owner now. Perhaps Andretha expected him to take a different view of social customs.

'No objection at all,' I said heartily. 'Aulus was just showing me a most ingenious hiding place. I wonder how he came to know of it?'

Aulus looked as if he would cheerfully have stuffed me into it, but he said, 'I heard about it from the slave who cleaned the place. It was not difficult to hide things there – the latrine is not used at night. Only Crassus ever came here after dark, and it was easy to avoid him. He almost always had an oil lamp, or had Daedalus carry one, to light his way.' He brightened. 'Do you think Daedalus hid Regina's body in here, while he dug the hole? Perhaps Paulus helped him. Obviously Daedalus had discovered the Druid connection and could force the boy to do anything, as his price for silence. It would not take long – the floor had already been dug over in preparation for a pavement.'

Of course, I thought. He was right. Even the disturbed earth would attract no attention. And then, in the morning, the slaves would pile the new earth over the hasty grave, to 'make a good foundation' and some foolish pavement maker, proud of his art, would conceal the evidence for ever. It was a humbling thought.

Aloud I said, 'Why do you think Paulus was involved in this?'

Aulus looked at me as if I were feebleminded. 'Regina's throat was cut,' he said. 'Paulus is missing. And you found a novacula, didn't you, citizen? In Paulus' bed, I'm told.'

I wondered where he had learned that. From the guard who had been posted at my door, perhaps. I had to admit it, Aulus seemed to be an effective spy.

Andretha had concerns of his own. 'I wished to ask your advice, citizen, about this body you have found. Should it, do you think, be given burial? And if so, how? After all, it has already been buried once, after a fashion.'

It was typical of Andretha, I thought, to agonise over the ritual niceties of reburying a corpse, when we were faced with a double murder and a runaway slave. Yet, strictly, he had a point. As a free woman visiting the villa Regina should be accorded funeral dignities.

'Cremation would be best,' he went on fretfully. 'But the land is Lucius' now. He might not welcome that. Christians do not like to burn the dead. Perhaps we should send to him for instructions. Or to her family. But we cannot wait for long. In the meantime we should wrap her up, at least. The sight is awful and the stench is worse.'

'I think you might lawfully do that,' I said. I had no authority, but somebody had to take command. 'Fetch in some bedding and lie her in the librarium. It is cold in there, and dark, and you can lock the door. In the meantime we will send to Marcus. He should be told in any case.'

'I fear to touch the body,' Andretha said. He looked ashen. 'She was not properly interred. I do not think her spirit could escape when it wished to. Her hair and nails have grown.'

If that was true, it was certainly horrifying. Andretha looked pale. More than pale, in fact. He had been living with acute fear for several days and this body under the pavement had been the last straw. I realised that this visit to the latrine had been born of necessity, not merely a desire to find me. If we had been equals, of course, there would have been no difficulty – the place was built for communal use. But since I was a citizen and a guest, and he was merely a slave, it was out of the question for him to 'insult' me. The least I could do was leave quickly.

I said, matter-of-factly, 'We have found Regina. Now perhaps I can look for Paulus. Come, Junio.'

Andretha let out a little whimper. 'Yes, I have lost Paulus, too. I shall be executed, I am sure of it.' He was already edging urgently towards the wooden bucket with the communal sponge-stick in it.

I could take a hint. I led the way outside and left him to it. 'He is right,' I said to Junio. 'Who would have dreamed that Paulus would run away? He was so timid. And where would he go? He took nothing with him – he had nothing to take. To his family perhaps?'

'He couldn't do that,' Aulus said, desperate to please me by offering information. 'His family are all slaves too. He told me so. Besides, he still has his neckchain, identifying him as Crassus' slave. I am surprised he has not been dragged back here before.'

Andretha came out of the latrine looking shaken, and hurried up to us. Now, perhaps, he might be in a position to assist.

I held out the head that I had been holding. 'Aulus found this. Have you seen it before?'

He looked at it. 'It looks like the missing *genius* from the household shrine; Rufus said it was broken. But who could have done this to it?'

'I wondered about that for a moment,' I replied. 'But I have changed my mind. I don't think this came from the shrine at all. From Crassus' collection of figurines, more likely. See where the stone has been broken? That is an old scar. It is too smooth to be recent damage, and not clean enough. This has a patina that comes with age. It has been broken for a long time.'

'It must be important, all the same,' Aulus said sulkily, 'otherwise Paulus would not have hidden it in the oak.'

'Paulus hid it in the oak?' Andretha said. 'A severed head?'

Aulus looked smug. 'Among the mistletoe.'

'Then that proves it. Paulus was a Druid.' Andretha made a despairing gesture. 'I suspected as much! A Druid! And in my household too. One disaster after another. I wonder if it would help if I denounced him to Marcus.'

'*We* shall denounce him to Marcus,' Aulus said hotly. 'I was the one who found the head.' He flung Andretha a mutinous glance. 'There may be a reward.' He turned to me. 'And we should find him quickly, before he goes running to Lucius. Lucius will claim him as a Christian convert, and the next thing you know they'll be blessing bread together and I shall lose my reward.'

I stared at him, taking in what he had said. Suddenly I had the missing piece, and everything made sense. What Aulus had said was surely the solution. It is no crime, even for a slave, to run away and find your master. Being a Christian is frowned upon, but it is not in itself a capital offence – not yet, at any rate. Far better than being under certain sentence of death. Paulus was no dedicated Druid, and he was so terrified of mere physical punishment – let alone execution – that a swift conversion would not bother him. He would sacrifice his own left arm to the emperor if it would help.

'Of course! He has gone to Lucius!' I cried. 'How could I have been so blind? Andretha, put that body in the librarium and have the farm cart readied. I must go to Glevum, and then to Lucius. And hurry! If I am right, delay could be fatal.'

'Fatal?' Andretha quavered. 'Fatal to whom?'

'To you, among others,' I told him brutally. It was not, admittedly, likely to be true but it ensured I had the farm cart readied in record time. In less than a hour Junio and I were at the gates of Glevum.

Chapter Twenty-four

I found myself in a quandary. Marcus, of course, had no idea that I had gone back to the villa, and I was faced with the rather unpleasant necessity of telling him, not only that I had done so against his instructions, but that I had also dug up his librarium floor without his consent and found a decomposing body under it. These were not tidings likely to improve his afternoon.

Under the circumstance, I felt, I would have to be more than usually persuasive to convince him that it was necessary to stop whatever he was doing and accompany me immediately to visit Lucius in the fastest available official transport. Yet that was precisely what was required.

My heart sank when, after enquiring at Marcus' lodgings, we discovered where he was. If I were to make a list of all the places where Marcus hated to be disturbed, a private massage room at the bathhouse would be very near the top of it. Lying there while a nubile slave rubbed his body with perfumed oils, before he strigiled off and went to join his friends for intrigue and gossip in the steam room, was one of my patron's most sacred pleasures. He would not welcome intrusion there.

I sent Junio. All right, it was a sort of cowardice.

Junio was willing enough – that is what slaves are for, he said – but I was rather ashamed of myself for it. Though there was a kind of excuse. I knew Marcus. He would think it below his dignity to lose his temper with a menial messenger. While he was getting dressed to see me he would have time to cool down a little, mentally as well as physically.

A little while later Marcus emerged in a tunic, looking pink and furious, and followed by a slave carrying his towel and cloak. He cut short my obeisance and greetings.

'There had better be an excellent explanation,' he said.

I swallowed. 'Your pardon, excellence, but I come on your commission. I believe I know now who our killer is.'

He made an exasperated sighing sound. 'I thought we had disposed of that. I suppose that you will tell me now that it was not Rufus? Although the slave confessed?'

I smiled, I hoped ingratiatingly. 'Yes, excellence. That is what I am going to say.'

'Very well, I am listening. But do not expect me to reprieve your little lute player. He is guilty of lies, if nothing else. No mere slave tells lies to me. I represent the State.' He took his wrap from his own attendant and flung it impatiently around himself as he spoke. He did, I thought, look like a dumb show in a spectacle, representing Imperial Justice.

'Not even lies, excellence. He thought he was to blame. He is a Silurian and worships Nodens. He went to the city shrine and put a curse on Crassus during the procession. When the body was discovered, he was horrified. He had not expected such a swift response. I

think he still believes he brought down divine justice on
Germanicus – you remember he thought the broken
statue was a sign? When no human murderer was found,
and the whole household seemed in danger of being
executed, he confessed – to save Faustina's life at least.'
I was talking too much, but there was method in it. If I
could keep Marcus interested, his mood might well
improve.

He was interested. 'You have seen the curse-tablet?'

'No, but I am sure it could be found. I should have
suspected something like this earlier. I found a lock of
hair under his bed. I'm sure now it came from Crassus.
Obtained from the barber slave, no doubt. Almost
certainly it was used to strengthen the charm – a piece
of the cursed man's hair is said to double the force of
any curse. He went back to get a strand or two, secretly,
while the other slaves were waiting on the farm cart
– probably intending to save the rest for further
imprecations. No wonder he was so troubled at its
effectiveness that he kept breaking his lute strings.'

'So, it was not Rufus. Do you know who it was?'

'I think so, excellence. But I need your help.'

'Someone else at the villa, I suppose? Libertus, you
have a generous spirit, but there is little point in this.
Merely one slave's life against another – and strictly, we
could execute them all.'

'Regina was not a slave,' I said.

He looked at me. 'Regina? I have searched for her, as
you asked. There is no trace of her.'

I told him.

There was less of an explosion than I was expecting.
He raged for a moment. 'Digging up the mosaic!
Without authorisation? I should have you flayed!'

'Should have you flayed' I noticed, not 'shall'. I began

to breathe again. 'Her throat was cut,' I ventured.

'Murdered?' he said.

I quelled any temptation to answer that ironically. 'It seems so.'

'By whom? By Crassus? Or by one of his household?'

'Her throat was cut,' I said carefully, 'with a novacula, it seems.'

That did it. I saw his eyes light with interest, and there was no trace of irritation as he said, 'With a novacula. Like the one you found?'

'The one Junio found,' I said. 'Yes,' I added theatrically, 'perhaps with that very blade.'

'Great Jove,' he said. 'And Paulus could not be found when I wanted him. Where is the barber now?'

'Missing,' I said. 'Although I think I know where to find him. And we should hurry, excellence. We shall find ourselves investigating the death of Lucius next.'

That roused him. 'Then I will put on a toga and come with you.' I had been hoping for that. It is always better if Marcus suggests these things himself. 'I will arrange a gig at once. Go and see to it.' This last to the slave who had been waiting patiently, and who trotted off at once at the command. Marcus turned to me. 'Why did you not tell me about this at once?'

Since there was no possible answer to this, I merely grinned apologetically, and followed with Junio to the building where my patron had his apartment. Like all wealthy men he inhabited the first floor, a spacious suite of rooms immediately above the wine shop. I had visited the place before and it was impressive: stone floors, painted plasterwork and real windows. There was even a balcony, although it was not a good place to stand. It was too vulnerable to anything thrown down from above. I have waited for Marcus on that balcony before, and can bear witness to the interesting varieties of refuse – and worse – tipped into the street from overhead. There were times when I preferred my own humble habitation. At least I rented it whole, 'from soil to sky' as the law went.

We were not invited onto the balcony today. Marcus left us to wait outside on the landing, to my relief, among a small crowd of 'hangers-on' who had collected to see Marcus, and a bunch of inquisitive inhabitants from the cramped, bug-infested and overcrowded flats upstairs.

It was not long, however, before Marcus himself reappeared, resplendent in patrician purple edging and spotless linen. It must have taken five slaves to get him ready so soon. He waved an imperious hand and the crowd melted away like frost in the sunshine. The gig was ready and waiting too, together with a driver and a few mounted soldiers as guards provided by the local garrison. I was obviously not the only one who respected the possibility that my patron might have real imperial lineage. Marcus got in and motioned me to follow. Junio stood beside the gig, hesitating.

'We need Junio,' I said, daringly, and Marcus nodded. Junio clambered in, wide-eyed, and crouched at my feet, where he remained uncomfortably for the whole jolting, breathtaking journey.

It took only two thirds as long in the gig. It was harder on the bones, but the lighter conveyance seemed fairly to rattle along the roads, and with our armed outriders other traffic moved smartly aside to let us pass. Even a troop of soldiers parted ranks to let the official carriage through. We stopped again for horses, at the posting station, but this time we were offered spiced meats and almond cakes, not the mere bread and cheese of my last visit – that was reserved for Junio and the cavalrymen. (The exquisite envoy would have been chagrined, I thought, to know what luxuries real rank afforded.)

It can barely have been three hours before we turned down the little lane and I found myself outside the Dubonnai roundhouse again.

The appearance of the soldiers created a far greater stir than my fashionable companion of a few days before. I imagine the roundhouse dwellers associated the military with land seizures or with tax. No sooner had the gig stopped than the entire household hurried to the entrance of the enclosure, and formed up in lines to greet us. Marcus smiled, but I could read the signs. Women and children at the back, shielded by their menfolk. The males deferential and polite, but armed. The family were ready for trouble.

Marcus descended from the gig. 'From your Roman governors, greetings!' They abased themselves appropriately. He turned to me. 'You talk to them, Libertus.' Obviously the envoy had told him that I spoke the language.

I stepped forward, allowing my face to be seen, and deliberately catching the eye of the woman who had provided the oatcakes. 'We have come to see the hermit,' I explained, in Celtic. Some of the tension vanished. 'We think there is a criminal in his cave.'

'There is a boy there,' the woman volunteered. 'He arrived about an hour ago. I was a bit worried about letting him go up there – he looked a bad type, dirty and wild-eyed, dangerous almost. I went up myself with my son, to take some barley loaf and cheese, just to make sure, but Lucius came out and told us not to worry. It was just a runaway slave, he said, and rightfully his.'

'That's true,' I said. 'It is a long story. We have come to take him away before any further harm is done.'

'And quickly,' Marcus said, taking his lead from me. 'You know the way, lead on.'

I hesitated. I thought I knew, now, what had happened, but I could not prove it – yet. I said, 'Give me a little time to talk to the fellow alone.' That was important. I would never gain his confidence while Marcus was there.

Marcus looked doubtful. 'But I want to talk to Lucius. About the villa.'

'A little while, that is all.' I looked around for some way to mark the time. 'Look at the tree. Wait till the sun has passed behind the highest branch, then follow me. That should give me time for my purpose. Junio, you stay here with Marcus in case you are needed. And do not fear for me, I'll take the soldiers with me.'

Marcus looked doubtful, but he agreed, and off we went. Great Minerva, they knew how to march, those men! They were not infantry, but they strode up that hill as if it were the merest ridge-furrow, with me struggling breathlessly after them.

'Wait,' I panted, as we reached the final slope. 'Let me go on ahead, I want to—'

I broke off. The hermit had seen us coming. He was standing outside his cave, hands folded at his belt, and was confronting us, his hood half-obscuring his face, very still, very solid, very determined.

I said to him, 'We have come for Paulus.'

The eyes beneath the cowl hardly flickered. 'He has come to cast himself on my mercy.'

'Then you know what he has done? It is an offence – you cannot shelter him. The price is execution.' I raised my voice. 'Paulus, come out. Come out or I will send the soldiers in.'

There was a silence.

'Very well,' I said, producing my best impression of an officer. 'Cavalry detachment—'

'All right,' said a little voice. Paulus came trembling out of the cave. 'I'm here. Don't beat me. I confess. The head—'

I silenced him. 'Yes,' I said. 'That misled me for a time. Heads. The head of a corpse in the hypocaust, the head of a statue hidden in a tree. And then of course I realised that it was intended to mislead. I was supposed to concentrate on the heads, to make connections between heads and Druid ritual. It drew attention to you, Paulus, but at the same time drew attention away from the brutal truth.'

'Which was?' the hermit said.

'It was a much simpler murder. We have found damning evidence. There was a woman's body buried at the villa – Crassus' bride, Regina. Her throat had been cut with a novacula. A novacula which Paulus admitted was his own. It was found bloodstained, hidden in his bed—'

'I didn't kill her,' Paulus interrupted. His voice was almost a shriek. 'I came to find my new master, because—'

I whirled on him. 'Quiet! How dare you interrupt a citizen. Silence him at once.'

One of the burliest soldiers stepped forward and seized the barber, one hand forcing his arms behind his back, the other clamped across his mouth.

'A novacula, you say?' The hermit had not heard of our find. He stared at me, white-faced under the beard.

'And there is more,' I said. 'The barber used

ointments in his work. Regina was an expert in herbs. She had a chest of potions, some of them deadly. That chest has not been seen since she died, but one of her phials was found, empty, on the rubbish pile, the day of the funeral.'

Paulus shut his eyes in anguish, but he could not speak.

'With fatal liquids on his tray Paulus would have a thousand opportunities to murder his master. One nick is enough to introduce poison, and he cut Crassus badly the day before the procession. I imagine he applied one of Regina's ointments, claiming it would staunch the bleeding. Not all poisons kill instantly – my own slave pointed out that if Crassus was poisoned, the murderer need not have been there when he died. Paulus hated his master. It would have pleased him to see Crassus die in public at the parade.'

The barber gave a little hopeless moan, but I carried on inexorably.

'Only, it was not Crassus in the procession, it was Daedalus, taking his master's place for a wager. Did Paulus slip away to see what had happened – he told me himself he had left the others at the festival – and stab Daedalus in the back with his centurion's dagger?'

The hermit was looking at me steadily, the grey eyes very glittering. 'Why should he kill Daedalus?'

'Daedalus died,' I said, 'because he knew too much. Just that. That is the problem with murder, one killing leads to another.' I turned to the soldiers. 'You may have Paulus now. Take him to Marcus. Bind him, gag him, and take him away. I have some business to conclude with Lucius. Tell his excellence I shall not be long.'

I watched them bear the slaveboy, struggling, down the hill.

Chapter Twenty-five

The hermit watched them go. Paulus was being half-dragged, half-carried, as if his legs had failed beneath him.

'Unfortunate young man!' My companion turned to me with genuine emotion. 'You did well, citizen, to fathom the truth. It was a subtle crime.'

'More subtle than I thought,' I said. 'I underestimated the lengths to which fear will drive a man. Perhaps you guess yourself what danger you were in when we arrived here. I think we narrowly averted another killing.'

'Mithras!' The smile grew graver. 'You think so? He meant to kill me? Citizen, I cannot thank you enough for coming here.' His eyes searched my face. 'But you have business with me?'

'About the villa,' I said.

He smiled. 'Have you the leisure to break bread with me again?'

I glanced down the valley, where the gig was just visible in the distance. There was no sign of Marcus. 'I think I might accept,' I said. 'My patron is being fêted by the Celts.'

I followed him into the cave again, and took my seat on the stool, watching as he poured out two goblets of watered wine. The woman's barley loaves were on the bench, a single slice of cheese, and two bunches of the same meagre herbs I had observed before.

'Wine?' I said, in surprise, taking the goblet he offered.

He smiled. 'From Crassus' cellar. I have three amphorae here, for medicinal use. I meant to give some to that unfortunate boy. I was preparing a meal for him. He was so consumed with terror, I felt a little sustenance would help.' He picked up a wooden platter on which a piece of bread, filled liberally with herbs and cheese, was already lying. 'Take it, citizen. It is not much, but it is all I have.' He went to the bench, carved an end from the barley loaf, and began to prepare a similar meal for himself.

I took a tentative sip of wine, and waited until he came to join me. Roman politeness demanded that, at least.

'So,' he said, cutting a slice of cheese with that handsome knife, 'what will you do now, citizen, since you have resolved this mystery? Go back to your pavements?'

'I have a commission for Caius Didio,' I said. 'I hope to start work on that again tomorrow. It leads me to a delicate matter, Lucius. The librarium pavement at the villa. Crassus commissioned it, but he never paid, and under the circumstances I can hardly ask Marcus . . .' I smiled hopefully.

'Of course.' He laughed. 'You have dug it up again. Well, I will see what I can do.' He came to join me, settling himself on the mattress as before.

'And will you pardon the other slaves, now Paulus is arrested? Even Rufus? As a Christian, I suppose you will? Marcus would be glad of your seal on these matters. I have brought a wax-book for the purpose.' I detached the small hinged tablet-book which hung at my girdle, opened it flat, and scratched a few words there with the stylus. Then I handed it to him and watched while he read what I had written and imprinted the wax carefully with his signet ring. The ring was so loose that he had to take it off to make the mark.

'There.' He folded the tablet in half again and gave it back to me. 'Marcus will be pleased, now that you have caught Paulus.' He took a sip of wine. 'You reason well, citizen. I would never have connected him with the murders. He is too timorous.' He raised his goblet.

I did the same. Carefully. It was important, very important, that I should not allow myself to drink too much. Roman wine did not agree with me, and if I was right about my companion I needed my wits about me. On the other hand, if I showed signs of inebriation, I would seem unthreatening. I took a gulp of wine, and appeared to savour it for a long moment. Then I put down the beaker again and took a deep breath before speaking again.

'Of course,' I said. 'You are quite right. The evidence looked overwhelming, but Paulus did not kill anybody. As you know.'

Silence. The hermit did not move. He seemed scarcely to be breathing.

'He did not have the subtlety for it,' I said. 'These killings were the product of a shrewd and clever mind.'

He was sitting very still. 'Then who?'

I crumbled a piece of my bread. 'I think you know the answer, my friend. And the reasons, too. Let us start at the beginning. A soldier, who wants to gain advancement and who is too impatient to wait for legal means. He has a toothache, and when he goes to a woman who makes herbal cures, she offers him a tiny dose of aconite. Faustina told me it was a common cure. He knows little about herbs himself, but he knows that one.'

The hermit nodded. 'Everyone does. A single draught is such a swift and effective poison that Trajan had to forbid the citizens of Rome to grow it on their property.' He was still sipping his wine.

'Exactly,' I said. 'Our soldier sees a chance. The woman is plain and thin, and has no dowry – her family was dispossessed. She will be lucky to find a husband. He courts her, promises to marry her as soon as he is legally able. But in return he begs a favour – a strong infusion of aconite.' I looked at my companion.

'Go on,' he said. He was eating his bread and herbs, now, but he paid the meal scant attention. He was watching me intently.

I produced a slightly tipsy smile. 'But our soldier has a brother, not unlike himself, a man who enjoys a drink and a wager. They have been in many scrapes together. With his help the poison is administered, at a gambling party perhaps – on an occasion when there are a dozen witnesses to swear that our man was a score of miles away.'

The hermit said softly, 'I admit nothing. But supposing the brother does not even know about the poison? It is explained to him as a practical joke. A laxative in the wine, perhaps, and when the man is taken ill, the brother goes home chuckling. Something like that? That does not make him culpable.'

'No,' I agreed. 'I do not think the brother knew of the aconite. He lacked his brother's ruthless streak. But the military court might not be so forgiving. The army does not forgive treachery in the ranks, even years after the crime.' I was slurring my words, and I looked at my goblet doubtfully. 'This is strong vintage, Lucius. It has gone to my head already.'

He poured a little more into each of our drinking cups. 'It is Crassus' wine. You may thank him for the quality. But go on. Your theory interests me.'

I took another sip. 'The soldier gained his promotion, but when the company was posted elsewhere, he left the woman behind. She must have suspected.' I took care that it sounded like 'shuspected', and that the hand that held my plate was trembling. 'But she could prove nothing, and if she spoke, would only imp – imp – licate herself.' I looked at my wine again, rather foolishly. 'This is very strong.'

'I should have given you more water with it.' He fetched me some from the ewer. He was beginning to move a little drunkenly himself. 'So, he gains a centurion's salary. A clever rogue.'

I laughed, a drunken little giggle, and tapped the side of my nose. I felt rather an idiot, but it seemed to be having the desired effect. 'A very clever rogue. Gets to be . . . shenturion . . . and make slots of money.' I shook my head. 'A lucky, lucky man.' I put down the cup and clutched at the table. ' 'S hot in here.'

The hermit was watching me carefully, crumbling bread in his turn. He said nothing.

'Then, suddenly, a dreadful thing occurs.' I was acting the story now. 'The brother converts to Christianity, and the sin of all those years ago rises to haunt him. He has killed a man. He wants to make amends.' I made a face which began as anguished contrition, and ended as a sort of vacuous smile. 'He gives the woman directions to the villa. Oh yes—' I raised my hand, like an orator on the forum steps, 'He knew where she was living – in Eboracum. You told me so yourself. She must have learned recently where the villa was – her appearance is too great a coincidence otherwise.'

The wine was beginning to affect me now. I must not drink much more of it. I stretched out a hand as if to lift the goblet, but contrived to knock the heavy vessel to the floor.

My companion retrieved it, while I picked up the plate of bread and herbs and began to eat.

'Go on,' he said. 'You interest me . . . a great deal.' His own voice was unsteady now.

'She comes,' I said, waving my hand like a drunken poet reciting at a banquet, 'poor stupid woman, older and plainer than ever, desperate because her father has died and she is faced with beggary. She threatens to tell her story if Crassus does not marry her. He agrees to have her in the villa. But she gets too friendly with the slaves. She might tell somebody his secret.' I rolled my eyes dramatically. 'She must be disposed of. He kills her custos, has her dismiss her maid, and promises to marry her. He sends her away, with money, supposedly to purify herself and prepare for the wedding. Then, on the appointed night, she comes. There is no dowry, so she needs no witnesses. She is dressed as a bride and thinking to fulfil her vows – and instead . . .' I drew an imaginary novacula around my throat. 'In the round-house, I think. There is a bloodstain there.'

The hermit shook his head mournfully.

'In the meantime he has prepared a grave. His brother is coming, so he buys half a dozen manuscripts – he did not even care what they were – and arranges for some poor fool of a pavement maker to lay a mosaic over the floor.'

He was nodding, stupidly. 'And no one knew?' It sounded like 'noanoooo'. He was not feigning, I thought with satisfaction.

'Aulus saw him in the lane with the body in his arms,

but our man was cunning. He pretended to be kissing her, and then smuggled the corpse into the villa while Aulus went to open the gate to come out and spy. Aulus, of course, thought it was Daedalus again. Crassus had sent the slave out with presents for her before, and Aulus had seen him.'

'Foolish Aulus,' the hermit said, staggering to the wine jug to refill my goblet. 'So, the killer was safe.'

'Safe enough,' I said. 'Until his brother comes. He is a changed man. Doubtless he asks about Regina, and will not be fobbed off with excuses. He is cleverer than I am; he guesses the secret of the pavement. He knows what Crassus is capable of.' I wagged a finger at him. 'Germanicus is a clever and devious man – we know he chose his punishments with care. Whatever hurt the victim most. A man who does that has intelligence.' I looked at him. I was slurring my words, but my brain was clear. 'Cruel, but intelligent. You knew that.'

He laughed uproariously. 'Crassus was not the fool that people thought him.' He stopped, suddenly sober, and eyed me thoughtfully.

'And doubtless his brother shared his cleverness. He tried to persuade Crassus to confess. Worse – he warned him that he proposed to confess himself. He wanted to found a church. Crassus tried to buy him off, with gifts and the promise of inheritance, but to no avail.'

'So?'

I cast a swift glance in the direction of the valley. The sun should be safely above the tree branch by now. 'So.' I drained my wine dramatically, and rose to my feet. I was genuinely swaying slightly, but I managed to speak coherently. 'You did it, didn't you? You agreed to meet your brother during the procession, while Daedalus impersonated his master in the march. Perhaps Crassus even promised to convert. He had poisoned the wine he offered. You are no fool. It is an elementary precaution to exchange goblets, when you drink with a known poisoner.' I lifted my empty goblet. 'As I exchanged my goblet with yours a little while ago.'

He said nothing, but a little smile played around his lips.

'When he died you arranged his body in the hypocaust and came back here, as quickly as you could. You had the mule, of course. It is a pity you tried to implicate Paulus, putting the novacula under his bedding and that bloodstained statue in the lararium. He panicked, of course, and hid the head, so it took a little longer than you expected for suspicion to fall.' I was wavering dangerously, and I clutched at the table for support.

He stood up himself, almost as giddy as I was. 'All right,' he said, 'that was foolish. But I swear I did not knowingly kill Crassus.'

This was my big moment. It was a pity that my heart was thumping so painfully and my head swam.

'Of course you didn't,' I said, with the careful deliberation of the drunken. 'Crassus is still alive. But you killed your brother. You killed Lucius.'

I just had time to utter the words before I pitched forward and tumbled onto the floor.

Chapter Twenty-six

Just in time.

The pretended hermit lunged at me savagely. He had given up all pretence, and he did not even raise his hand as his hood fell back, exposing that unmistakable bull neck and the tell-tale scars on his cheekbones – visible even under the new beard – where Paulus had trembled in his shaving.

I had little time, however, to think of anything so mundane. He had turned around, seized the stool on which I had been sitting, and was now whirling it around his head with the evident intention of bringing it down on mine, and bashing my brains out.

This had not been part of my plan. I had intended to feign the early symptoms of aconite poisoning which I had learned of from Faustina: thirst, headache, giddiness, stomach pain. He would give me time to die, I reasoned, before running off, pretending to seek for help. A poisoning he could explain; doubtless he would pretend to be ill himself and blame Paulus for bringing poisoned wine. He would hardly finish me off violently, and leave tell-tale wounds, with Marcus and his soldiers waiting in the valley.

I had misjudged my man.

He brought the stool down with a crash that

reverberated through the cave, and which would undoubtedly have seen me laying mosaics for Pluto if I had not managed to roll under the table. The stool, mercifully, snapped into several pieces.

It hardly slowed him, however. A moment later he was attempting to perform a similar trick with the table. If he managed to lift that there would be no escape.

I had to do something, fast. I clutched at the table leg. I considered crawling up it, moaning and twitching as if in the final throes, but I doubted that would be very convincing. I had taken an enormous risk, as it was. I am no thespian at the best of times, and I was in the company of a man who had learned his acting from Daedalus – one of the greatest mimics in the empire.

It is not easy, either, to imitate the symptoms of poison convincingly to a man who has watched at least one victim actually die of it. And I had done the easy part; according to Faustina the next step was vomiting and haemorrhage, and that was going to be much more difficult to manage.

I saw Germanicus pick up the knife. Soon I might not even have to pretend, I thought. If Marcus did not arrive soon, I was going to expire in good earnest.

I twisted round the table leg and tried to leap past him and run away – not very honourable, but I could see no alternative. A trained centurion with a knife is more than a match for me, especially with several goblets of wine inside me. It may have been the wine, indeed, that did it. I misjudged the distance, and leapt up, rapping my head sharply on the table edge. I let out a roar and fell back, holding my head.

I lay there trembling, waiting for the knife.

It did not fall. I suppose a man sees what he expects to see, and my abrupt collapse looked like the effects of poison. I was aware of him standing over me for one breath-stopping moment, and a finger lifted my eyelid.

I let my eyes roll back into my head – I was so faint with fear I do not think I could have prevented them!

'Not long now,' Crassus grunted. The disguising whisper was gone, and it was his own voice now. 'You thought you were so clever, pavement maker, changing the goblets. A pity you did not change the platters too!' Then, sharply, 'What's that?'

I knew what it was. Footsteps at the door. Marcus at last, and not a moment too soon. I heard the knife clatter to the floor.

'Must keep them away. Too much wine,' Crassus muttered, indistinctly, and I heard him as he went outside, calling, 'Help! Help up here! A terrible misfortune has befallen Libertus. We need a litter, quickly.'

'What is it?' Marcus' voice at the entrance, sharp with concern.

'Someone has sent me poisoned wine.' The ecclesiastical whisper was back. 'Do not go in there, excellence. There may be vapours in the air. I have made him as comfortable as I dare. But fetch a litter, quick. I will come with you.'

He was playing for time, of course, waiting for the poison to take effect. I opened one eye gingerly. I could see him, hurrying down to the valley with Marcus, pulling his hood back over his head, and already the very personification of a hermit. 'He did a merciless and deadly accurate imitation of Lucius,' someone had said. It was true. At least, I thought, this little piece of acting vindicated mine. I would have looked particularly stupid if I had been wrong, and the meal he had prepared for me had been innocent. There is nothing likely to make a man feel more foolish than pretending to be poisoned by an innocuous plateful of bread and herbs.

I presumed it was the herbs. I had taken the precaution of exchanging our goblets while he signed the tablet, just in case it was the wine, but I had let him know that I had done that. 'It is an elementary precaution to exchange glasses when one is drinking with a poisoner.' It had not prevented him from draining his cup.

He had been very anxious, however, to give me the meal that was prepared for Paulus. The boy, obviously, had posed a threat to him. No doubt, like Daedalus, he had served his master in the bathhouse and would soon have seen through the disguise. So Germanicus had prepared a deadly meal for him, and then given it to me, and watched like a hawk as I pretended to eat it. I had been obliged to ask for water in order to distract him long enough to exchange the plates, and then to knock the beaker flying – I dared not risk a drink he did not share.

I carefully collected up the few fragments of leaf which still lay upon his plate and wrapped them in the square of cloth in which the woman had sent the loaf. I was careful not actually to touch them; according to Faustina the poison can be absorbed through the skin.

They did look like parsley leaves. Mentally I blessed that blow on the head I had received at the villa. It had saved my life. If it had not been for my conversation with Faustina then, I should undoubtedly have eaten those leaves unsuspectingly. Aconite or hemlock, I was sure. The herbs which had leaves very like parsley. There was no way of testing the fragments here, but if it was absolutely essential, Marcus would order that they be

given to condemned criminals. That would prove that
the herbs were poisonous.

However, I hoped that the matter would soon be
proved by more immediate means. Crassus was a bigger
man than I was, and strong, but he had eaten his
meal greedily. I hoped he had provided himself with a
sufficient dose.

He had.

It was Junio who came bursting up to find me,
breathless and wide-eyed. I was searching through the
chest-cupboard and cave when he arrived, collecting
together the treasure which was hidden there.

'Master!' Junio blurted breathlessly. 'You are un-
harmed! Thanks be to Jupiter. They said you were ill.
Marcus is sending a stretcher party. Something has
happened to Lucius. I was afraid . . . ' He broke off,
goggling at the array of gold and silver, precious oils and
gems, fine dishes and expensive ornaments which I had
piled up upon the bed. 'What in the name of Mercury is
that?'

'The treasure of Crassus Flavius Germanicus,' I said.
'The treasure for which he lived and died.' I was aware
that I sounded like a candidate for some schoolboy
oratory competition, but I felt that the occasion
warranted a little dramatic rhetoric.

Junio was duly impressed. 'Great Olympus!' he
exclaimed. 'I knew Crassus had been generous to his
brother, but this is astonishing. No wonder Lucius
required the mule to carry it all home.' He looked sober.
'Poor man, his legacy will do him little good, I fear.'

I took a deep breath. 'Oh?'

'He staggered down the hill, saying you were ill,' Junio
said. 'Said you had been drinking poisoned wine that
Paulus brought from the villa.' He looked at me. 'It is as

well you do not care for Roman wine, or it would have killed you too. Lucius is dead.'

'I know,' I said. 'His brother murdered him – as he murdered everyone else who stood in his way. Murdered him, and then subjected him to the ultimate betrayal anyone could inflict on a sincere Christian convert. He had his body burned and his ashes buried in a pagan funeral.'

'But . . .' Junio began. 'I don't understand. His body is being taken into the roundhouse now.'

'That is not Lucius. It is Germanicus. He was disguised under the cowl and the beard, and that was good enough when no one knew him well, especially in the dim light of the cave. But I have no doubt Paulus would have recognised him soon.' I looked at Junio's astonished face and laughed. 'I know. I only lately worked it out myself. I almost left it too late—'

I broke off as two soldiers stumbled in, bearing an improvised litter of boards and cloth. They goggled as they saw me.

'I shan't be needing that,' I said, 'but you could carry some of this down the hill.' I picked up two silver figurines and led the way out of the building and down the path, leaving them staring after me open-mouthed.

They had taken the body into the roundhouse, and the whole family was gathered around, white-faced. The woman was openly weeping. The carved stool had been set by the fire for Marcus, but he was not sitting on it, he was pacing the uneven floor, a striking sight in his patrician toga and scarlet cape, but looking anxious and discomfited. There was no sign of Paulus and the rest of the soldiers.

Marcus came bounding over when he saw me. 'Old friend. You are recovered!' His evident relief was

flattering. 'The hermit is dead, poor fellow.' He looked
at the figurines in my hand. 'But how . . . ?'

'It is a long story,' I said. 'I was not ill, only stunned.
I will explain later. Let us first deal with matters here.' I
walked over to look more closely at the dead man. The
hood had fallen back from his head again. I looked at
the tell-tale scar on the cheek – I should have noticed it
earlier. I turned to the woman. 'You have seen that scar
before?'

She shook her head tearfully. 'No, until the feast of
Mars I had never seen him shaven. He only cut his hair
and beard as a sign of mourning for his brother.' She
looked at me helplessly. 'Will you speak for us, kinsman?
You have influence with this Roman. Must you take the
body away for funeral? He told me once he longed to be
buried here – a simple burial with Christian prayers. In
an unknown spot, he said, with no memorial. God would
know where he lay and he did not wish the place to
become a shrine, which it might do otherwise. He has
brought down many blessings to this place. He was
good to my son. I should like to do this for him.'

I translated this to Marcus, who frowned doubtfully.
'What do you think?'

'It seems to me,' I said, 'that it would be, in many
ways, peculiarly apt. No, not a word.' That was to Junio,
who had just come in, his arms full of treasure. He had
the missing ring-key on his thumb and seemed about to
say something. I said, 'I will explain it all to Marcus
presently.'

Marcus looked at the armsful of golden artefacts.
'Should we . . . ?'

'Bury them with him? I don't think we should. You
have heard what he told this woman. A simple funeral.
Besides,' I went on in rapid colloquial Latin, in case the

young man from the house should be trying to understand, 'these items came from Crassus. Are you not the
named substitute heir, since Lucius cannot inherit?'

Marcus looked at the priceless figurines, at the dead
man on the bed and back to me again. 'Sometimes, old
friend, I am grateful for your advice. Of course, as a
representative of the governor, I do not wish to upset
these good people by depriving them of their dead
friend. It shall be as you suggest. Meanwhile Lucius'
possessions shall be returned to the villa.'

'There is a great deal more of it,' I said. 'Perhaps the
soldiers could help to fetch it down.'

'They are outside guarding Paulus,' Marcus said. 'I
suppose they can be spared since he is tied to the gig. I
was going to have him dragged back to Glevum at our
wheels.' He led the way to the door.

'I think it would be better to release him, excellence,'
I said in an urgent undertone, as I followed him. 'Paulus
had no hand in this, or in any of the other deaths.'

Marcus looked at me sharply. 'Who then?'

'I think discretion is called for,' I went on, pressing
my advantage. 'There is a soldier involved.'

Marcus nodded slowly. 'I see. Well, what am I to do
with the prisoner? We cannot take him in the gig with
us.'

'If I might suggest it, excellence, Lucius had a mule.
Let Paulus ride on that. You could ask the household to
provide another, to carry the treasure. Or an ox cart
would be even better. Then one of your cavalrymen
could escort everything back to Glevum under guard.'
We were out of earshot of the others now and I added
quietly, 'And you could get your soldiers to bring down
the rest of the wine – I believe it is a fine vintage and
there is nothing the matter with it. But tell them to be

very careful not to touch anything wrapped in the blue cloth. I would prefer the Dubonnai household not to know this, but it contains the herbs he managed to kill himself with.'

Marcus turned and stared at me. 'You jest.'

'I do not jest at all, excellence,' I told him. 'It is scarcely a jesting matter. He was trying to use them to poison me.'

Chapter Twenty-seven

Matters were soon arranged. The Dubonnai woman was so delighted at being able to keep her 'hero' for burial, that she agreed to lending the precious ox cart without the slightest demur, although others of the family were visibly less enthusiastic. The young osier cutter, in particular, seemed to feel that it was a very bad exchange.

Which it was, I thought, although Marcus still had no idea how bad. I would have to ensure that he was scrupulous about returning the cart. I allowed him to supervise the loading, while I set about freeing Paulus.

The barber was so frightened he was almost unable to stand, and when I undid the ropes and gags he burst into tears and blurted that he did not know how to thank me. It made me feel uncomfortable; after all, I had been instrumental in having him bound in the first place.

'Thank me,' I said severely, 'by saying nothing – nothing at all, on the way home. I will leave Junio with you to make sure you do not.'

'But, citizen—' he began.

'If you hope to escape with your life,' I said, 'say nothing. Except, you can tell me where you went during the procession on the feast of Mars. I know where the

259

others were. Andretha went to the moneylender, Rufus visited the temple, and Aulus followed him. That leaves you. I presume you did not merely roam the streets.'

The boy coloured. 'I went to a barber's shop, citizen,' he said meekly. 'I had used almost all of Regina's herbal ointment for cuts, and I wanted something to replace it. I bought the concoction of spiders' webs you saw. Crassus would never permit me to buy such things, but they eased my task. If I could staunch the bleeding, Crassus hit me less.'

'And?' I said. I remembered how terrified the boy had seemed when I questioned him.

He looked at me helplessly. 'I took it to one of our priests to have it blessed, to make sure it worked. Some of these potions are useless. But the man is a known Druid. I knew where to find him . . .' Paulus shuddered. With reason, I thought. If the authorities ever heard of this, they would beat the information out of him first, and execute him later.

We were already out of earshot, but I took him by the arm and led him further off. 'And the head? No – this is no time for denials. You hid the head of a statue in your hollow tree. Aulus saw you.'

He had turned chalk white again. 'It was in the lararium when we came back from the festival. The statue was broken – the head was severed and there was a bloodstain on it. And my master had been murdered, with his head in the furnace. I thought – you can see what I thought. People would think that I had done it. The body of the statue was no problem. It was only roughly carved to suggest a toga, and without the head it just looked like a piece of weathered stone. I simply threw it away. But the head! I was terrified someone would find that! I took it away and hid it in the tree.'

'Where Aulus found it,' I said.

Paulus gaped. 'He had it?'

I nodded.

'In that case . . .' The barber trailed off helplessly. 'But it would have done no good, I had no money to bribe him. When I found the head had gone, I panicked. I ran away to Lucius. You cannot be punished for running away to find someone to plead for you, and I thought if I confessed he would protect me. He would believe me in any case. I had done nothing.' He gulped hard. 'But Lucius was angry – I suppose because he thought I had dealings with idols.'

'That was not Lucius,' I said. 'Lucius was already dead.' I explained, briefly. 'And no suspicion for any murder now attaches to you. So, keep your mouth shut about Druids and you may yet escape from this alive. You came to find your new master, that is all you need to say. Keep your own counsel and do not run away again. Now, here is Marcus coming. I must go.'

I got back into the gig with my patron and we bounced uncomfortably back towards Glevum. Even then, I did not try to explain until we were past the staging post. I did not want Marcus to go back to the roundhouse and start demanding the body.

When I did explain, he was thunderstruck.

'The hermit was Crassus!' he kept exclaiming. 'I can't believe it. How did he get away with it?'

'He looked much like his brother,' I said. 'And you heard the woman, no one at the roundhouse had seen Lucius shaved. When Crassus took his place, he claimed that he had shaved his head and beard in mourning for his brother. Equally, none of us had seen Crassus with a beard. His plan was to hide himself away until he had time to grow one. It would not take him long. With that cowled hood and the dim light of the cave, he came close to getting away with it.'

'I see,' Marcus said. There was a silence, during which we bounced along more perilously than ever. 'At least . . . no, I don't see. Lead me through the arguments again. Crassus killed Regina and buried her under your pavement. And then he got Daedalus to take his place in the procession so that he could meet his brother at the villa unobserved; that much I understand. I suppose that is why he gave all his slaves a holiday to Glevum. I thought it was unlike him at the time.'

'I doubt he even went as far as Glevum himself,' I said. 'It is more likely that he just went to the ruined roundhouse, where Daedalus changed into his old uniform. They must have hidden it there.'

Marcus said thoughtfully, 'That would explain the piece of scale-armour which you found there. I suppose Crassus simply waited until the villa cart had left and then went back to the house to await his brother. But how would he get in? The gates were locked. You think he scrambled up the path past the nymphaeum? That would be quite a feat, in full armour.'

'Yes, but he was very strong. He was getting fat, but he was a centurion after all. He had been trained to march twenty-four miles non-stop in a day, carrying his kit. Besides, we do not know that he was wearing armour then. It would have been an easy matter simply to come back in his tunic. That would have impressed his brother, too. Lucius must have believed he had a true convert, a veteran centurion who chose to miss the festival of Mars. It was on those grounds, perhaps, that they shared a celebration drink.'

'Into which Crassus had poured Regina's aconite,' Marcus finished. 'I wonder why he did not use some of that to try to poison Regina herself.'

'She was too familiar with poisons,' I said. 'She may even have carried antidotes – if there are any. No, the novacula was safer. Crassus was strong, it was no problem to tie her and slit her throat.'

'That is why the blade was bloody?'

'I don't think so. I think he cleaned it, that time. He had more time after all, and he took the body to the latrine; he could have cleaned the razor in the running water there. He told me himself how easy that would be. He blunted the blade, though. Paulus said he had to buy a new one, recently.'

'Much riskier than poison.'

'But more certain. She probably tested any food he gave her, especially after her custos died. She must have been suspicious of Crassus. He was certainly suspicious of her – look how he got Daedalus to taste everything he ate and drank while she was in the villa. It wasn't love potions he feared, of course, it was hemlock and aconite.'

'Yet he did not use her potion to poison you,' Marcus said. 'I wonder why?'

'Perhaps he sprinkled some on the bread, but I doubt there was any left. He would have used a heavy dose to be sure his brother died quickly. There was not a lot of time.'

'No,' Marcus agreed. 'His brother cannot have arrived early; he lived a long way from the villa. And there were no strangers in nearby inns. We established that.'

'He had a mule,' I pointed out, 'Crassus saw to that. And no doubt Lucius left his cave the day before. No one would think it odd – he was known to spend whole nights in prayer with the sick. And he would not stay in an inn. Doubtless if we enquired among Christian sympathisers we would find someone between here and Glevum who offered him shelter for the night.'

'So Crassus murdered him, dressed him in his own armour, and stuffed his head into the hypocaust?'

'And his hand,' I said. 'I should have seen the force of that. It was only today, as Crassus was imprinting his seal on a wax tablet, that I understood. It was Lucius' ring, and it was too big for him. Lucius' hands were fleshier. His finger had to be made smaller before Crassus' seal ring would fit. It was tight, even for Crassus, I saw the mark it made. It would not fit Lucius. I think he cut away a little of the flesh with the novacula – the blood on the blade must have come from somewhere, and the cuts in the legs did not bleed.'

'Why did he shave the legs?'

'He had to, of course, because he had shaved his own. He did that so that Daedalus could impersonate him in the march. Ironically, he was an even worse barber than Paulus was.'

Marcus thought about that. 'So he forced the ring on, and then thrust the hand into the furnace so that the fire would disguise the wound?'

I nodded. 'He must have done it early, before the fire died down. He tried to rinse the blade again, but he was in a hurry and the handle and pouch were blood-soaked. He had a better idea. He decided to hide it, as it was, in the barber's bed. If it was found there, it would incriminate Paulus. I think that's why he chose the broken *genius* to replace his own. The fact that it had no head would make us think of Druids.'

'Why take the statue from the niche at all?'

I laughed, a little shakily. The breathless ride in the gig was taking its toll. It had been a long day. 'If he left the statue behind it would be ritually broken and charred with the corpse. He was too superstitious for that.'

Marcus said thoughtfully, 'He must have hated Paulus, to single him out in that way.'

I shook my head. 'I'm not sure that he did. He chose Paulus just because the slave was inclined to nervous talk; he was likely to blurt out that he'd found the razor, and so implicate himself. If one slave was blamed, the whole household would be executed. That was what Crassus hoped for. After that there would be no one alive who was a real threat to him. By his own will his money came back to him. No doubt he would soon have moved away, renounced Christianity, and begun again.'

'A complex plan.'

'It was. It must have taken time and money to accumulate a second set of armour. Breastplates and greaves are not so difficult to buy, but he required a full set of everything, including his torcs of office and his mask. But he had a lot to lose. He was terrified that the real Lucius would "confess", and he would be charged with poisoning an officer. If that had happened, he would have been put to death. The army does not forgive treachery.'

We were bowling up towards riverside farms and the walls of Glevum were almost in sight. It was getting late, and such other transport as was still on the road was lit with torches. Marcus paused and simply commandeered a light, and then a slave to carry it. If I had attempted that, it would have cost me twenty sesterces – even supposing I did not get my nose punched, or have my purse stolen for my pains. Marcus, to whom twenty sesterces was the merest trifle, did not expect to pay anything. It astonished me.

Marcus, though, was unmoved. 'Well,' he said, as

if nothing at all had happened, 'it was clever of you to realise what had happened.'

I said nothing. I was abjectly aware, in fact, of how peculiarly stupid I had been. Everything had pointed to Crassus from the outset. The rings should have given me a clue. Lucius was the same size as Crassus, but a flabbier man. Of course, on a body without a head, it looked like puffiness. I noticed it at the time. Andretha sensed the corpse was subtly wrong, somehow. That's why he thought it might be Daedalus. The armour had marked the flesh, but I did not see the significance. That is doubtless also why Crassus could not put his sandals on the corpse. The leather would not stretch enough, even on a dead foot. Andretha noticed the sandals were missing. The dead hermit, presumably, was still excellently shod.

I should have sensed something too, when the woman told me that Lucius would not eat, and was getting thin. Of course, Crassus could not feed himself from nature, as his brother did. That must have been the hardest thing for him, surviving on berries and dry bread instead of lunching on seafood in lovage, or warmed sweet cucumber with sage and egg.

There was the question of the mule, as well. It had actually been reported coming and going on the day of the murder, but I had not noted it. Crassus would have thought nothing, of course, of walking fifteen miles back to the cave himself, but the mule was useful to transport the treasure – and no doubt something in the way of comforts too. Crassus would not willingly have gone to a cold, miserable cave in the mountains, even to save his life. The woman and her son noted a change in his habits. I should have spotted that too. He started 'grieving' on the feast of Mars, yet Lucius should not have known the news until the day after.

I did not say any of this to Marcus. Better that he continued to think I was very clever.

'Yes, very clever,' Marcus said. He was tapping his palm with his baton. 'I don't know how you did it.'

I gave him a smile.

'It was the oatcakes,' I said. 'Among other things.'

Marcus raised an eyebrow. 'Oatcakes?'

'He simply laid them before me and started to eat. I knew there was something funny about it, but I could not lay my finger on it. And then, when I began to think about it, I remembered other things too. The first time that he saw me, he asked if I came from you. How would Lucius know that? Then he called me by my name. He should not have known it – he had never seen me before. And later, when I told him about Regina's body, he concluded that I had dug up the pavement. When he said that, I was certain. I had not mentioned the librarium. Why should he guess that her body was buried there?'

Marcus was tapping the baton again. 'But what about the oatcakes?'

'Why, any Christian would have blessed the bread. And he had a figurine in his cell – he gave an explanation, but I should have suspected then. No Christian will admit the presence of idols. That was when the last pieces of the mosaic fitted into place.'

'So when you came to fetch me at the baths, you knew this already? When you spoke of the risk of another death . . . ?'

'It was Paulus I feared for.'

Marcus frowned. 'But you said . . .'

'I warned you we might find ourselves investigating the death of Lucius,' I reminded him. 'Which of course, we did.' I had been rather pleased with my oblique comment at the time, but glancing now at Marcus' displeased face, I added quickly, 'Although of course, I didn't know then for sure.'

Marcus nodded. 'So, the body we have left at the roundhouse is not the hermit. They will give it burial.'

I smiled. 'A simple burial in an unnamed grave. Something that Crassus would have hated, but exactly what Lucius desired. Instead his brother subjected him to the ultimate indignity: a pagan ritual and cremation. There is a certain justice, don't you think?'

Marcus gave me a rueful grin. 'Perhaps. But what should I report to the governor? Or perhaps he will not care, since it does not affect him. It was nothing to do with the army, or those soldiers at the gate, after all.'

'On the contrary,' I said, 'it had everything to do with them. All the murders were a direct result of Crassus killing his superior. He was afraid that Lucius would confess, and then his crime would come to light. He simply killed his witnesses. And as for the centurion at the gate, I am surprised that Aulus did not work that out. It was Daedalus, dressed in his uniform. Armour is heavy, and a man must train in order to wear it easily. It has been said many times that Crassus was trained to march. The wager at the procession would be lost if Daedalus could not maintain the pace or failed under the weight. Aulus reported that the man seemed stronger and more confident the second time.'

We had reached the West Gate now. Other carts and carriages were being refused entrance; wheeled transport was permitted inside the town in the evening, but the gates closed relentlessly at dusk. The soldiers, however, stood aside to let Marcus pass. Junio, on the ox cart, would have a longer wait.

'What should I tell the governor?' Marcus said, anxiously. 'Such plottings, and in a villa I have visited.'

It occurred to me for the first time that slaves and pavement makers are not the only men to fear their betters. I said, softly, 'I do not presume to advise you, excellence, but suppose that Lucius *had* killed his brother, knowing of his crimes, and then taken his own life in remorse?'

'That would have made things easier,' Marcus scowled. 'But he did not.'

'I know that, excellence, and so do you. But no one else knows it. And are you and the governor not, after all, residuary heirs to Crassus' fortunes?'

Marcus looked at me. 'Are you suggesting . . . ?'

I smiled. 'Excellence, I could not possibly advise. But there is one thing. I do have here a statement sealed by Lucius' ring, promising amnesty to the slaves and payment for that librarium pavement.'

Marcus' sudden laugh was joyous. 'Libertus, I always knew I was a brilliant man. Employing you has proved it.'

Chapter Twenty-eight

I was at home, sitting in my workshop. Junio, who had finally arrived home halfway through the morning after a miserable night spent on the ox cart, had warmed up by the fire and brought me a goblet of spiced mead. I was looking gloomily at the pieces of tile which were still waiting my attention, and which I would have to finish cutting by tomorrow. The prospect did not fill me with enthusiasm.

'So, master,' Junio said. 'Marcus was pleased.' Despite what I had said to Marcus I had, naturally, told Junio everything.

'Marcus was delighted,' I replied, 'He has even agreed to pay us for the pavement – fortunately I had Lucius' seal on that – and has offered me two of the slaves as a reward. He says he would not insult me by offering money.' I grinned. It was a little joke between us, that when I worked for Marcus I often wished he would be more insulting.

Junio though, did not return my smile. He looked quite downcast. 'Two slaves? Who will you take, master?'

I knew what he was thinking. I winked at him. 'Don't worry, Junio. I shall have no more slaves here. One hungry mouth is quite enough to feed and clothe.' I could see him debating whether to remark on the difficulty of clothing a hungry mouth, and I went on quickly: 'I shall ask for Rufus and Faustina.'

'And sell them together?'

'And let them go. Rufus is only a contracted slave, he can have his contract cancelled, even if he is too young for manumission. Then he can take Faustina as his own slave. I daresay he can make a living, with his lute, and she has learned skill with herbs. They will not starve.'

Junio smiled.

I picked up a piece of marble. It had a good vein in it.

'And Andretha?' Junio asked. 'He will not be able to present the accounts, and he will go on to menial slavery.'

He handed me my light hammer and a spike. I hadn't asked for them, but it was a good idea. If I just rested the marble . . . so . . .

'Most of the shortfall is accounted for now,' I said, when I had chipped off a perfect piece for Didio's border, 'thanks to Crassus' treasure. Fortunate for Andretha that Germanicus was so greedy. He could not resist keeping the hundred denarii that Daedalus had – and that was most of what was missing. Andretha will have to pay the moneylenders, of course, but it will not be a great sum.' I started work on another tile.

'Why did Daedalus need that money?' Junio said. He squatted beside me on the floor and began cutting tiles of his own. 'I have wondered about that.'

'Crassus would not take a bet without a stake,' I said. 'Daedalus was to get his freedom if he won. He didn't know Crassus' plan, of course; he thought it was a simple wager – a sort of daring, like that performance at the banquet. I thought so too at one stage, though I was wrong. But Daedalus had the money to offer Crassus if he lost. He did not know that Crassus meant to murder him. That was always the intention, of course. Germanicus could not risk a living witness, he needed the world to think he had been in the parade. I think he met Daedalus after the procession, but instead of arranging for manumission, he stabbed the slave and pushed the body into the river where the currents are strongest. He probably didn't expect it to be found. Daedalus was promised freedom in his will, so, as Lucius, he could call off the search for the missing slave.'

'And the purse?'

'Oh, he stole that, just in case the body was found. It made it look like robbery, and besides Crassus could never resist a chance of money. We found most of it in the cave. It will go back in the coffers now, and the books will almost balance. Andretha will be a slave, but not a menial one.'

'Better than he deserves, perhaps.'

'Much better. After all, he hit me on the head. I still have a lump.'

'He did?' Junio looked surprised.

'Oh yes, it must have been Andretha. I should have realised it before. He was afraid that I would find that empty chest under his mattress – I had told him I was going to search the slaves' quarters. He watched me closely after that. It must have been Andretha who followed me to the nymphaeum: only he could have kept the other slaves away from that path.' I stopped. 'That's a good tile,' I said. 'We'll have three more of those.'

Junio looked pleased.

'And when I went into the slaves' quarters, and started searching the beds,' I continued, 'Andretha was right there outside, supervising the loading of the cart. I saw him there myself. I imagine he picked up one of the logs and hit me before I could reach his sleeping room. Then he sent in Aulus to "find" me. Aulus then reported to Andretha, who was still outside the door. I don't think he meant to hit me so hard – he was terribly apologetic afterwards. He almost split his sandals running about trying to help. Thought that I suspected him, and was about to report him to Marcus, I suppose.'

'And Paulus? I thought you might have felt sorry for Paulus.' Junio finished the third tile and stood up. 'He almost died of fright yesterday, thinking he was to be executed. And all the time he was innocent. I thought you would do something for him. Will you commend him to Marcus as a barber?' He brought me another beaker of spiced mead.

I put down my tools and sat back on the stool to drink it. 'No. Commending him to Marcus would not help. He is not as innocent as all that. Paulus is not a murderer, but he has been flirting with the Druids. That is explicitly forbidden, you remember, on pain of death. That was why he ran away, of course. He ran to Lucius because of the head.'

'I had forgotten about the head,' Junio said. 'You did not mention it yesterday, to Marcus.'

'Of course I didn't. Paulus nearly did. I had to have the soldiers gag him, so that he didn't blurt it all out to them in a panic. Then he would have been executed, murders or not. I haven't mentioned Druids to Marcus. No, better that Paulus is sold, and goes somewhere as far from here as possible.'

Junio took my drinking vessel and refilled it without comment. Sometimes he seems to read my mind.

'And the poison phial on the kitchen heap? Was that Crassus' own?'

I grinned. 'No, it was Faustina's. Only it wasn't poison. It was Regina's cure for the flux, as Faustina always said. She took it, of course, once Crassus was dead. She wanted to get back to Rufus. Only he didn't believe that when she told him. They will have some making up to do, those two. Never mind. I think they will enjoy it.'

'So,' Junio said. 'That solves everything. Except that there is no librarium pavement in the villa. Although Marcus may commission a proper one, in time . . . What are you smiling at?'

'I was thinking how apt your design was, in fact. *Beware of the dog*. Perhaps I should have left it as it was.'

Junio glanced at me. 'Your alteration wasn't very apt, was it? *Art is long*. It only lasted a few weeks.'

I laughed. 'Well, next time you design a pavement, let's hope the art lasts a little longer.'

He grinned. 'So what will you do now, master?'

I stretched out my feet luxuriously and took a long sweet sip of mead. 'Tomorrow,' I said, 'I shall try to finish Didio's border, and then, perhaps,' I gave a deep contented sigh, 'we can go to Corinium.'

A Pattern of Blood

Rosemary Rowe

In the Britain of the second century, Corinium (modern Cirencester) is a bustling town, frequented by vagrants and pickpockets. So pavement-maker Libertus is not entirely surprised to witness a stabbing on the street. Luckily the victim, the wealthy decurion Quintus Ulpius, has a personal physician on hand, and tragedy is averted.

But Libertus has not heard the last of the incident. Commanded by his wealthy patron Marcus Septimus to investigate the attack, he arrives at Quintus's sumptuous mansion only moments before the decurion is knifed again, this time fatally. Was he killed by the loutish Maximilian, his son, who feared disinheritance? Or Flavius, the jealous husband from whom Quintus stole the enchanting Julia? Or was it Lupus, a shifty old fellow forced to depend on Quintus's goodwill, despite their long-standing quarrel?

When one of Quintus's enemies is found with bloodstains on his toga, for Marcus the case is closed. But Libertus is not convinced the solution is so simple. When a second body is found, he knows he must act fast before other lives are threatened . . . including his own.

The Germanicus Mosaic featuring Libertus is also available from Headline:

'Lots of local and historical colour . . . The story is agreeably written, gets on briskly with its plot, and ends with a highly satisfactory double-take solution' Gerald Kaufman, *Scotsman*

0 7472 6102 4

headline

Murder in the Forum

Rosemary Rowe

When Perennis Felix, favourite of the Roman Emperor and would-be enemy of all, heralds his arrival in Glevum (modern Gloucester) with the arbitrary execution of a slave, there are few who dare question his actions. Indeed, a feast in his honour is universally approved in the cause of self-preservation.

Libertus, freedman and pavement-maker, and his patron, Marcus Septimus, are among the reluctant citizens at the celebration. It is one occasion on which Libertus is thankful for his lowly status – he revels in his anonymity while more esteemed guests, his patron among them, are subjected to Felix's misplaced humour. But the festivities come to a sudden end when Felix appears to choke on a nut and dies in front of a stunned gathering. And soon the ever-vigilant Libertus notices the mysterious disappearance of at least two guests – one of whom he has very good reason to suspect is not all he seems to be. Is it possible that behind Felix's apparently accidental death lies a much more sinister explanation?

The Germanicus Mosaic and *A Pattern of Blood* featuring Libertus are also available from Headline:

'Demonstrates Rowe's pithy command of the Roman sleuth genre . . . a considerable achievement' *The Times*

'This engaging and sympathetic character once again has a date with danger and double dealing . . . Rowe's pacy writing style ensures that the action never flags' *Western Morning News*

'Lots of local and historical colour . . . The story is agreeably written and ends with a highly satifactory double-take solution' Gerald Kaufman, *Scotsman*

0 7472 6103 2

headline

Now you can buy any of these other bestselling Headline books from your bookshop or *direct from the publisher*.

FREE P&P AND UK DELIVERY
(Overseas and Ireland £3.50 per book)

An Evil Spirit Out of the West	Paul Doherty	£6.99
The Outlaws of Ennor	Paul Doherty	£6.99
The Templar's Penance	Michael Jecks	£6.99
Seven Dials	Anne Perry	£6.99
Death of a Stranger	Anne Perry	£6.99
The Legatus Mystery	Rosemary Rowe	£6.99
The Chariots of Calyx	Rosemary Rowe	£6.99
Badger's Moon	Peter Tremayne	£5.99
The Haunted Moon	Peter Tremayne	£6.99

TO ORDER SIMPLY CALL THIS NUMBER

01235 400 414

or visit our website: www.madaboutbooks.com

Prices and availability subject to change without notice.